THE RACE IS NOT TO THE SWIFT

THE RACE IS NOT TO THE SWIFT

A novel by Tu Jì Fun

RESOURCE *Publications* · Eugene, Oregon

THE RACE IS NOT TO THE SWIFT

Resource Publications
An Imprint of Wipf and Stock Publishers
199 W. 8th Ave., Suite 3
Eugene, OR 97401

www.wipfandstock.com

PAPERBACK ISBN: 978-1-7252-5092-5
HARDCOVER ISBN: 978-1-7252-5093-2
EBOOK ISBN: 978-1-7252-5094-9

Manufactured in the U.S.A.   11/25/19

"There are times when you can only take the next step.
And then another."

—William Gibson, *Pattern Recognition*

The race is not to the swift, Steve thinks as the a.m. bell crows Hwæt hwæt hwæt signaling the start of the day. Most of the kids are already inside, having begun the playground-to-classroom procession five minutes earlier when the first bell sounded. Most, but not all, and not Sam, who if she's not quite running is striding anyway, sylphlike, at a faster than normal clip—striding and smiling—she's almost never without a smile—holding his left hand in her right, one of her incisors wiggling like a worm emerging from the earth oblivious to the hungry golden-crowned sparrow perched on the branch overhead. By the looks of her she cares as much about being late as any first-grader would, which is to say not at all. Which is as it should be, probably. The same can't be said of Steve, who despite his best efforts at keeping calm and carrying on, is feeling pretty anxious, to tell the truth. How's a person supposed to keep calm anyway? Because it's already nine o'clock, if not 9:01, the bell has gone and they're still half-a-block away. Other tardy students are jogging: some in a dead sprint: some alongside or just slightly ahead of an accompanying parent or guardian. Though it is rather remarkable how few of these late-arriving girls and boys there are. Most Bluffwood kids are probably seated by now, giving their teachers their undivided attention. Steve is every bit as concerned about his daughter being late as the handful of mothers and fathers passing him are about their own children and it shows a little in how enlarged his pupils have become and in the way his lips are parted just so, as if he's doing everything in his power to stifle an atavistic scream. But whatever. He refuses to hurry any more than he & Sam are already hurrying. To go any faster would be a sign of not weakness exactly, but something resembling weakness. He's not sure what he'd name it or why he thinks whatever the appropriate term for it is, this strange feeling he's feeling, is near to weakness, except he knows it's not anything positive. It's not the kind of thing that gives people a good impression. They continue hand in hand going their brisk-but-not-too-brisk pace, cut across

1

a shoe-trampled dirt path worn in the middle of the grass lawn, up four cement steps—

four
three
two
one

—Sam wrenches her hand free from his grasp. They're through the hunter green side doors. Her classroom is down the short flight of stairs leading to the basement, at the beginning of a longish hall, second door to the right, and the door is still open, hurrah, meaning Mrs. Canard hasn't started teaching yet, hasn't taken attendance; i.e., technicality or not, Sam isn't late. Sam is on time. Sam will be marked same as if she'd been two minutes early. Steve hums. *Though my weary steps may falter, grace for ev'ry trial.*

A foot from the door Sam stretches out her arms. "Bye, Daddy."

Steve bends down, rests his knees on the tile floor, but gingerly because he has not the best knees in the world. Hug. A line from a song whose title he can't remember, one of those once-popular praise-and-worship numbers he used to sing with two hands raised roofward at the small-p pentecostal church he attended seventeen years ago when he was in high school, appears then disappears like mere breath, vapour, like a phantasmagoric scrolling text. He wants to hold her close, close and forever, or at least a little longer, but their embrace lasts a couple seconds at most. It's already over. A metaphor for life if there ever was one. Not an especially trenchant observation. He stays genuflecting a second longer before standing up, dusting the hallway detritus from his pants as Sam strolls inside, 100-percent content, and why shouldn't she be? Why shouldn't she feel entirely unencumbered, as filled with joy as a powdered sugar donut is with strawberry jelly or grape? Steve likes jelly-filled donuts: strawberry, grape, raspberry even. ABC: Anything but Boston Cream. Come to think of it, he could go for a jelly-filled donut right about now, and a cup of coffee. He dips his head in after Sam, peeking beyond the doorframe as she approaches the 4.5-foot tall cubby rack, hangs up her midnight blue, 19L Tom Bihn backpack. It was Steve's idea to get her this backpack, he occasionally likes to remind whichever of his kids will listen—usually just Sam, who apparently goes by Sammy now, is what Mrs. Canard told him last month. Daphne and Gillian are too young to understand the practical wisdom of using an adult-sized backpack in elementary school. They'll learn. Other girls in the first grade have pink

Barbie-themed packs that will have to be replaced the summer before second grade because their nylon bottoms will be falling apart, assuming the kids with these twee packs matriculate, or else they've got ones sporting pictures of this and/or that Disney princess or fairy; also two-season accessories, three at most. Sam's backpack will last through high school, even university if she takes care of it. Though it was made in China. So was he, though. Well, Taiwan, technically, which isn't a political statement. Steve would like her to go to Penn, follow in his footsteps. But would he, really? It's all the way on the other coast, in another country, another world. Sam removes her hound's-tooth coat of many shades of mulberry and hangs that up, too, on the same hook as her pack.

Steve exhales, relieved for the first time since he opened his eyes earlier this morning to the sight of Gillian sleeping peacefully in her crib, her chest rising and falling like a beluga repeatedly surfacing and submerging in the frigid Arctic waters. He may have only ever seen belugas at the aquarium, but they go up and down in their tank there, it can't be all that different in the wild can it?

He waits by the door because he wants to wave goodbye before he leaves.

Sam doesn't go immediately from the cubby to her desk. She's talking to Adi, who looks like she's crying. Her head is turned in such a way that she's half facing the door, half facing Sam, who's standing by the coats and packs so Steve can't make out whether or not Adi's crying, though it sure looks like she's sad. Sam gives her a longer hug than the one she'd just given him, her arms not quite making it all the way around Adi's stuffed-to-capacity carnation-and-periwinkle Moomintroll pack, which she's wearing over both shoulders, arms dangling by her side. It's Moomintroll, but chances are it was made in China, too.

Her mother is at the back of the room, Steve suddenly notices. Mary Cale is a Chinese woman of above-average height and looks somewhere between about 35, say, to 44, it's hard to tell with any more precision than that even for a fellow Chinese like Steve. She's definitely older than he is, that's for sure. Marigold is her actual first name. A slender woman with chubbyish fingers and a high forehead. Steve has always found women with high foreheads to be more open-minded.

Mary is talking to Mrs. Canard about Adi. There's no doubt they're talking about Adi. What else could they be discussing? Plenty of things actually, he knows that. But it can't be a coincidence: Adi crying by the coats and backpacks, Sam trying to console her while her mother and Mrs. Canard are over by Mrs. Canard's desk. The two events are definitely related. How?

Mary shakes her head as if disappointed and turns to face the front of the room. She begins walking away from Mrs. Canard, who remains in the same spot, statue-like almost except she rolls her shoulders.

Both women sport sizeable frowns.

Mary places a hand on Adi's back, directing her toward the door.

Adi obliges meekly.

Mary sees Sam and smiles as if all is right with the world.

Adi sniffles.

Steve shuffles out of the way, allowing the two of them to step into the hall. He waves at Sam who doesn't notice.

She's sitting between Hailey and Dante, having joined the rest of the class at the rug, the one with a map of North America that Mrs. Canard asks the administration at the start of every academic year about replacing because there's no Nunavut on it, it's that old, but there's never any room in the budget, the budget is running at a perpetual deficit, so there it still is in all its pre-1999 glory, the same old fraying Nunavut-less rug. That's what she told Steve at their most recent parent-teacher conference, right before telling him his daughter prefers to be called Sammy now.

Sam is sitting closer to Dante than Steve would like, but what can he do about it?

He can't do anything.

"What's wrong?"

Adi uses the sleeve of her jacket to wipe her cheeks, which Steve can clearly see now are damp and wan.

Mary tilts her head in the direction of the stairs, the ones leading outside. She means to tell him what's wrong, Steve understands by the gesture, but not until they're out of earshot. Not until they're some place Mrs. Canard with her fox-like audioception won't be able to hear what she has to say.

The door to the classroom shuts and the three of them make their way up and outside, silent save Adi's sniffling and the squishing of rubber-soled shoes and clopping of heels against lurid linoleum.

Mary squints the moment they exit the building.

It's sixteen average-sized paces from the door to the top of the cement steps.

"She had a little cold yesterday."

Steve nods, paying only partial attention to what Mary continues to say, remembering instead how he'd seen Adi looking a little out of sorts yesterday when he was in the cafeteria helping with lunch distribution.

Once a week Bluffwood serves lunch to all its students. Not Bluffwood exactly: the Bluffwood Parents' Association: the BPA, but no one says all three letters aloud. Everyone pronounces it *bee-puh*. Yesterday was Hot Dog Day. Steve doesn't have to cook the wieners or assemble them in their buns on HDDs, which are the first Tuesday of every month—subsequent Tuesdays feature other foodstuffs; Mondays and Wednesdays through Fridays parents are left to sort it out on their own—two moms from other classes do the boiling and bun-fitting. He merely distributes them, and even that he does only for Sam's class. It's not a complicated job: hand out the hot dogs and squirt small quantities of ketchup or mustard on them for whoever asks, ketchup and mustard being the only condiments the BPA provides. No relish or sauerkraut or banana peppers. No jalapeños. Also pass out juice boxes. That's what he was doing yesterday. Adi, who normally wants her hot dog, a veggie dog the last couple of times, smothered in mustard, and mustard only, never ketchup, shook her head no when Steve asked if she wanted any, any mustard, which surprised him a bit. It makes sense now. Nobody likes the taste of mustard when they aren't feeling well.

"And apparently Mrs. Canard told her to stay home today if she wasn't feeling better." Mary looks at Adi, who's staring at the ground. "Right?"

Still staring down.

"She's not even that sick, though," rubbing Adi's head. "And anyway it's easy for Mrs. Canard to say stay home. Is she going to babysit? I have to teach today and Hawthorn is still out of town."

That's right, Steve remembers: Mary is doing her post-doc at the university. "I could watch her."

"She was fine when we left home. I mean, she had a bit of a cough, but she was running around, really active, you know? I think she's just afraid if she coughs she's going to be on the butt end of Mrs. Canard's death stare." Mary does an approximation of the stare.

"Honestly, I don't mind. I'm happy to watch her if you want."

Mary leans over. Steve can't hear what she's saying to Adi.

Some of Sam's friends' parents when they find out Steve is a pastor—never mind what an absolute angel Sam is, which is a fact, all Sam's teachers have said so—their kids instantly stop talking to her, which Steve has always assumed was because of him even though he's not that kind of pastor, like for example of the Barths, John has had a greater influence on him than Karl, which concerned parents would know if they gave him a chance, and even if they don't want to, what does that have to do with Sam? Adi's face is a footnote.* Mary and Hawthorn hadn't appeared bothered when Steve told them what he did for a living after they'd asked, though they themselves volunteered they weren't a church-going family. Made no difference to Steve. Some of the best people he knows aren't Christians, don't go to church. Many of. Most? This was six months ago at Sam's birthday party. Anyway, he and Mary get along fine enough. Him and Hawthorn, too. It's just that it's usually Mary he sees, Mary who does the drop-offs. They exchange pleasantries whenever they see each other at the school. Each has had the other's child over for playdates. Once they had a long talk while sitting in the bleachers of the Kerrisdale Play Palace watching their kids on the bouncy equipment. They're not exactly close, though, not close-close anyway, so Steve isn't certain if Mary is going to take him up on his offer. In fact if he had to guess what she was going to say, he'd guess she'd say, Thanks but no thanks, which is possibly why he offered in the first place.

Mary fixes her posture. "Are you sure? Don't you have to work?"

Adi tugs on the bottom of Mary's coat.

Steve shrugs.

Mary leans down again.

What is he supposed to say? "It's alright."

Adi is whispering something in her mother's ear.

On the one hand he's always working. A pastor's work is never finished, not really. Not until death. Is anyone's? On the other hand he does have a fair bit of actual work to do: prep for tonight's evensong service; Maundy Thursday tomorrow; Good Friday the day after and he hasn't finished his sermon; Easter; his sister's wedding in Maui two Saturdays later which, sure, he's not officiating because he doesn't have credentials to officiate a wedding in Hawaii, but she did ask him to write something and read it during the ceremony and he hasn't finished that yet either; a stack of emails to respond to; what else? Probably shouldn't have offered to babysit then.

"As long as Adi doesn't mind coming to a lunch meeting with me and maybe waiting at the office while I get a few things done." He has to prep for next week's elders' meeting, too. "The car is in the shop today so we'll have to foot it."

* ^_^

6

"What about it, Adi?" Mary runs her fingers through Adi's fine russet-colored hair. "Do you want to hang out with Steve?"

"Please," sugary with zero hesitation. She cocks her head back and looks up at Mary, smiling with alacrity.

"You sure it's okay?"

"I wouldn't have offered if it weren't."

Mary thanks Steve, looks quizzically at Adi, shakes her head, sighs, kisses her on the cheek. She takes the Moomintroll pack from Adi's back, thanks Steve again. "You're a life-saver," she says and offers him some money to cover the cost of Adi's lunch. "Or she could just take the one I packed for her."

"It's fine, don't worry about it," refusing to take the money. "It's nothing. Lunch is going to be potstickers."

"Sounds delicious." Mary puts her wallet away and thanks Steve again, then follows the cement path from the side of the school to the sidewalk toward her car, a silver VW Tiguan, parked on the other side of the street, sunroof open. Steve and Adi remain between the heavy doors and the cement steps waiting until Mary has looked both ways and safely crossed the road at the designated crosswalk, and now she has. She remotely unlocks her car, gets behind the wheel, starts the engine, pulls on her seatbelt, almost certainly fastening it, though Steve can't know for certain whether she's fastened it or not. He can't see from where he's standing. As sure as he might be that she's buckled in, a person can't know a thing for certain if he hasn't verified it with his own eyes. Mary gives a casual wave from behind the window. Steve waves back. She checks the sideview mirror—judging by the tilt of her head—then the rearview. All clear. She's driving off.

Wait.

A U-turn first so she can face the other direction. She'd been facing the wrong way. Annoying how people do that. A sign of entitlement, though Steve tries to ignore it in her on account of Sam and Adi being friends.

Not a U-turn. A three-, no, make that five-point turn. Watch out for that lousily parked BMW, though. Aren't they all? Yes that's it. Careful, careful. Careful. There.

Mary shifts back into drive and approaches the traffic lights where no other cars are waiting because it's so long after school has started the drop-off queue is no more. Then a sharp left joining the other westward-bound vehicles.

Steve takes his phone from his pocket and checks the time. It's 9:14. He shifts his attention from the road to Adi, who's eyeing the empty playground. "Did you have breakfast?"

She shakes her head, her ponytail swinging side to side.

"Me neither. Should we go to Starbucks? Get something to eat?"

"I don't have any money, though."

"I have a loaded gold card."

Adi shrugs.

"You can get a kid's hot chocolate," thinking what else might Sam get. "And a muffin?"

"Let's play." Adi extends an arm, pointing a budding pianist's finger toward the playground.

"Probably not a good idea to play right here." Steve grits his teeth. "What if Mrs. Canard comes out? Or worse, Mr. E.?"

Adi's chin is a contemplative scrunch, her head at a five-degree angle. "Alright."

They head off the school grounds, a slow march. Steve leads the way, retracing the route he took some fifteen minutes ago with Sam, down the four cement steps—

four

three

two

one

—across the shoe-trampled dirt path worn in the middle of the grass lawn, back onto the deserted sidewalk. It's been maybe eighteen seconds since they started toward Starbucks and already there's that awkward silence, that discomfiting quiet, punctuated by two birds chirping it sounds like—European starlings? Red-winged blackbirds?—and a lawnmower and cars zipping by in the distance on King Ed.

"Sorry you aren't feeling well."

"Look, a silkworm." Adi has stopped beneath a cherry blossom sapling, her nose tipped skyward. Suspended at the end of a wispy thread dangling from a crooked branch is a single shamrock-colored, toothpick-sized silkworm. It wiggles, contorts its body into a pilcrow.

"Neat," for want of anything cleverer.

"Did you know silkworms become moths?"

"I did."

Adi wrinkles her nose. "Well, did you know there are people who eat silkworms?"

"It doesn't look very appetizing to me, but if you want to give it a try."

"Eww."

Steve laughs.

"You shouldn't encourage a kid to eat moth larva."

For a moment he thinks about telling Adi the grossest thing he's ever eaten, some Vietnamese delicacy, then asking her what disgusting food or foods she's tried.

They resume walking, Adi next to him now, on his right.

Steve, his hands in the front pockets of his jeans, is trying to compile a mental list of things to talk to her about—the weather—the Canucks' game last night, a 5-4 shootout win—talk about school—about how he used to walk to school every day when he was a kid—what else? The Vietnamese dish he ate that one time, and why he forced it all down—other disgusting things he's eaten—traveling—places he's been: India, Switzerland, Toronto—places she's been—has she been to Wales? Hawaii? Disneyland?—books she's reading—music—activities she does: piano lessons and what else? ballet? gymnastics? swimming? art? Chinese school? Spirit of Math?—who her other friends are at school—what about the boys in her class?—would she want to come with Sam to church one day? Should he ask that? The most important thing is to keep her safe. And what with all the inattentive, distracted, flat-out incompetent drivers in the city, especially this part of the city it seems, here and in Richmond and Delta and Burnaby and Surrey, that should be enough. Safe and fed. They cross the street. No talk of God unless it comes up organically and she's the one who brings it up. He could talk about how Adi is a Jess McConnell look-a-like. Does she know who that is? He could ask her. Does she have any American Girl dolls? He could ask her that, too. Sam wasn't named after Samantha Parkington. Someone asked him that once. What kind of parent would do a thing like that? It's better than being named after an athlete. Not by much. She does have a Samantha doll, though. They've both been archived now, Samantha and Jess, but they're still possible to find on eBay. He could tell her about these dolls. Jess might even be half-Welsh like Adi. If not Welsh, then Irish, maybe. He could tell her a joke. Steve slows, allowing Adi to pass him. He moves to her right, forcing her a stride to the left where she'll be safer, farther from the road.

"Where do the happiest people work?" shifting his eyes from the street to Adi, just for a moment.

"A satisfactory."

"Hey," not trying to hide his disappointment. "How did you know?"

"Sam told me it before."

"Oh."

"It's not that funny."

"Sure it is."

She looks unconvinced.

"Do you ever walk to school with your mom or dad?" He knows they don't. She lives cross-boundary, a ten-minute drive in decent traffic.

"Once we rode our bikes."

"Sam and I don't walk that often either. Only when we're running early," which is almost never, "and on days like today when there's something wrong with the car."

Adi's face is vernal.

"But when I was your age I used to walk to school everyday with my grandma." Over by the curb a landscaper reaches into the back of a gray pick-up, grabs some gardening tools Steve recognizes, but can't identify by name. "Whatever the weather, hot, cold, rain, snow, we'd walk there and back, half-an-hour each way."

"Snow?"

"This was in Toronto. Have you heard of Toronto?"

"Of course," her pupils enlarging as if in annoyance.

"Some kids have never been out of British Columbia. Anyway, I lived in Toronto, briefly. Some of my aunts and uncles still do. There are as many snowy days there as there are rainy days here."

"I know that."

"You know a lot of things, don't you?"

"I *am* six-and-a-half."

"I was living in Toronto when I was about your age. We'd just moved from Taiwan where I was born, to this beat-up, janky two-bedroom apartment on Bleecker Street in this pretty rough part of the city called St. James Town. It's probably gentrified today. Me, my parents, my grandmother on my father's side, and my sister Emily. She was a newborn then. My first year in Toronto, I was in grade one at Rose Avenue Public School in Mrs. Knight's class. She was the best, but I used to hate going to school. I had no friends. I was biblically shy back then, too. So my grandma and I would walk across this big grass field"—had he pronounced the R clearly?—"to get from home to school and vice versa, and in the winter it would freeze over so we'd have to go around it, and kids from the neighborhood would be there skating, playing hockey, most of them wearing blue and white Maple Leafs jerseys, which were unaffordable even then, but somehow these kids had them. I had no friends, couldn't skate, was too timid to ask anyone to teach me, and I didn't have a Leafs jersey. All I could do was watch the other boys play while we trudged back to the apartment."

"Sometimes I'm shy."

"Kind of sucks."

"Yeah, but sometimes I just don't feel like talking."

"Nothing wrong with that." They turn a corner. "I preach every week now, but believe it or not, I used to hate public speaking. At recess and lunch, you know how you and Sam and Hailey and everyone else go out to play? Mrs. Knight used to let me stay in and read. Once she even gave me a book."

"Which one?"

"*The Hockey Sweater.*"

"Hockey is boring."

"Blasphemy," shooting her a look of faux indignation. "Even if you don't like hockey, you'd like the book. *The winters of my childhood were long, long seasons. We lived in three places—the school, the church and the skating-rink—but our real life was on the skating-rink.*"

"What are you even talking about?"

"That's how the book begins."

"You memorized it? Sounds boring."

"It's on the five dollar bill." Steve pulls his wallet out of his back pocket, checks the billfold. No fives. No paper money of any kind, only tattered receipts. "It's about this boy in Quebec." He stuffs the wallet back. "All the kids have Montreal Canadiens sweaters, so naturally he wants one, too, more than anything else. Instead, his mom orders him a Toronto Maple Leafs sweater."

"That's mean."

"I guess," discreetly adjusting his boxers, which are riding up in the back.

"Why would she do that?"

"I can't remember. It was an accident or something. Anyway, like it or not, it's what he got. You get what you get."

11

"And you don't get upset."

"So he wears it," nodding, "reluctantly, and all the other boys kind of tease him about it. And that's the story. Anyway, my mom, who couldn't really understand English when I was six, six-and-a-half, she saw the book in my backpack, flipped through it, trying to follow along by looking at the pictures. Occasionally she'd ask me to explain something. And she thought what better gift to get me for my first Canadian Christmas, which was my first Christmas ever, since we never celebrated it in Taiwan—we were Buddhists in Taiwan—what better gift to help me make new friends than the same sweater that all the popular boys in the book were wearing. So Christmas morning, I wake up, run to the gold Buddha statue on one of our ratty living room tables, and under the table there's this box wrapped in this garish snowman-pattern wrapping paper, and my name is written on it. My Chinese name. Tu Jì Fun. I rip it open," Steve mimes the gesture, pauses for effect. "It was a Montreal Canadiens sweater. My mom thought I'd be more popular if I wore what all the boys in the book wore. I told my parents I wouldn't wear it, but my dad said red is a lucky color." Steve pats the top of a mailbox at the northeast corner of Angus and 29th, checks to make sure there aren't any oncoming vehicles, leads Adi across the street. "Then he said it was an expensive sweater so I had to wear it."

"Did you ever get the one you wanted?"

"End of that school year. My grandma was moving back to Taiwan. Her daughters—my aunts—they still lived there and my grandma missed them. Before she left she gave me a present in a box wrapped in newspaper. I didn't think there could possibly be anything special inside so I didn't open it right away, not until she was already on the plane, but when I did, there it was: my first ever Leafs jersey: a kid-sized Allan Bester, number 30. He was my favorite player. We moved to Vancouver the next year, in part to be closer to Taiwan."

"That didn't really happen."

Steve nods. "I still have the jersey." He's saving it to give to Sam when she's a bit taller. They'll get tickets to see the Leafs when they're in town and she'll wear it to the game.

"Does your grandma still live in Taiwan?"

He shakes his head.

His grandmother, the one who gave him the Leafs sweater, last visited Vancouver five years ago, 2007, before Daphne was born, when Sam was still a baby, when they were still renting in Kits. She came with one of Steve's aunts. Her dementia was advancing. Steve gave them a tour of the city in a white Dodge Caravan he rented for the week, and every twenty seconds his grandmother would pipe up from the passenger seat, ask where they were, and every time Steve would answer truthfully, Vancouver. But what difference did it make, it's not like she knew what they were talking about, so on about the seventh or eighth time she asked, Steve said we're in Taiwan, and her eyes got all big and buggy in a good way, full of wonder, and they glistened and she smiled a bigger smile than Steve had ever seen her smile before, which is the truth, trite as it sounds, and she said again, Taiwan? it looks different but yes yes oh my Taiwan. Which is a translation; her actual words had been in Mandarin.

"My grandma died on Valentine's Day." Adi tucks some stray hairs behind her ear.

"Valentine's just a couple of months ago?"

Nodding.

"Your mom's mom or your dad's?" What a stupid question, but it's too late now.

"My mom's."

A black Escalade, tinted windows, drives past them, slows up ahead at Maple, makes a right.

Steve isn't sure if Adi is telling the truth and he feels bad, a little, about his distrusting spirit, but kids lie. Not as much as adults, sure, but they make up stories and sometimes those stories have an air of credibility to them.

Adi's face is sepulchral.

"You must be sad."

"I'm always sad."

"It'll get better."

"That makes me more sad."

"Why?"

"Because it means I won't remember her. Being sad is proof that her life mattered. If I feel better, it means she didn't really count that much."

Adi does seem to be more sensitive than the other first-grade girls in Sam's class. It's not like he knows any of them very well, though. He doesn't know Adi that well either. Besides: always sad? That's all-or-nothing thinking and overgeneralization. Also magnification.

"Is your favorite *Winnie the Pooh* character Eeyore?"

She thinks for a second. "Rabbit."

They cross a no-longer-used railroad track running along the ridge of the low-grade hill they've been descending since leaving the school. Overgrown wild grass and not a few weeds springing from the spaces between the rotted wood and rusted steel bristle against their legs, and there's ballast poking at the underside of Steve's feet through the thinning-but-still-intact rubber soles of his shoes, which are only a few months old, from Aldo. He thinks they're rubber, anyway. What are soles made of? Across the tracks, two roughly parallel routes present themselves. To the left, an unpaved path coiling around a handful of massive firs turning a little ways from here into a 1.3km-long gravel trail that encircles Quilchena Park; to the right, an asphalt alleyway leading to a residential street that bends around the west side of the park. Both routes will get them where they want to go: down to Valley Drive, a small two-lane residential road where Steve and his family live in a too-small condo, then from there a short walk across Arbutus to Starbucks. He & Sam almost always take the path through the park when they walk to school or back home even though it takes a little longer, so that's what he and Adi do—they go left. He's about to ask her why she's always sad, when Adi spots the park's dilapidated playground a hundred yards away, through the trees, beyond the buildings that house the washrooms and the maintenance supplies. She wants to go. She's tugging at Steve's navy windbreaker, saying, Playground playground playground playground playground playground, and she's jumping as she says it and pulling at his jacket and she's not doing this delicately either, she's practically dragging him. A four-legged tuft of mottled chestnut-colored fur darts down one tree, scampers over some raised roots, races up another, claws scratching bark.

"Chipmunk." It scurries up one of the cedars.

Adi slows her pace, watches until it disappears in a thick cluster of needles. "Playground."

"How about after we get some food?"

"Playground."

"Don't you want to eat something first?"

"Playground pleeeeeeease," elongating her supplication all syrupy-like.

There's no sense resisting. Kids like Adi, once they've got their minds made up about a thing, good luck changing it. Reminds him of a verse from First or possibly Second Samuel. Men and women change their minds willy-nilly. God is not a man. Children aren't prone to vacillation like their parents. They're like God. They're like mules.

Steve and Adi are through the trees now, on the main trail perambulating the park. A Lululemon-clad jogger pants by. Steve needs to take up jogging again. Maybe next Monday once the busyness of the season is over. He hasn't been for an outdoor run yet this calendar year and it's starting to show around his hips and neck. He's so fat now the waistband of his boxers folds over itself when he's not doing anything, when he's just standing still. Time was he'd do four laps around Quilchena Park every day, first thing in the morning, 1.3km per lap, 5.2km total. The proximity to the park was one of the major selling points of the condo they purchased when Daphne was born. It took him twenty-odd minutes to run these four laps, less on days when it was raining or cold, when he'd move a few steps faster. He used to stick to his schedule like clockwork: wake at the first chime of his phone alarm, 5:43a, never hitting snooze because there are two kinds of people in the world, those who hit snooze and those who don't and Steve is the kind who doesn't, a habit he began to form senior year at Penn when he kept a passage from Proverbs framed on the bedside table next to his clock: A little sleep, a little slumber, a little folding of the hands to rest, and poverty will come on you like a thief, and want like an armed man. Then a quick coffee, or tea, if he'd neglected to clean the French press after he'd used it last, and out the door, across the street to the park. Most mornings he ran alone, though occasionally some other joggers were there. Chances are, the weather being what it has been these last couple days, sun rather than rain clouds, there have been more people outside running. He used to finish his run and be home by 6:30, 6:35, then make breakfast for the family, rouse the kids, help them get washed and changed into the clothes they hopefully picked out the night before but probably didn't, then fed. What changed? Why hasn't he been out for a run in over four months? Steve doesn't know why exactly, but whatever the reason, it's about time he runs again. He resolves to do so. It might take him a few consecutive mornings to get back to the low-twenties. No matter. He needs to lose some weight, some fat. Fat will kill a man before his daughters are married, before he's walked them down the aisle or officiated their weddings if this man is also an ordained minister. God, he could go for a jelly donut and coffee right now. Adi, skipping, navigates the unoccupied skateboard ramps, Steve right behind her. Three leaps to ford a narrow patch of dewy grass—hop—skip—jump—and they're at the playground.

"Monkey bars!" Adi runs past the chain-link ladder, ignores the wooden foot bridge, the plastic tube tunnel, the slide, the swings, and darts straight for the monkey bars. "Help me up," jumping, arms raised, palms open, a grunt.

"Later." Still a few feet away, Steve moves to one of the two swings. He takes his phone from his pocket and sits on the narrow black seat. "Why don't you play on some of the other equipment first?"

She glares, hands in fists at her waist. "Fine."

Steve slides his thumb across the glass screen of his phone. There are no new texts, and the red oval above the envelope icon reads 6,538, same as when he & Sam left home. Exhale. He launches a Bible app, scrolls to find the text he's scheduled to preach from on Good Friday. Both his feet are on the ground, but the swing he's resting on is swaying a little and it's making him queasy so he stands and as he does he looks for Adi who hasn't gone to play on some other piece of playground equipment after all, but has somehow managed to shimmy up one of the monkey bars' wooden support beams. Her left hand is on the first rung, her legs knotted around the post.

"Careful up there."

She smiles mischievously, releases her legs and swings chimpanzee-like, making quick work of the bars. Seconds after starting she's already at the other end. "I can skip, too," shouting. "Watch."

"Be careful."

She swings from the first bar to the third then tries for the fifth, but her hand slips or she misses it, it all happens so fast, too fast for Steve to catch exactly what went wrong, and before he can react there's a cavernous thud and Adi is on the ground, face down, struggling to get to her elbows and knees, and she's whimpering.

"Are you okay?" running toward her, sliding his phone back in his pocket. For a moment he wonders whether he'd be more worried if it had been one of his own kids who'd fallen, but it's a logically impossible hypothetical. If it had been one of his own daughters, wouldn't he have been a foot away the whole time, arms at the ready, prepared for the worst? He crouches by Adi's side. Her face is awash in tears and there's a scrape on her chin, but no blood, thank God.

"Am I bleeding?" She flicks loose a few pea gravel pebbles that had been stuck to her palms.

"Doesn't look like it," giving her the once over.

She scoots up, sitting on her bum. "I'm going to try again."

"Not a good idea."

Adi is that interstitial age between doesn't-know-better naïveté and danger-be-damned daring. Put simply, she needs direction.

They stand. For no particular reason Steve reaches for the metal bar that Adi had missed.

"It's wet." He wipes his palm on his pants. "That must be why you slipped."

"Captain Obvi."

"You're lucky you weren't hurt."

"You're lucky, too," blinking back the last of her tears. "My mom would have been so mad."

"It could've been a lot worse. Dante in your class? Sam & I were here with him last year. Well, we didn't come together. We happened to be here at the same time. He lives in one of those condos across the street," pointing in that general direction. "He was running around not that far from this spot, playing freeze tag or grounders, something like that, and he wasn't paying attention and out of nowhere he tripped and fell flat on his face just like you did. Except two of his teeth fell out and were lost in the rocks."

"I don't like the playground when other kids are there."

"Blood was everywhere."

"Cool."

"It was scary actually. Especially for his mom. Plus we never found his teeth so the tooth fairy never went to his place," pointing at the condos across from the park again, as they walk toward one of the logs enclosing the playground. Steve checks to make sure there aren't any ants or other insects—pill bugs, silverfish, earwigs—crawling by the spot he's about to sit on. There aren't. Satisfied, he sits.

Adi sits, too.

"Actually, I wrote a poem about what happened to Dante. Sam brought it for Drop Everything And Read Day."

"I don't think so." Adi is slouched over, staring at the grass just beyond her feet.

"She read it to the class."

"Probably not."

"She told me she did."

"I'd remember."

"I think I have it on my phone." Steve transfers his weight from one leg to the other so he can more easily take his phone from his pocket. "Do you want to read it?"

Adi exaggerates an eye roll. "Fine."

It's 9:34.

Steve opens his email, thumb-types the full title of his poem in the search bar, minus punctuation and capitalization even though a well-chosen titular fragment like the style guides recommend/insist upon will likely serve just as well. *Dante's eyes a rhyme.* The spellcheck algorithm recognizes *dantes* is missing an uppercase D and an apostrophe, and autocorrects. There is no automatically generated colon between *eyes* and *a*.

The search yields a single result.

Steve taps it and passes the phone to Adi.

He clears his throat as she begins reading, her eyes moving left to right across the 3.5-inch screen. Steve shifts his gaze, landing on a woman walking a half-dozen leashed dogs in the distance at the other end of the park. She's wearing one of those cyan volunteer jackets from the 2010 Olympics. Adi is still reading.

If she has a more plaintive temperament than most kids, maybe it has something to do with how she was conceived. On their first date her parents had gone for coffee after dinner. Mary had told Steve the name of the coffee place that day the two of them sat together at the Play Palace, but he'd forgotten almost as soon as she'd said it. He doesn't remember the restaurant name either. That island-themed place near the Public Market he wants to try, where every dish on the menu is from some island or another—PEI steak, Jamaican curry beef, Tasmanian abalone with black truffles, etc. Whatever the names of the places they went, Mary and Hawthorn had gone for coffee, that's what's relevant. She'd emptied a pack of sugar in her cup. He'd opted for Sweet'N Low. He poured it in his drink and continued delicately tearing away at the paper. Mary told Steve she'd thought it was a nervous tick or a bad habit, like Hawthorn didn't know what to do with his hands except rip, which was a major turn-off. But then he handed her the tiny paper rectangle he'd carefully torn from the pink packet. In baby blue ink it read: the sweetness of two. They were engaged one month later. After Mary told Steve this story he did the same thing for Lola thinking it would lift her spirits. Instead she was worried he'd accidentally spilled artificial sweetener on their carpet, which would have led to all manner of insects—ants, pill bugs, silverfish, earwigs. He hadn't spilled any, though. He'd blown on the piece of sweetener paper when he was still outside, and again in the condo hallway just to be sure. Mary's parents were furious when she and Hawthorn told them they were engaged, and not because he hadn't asked for their blessing. That wouldn't have helped. They were furious because he was a *gwai lo*. If she went ahead with the wedding, they wouldn't be there. Maybe Mary was exaggerating, but it sounded plausible. Of course she'd hoped they'd show up. Not that their being there would have meant they'd finally come around and given her and Hawthorn their blessing necessarily, but at least the four of them would have been in the same room, and there's something to be said for the father and mother of the bride being physically present at their daughter's wedding even if said parents were splenetic about the relationship, even if they remained inimical to her choice of partner, better them there than not. If Sam marries someone he doesn't approve of, Steve will show up at the wedding. Won't he? He wouldn't officiate it, but he'd still turn up, still hold his peace, right? So when minutes before Mary and Hawthorn were to exchange their vows and both her parents arrived and her father even said he'd walk her down the aisle, she was understandably ecstatic. It didn't matter that they were only there to save face or that her father had called Hawthorn her husband *pro tem*. All of that was forgivable, changeable, fixable. There was no bruising her spirit. And anyway, they'd see in him what she saw, it was only a matter of time and maybe grandchildren. They'd grow to love him as she did. Mary was sanguine about the whole thing. Life together with Hawthorn was off to the auspicious start she'd dreamed of. The whole time she was telling this story to Steve her face was ashen so he had a pretty good idea it wasn't going to have a happy ending. Real lives never end happily ever after. The battle is not to the strong. Then came the reception. Mary had feared her father would drink too much, say something inappropriate, but he was unusually abstemious all through dinner, which eased her worries. It wasn't until everyone was dancing that he made a commotion. She hadn't noticed at first, but as more and more of her guests crowded around the table where her parents were seated, she knew he was at the center of it and feared he was about to embarrass her. What he was doing, though, was clutching his chest, which she saw once she'd made her way through the crowd huddled around him. Someone called 911. It was a blur. Surreal is the word she used, of course. It was surreal. The doctors told her later that night that he'd suffered a heart attack; a minor one as far as heart attacks go, but a cardiac episode nonetheless. He looked alright, though, when Mary and Hawthorn saw him in his hospital bed, and the attending physician had reassured them that they'd keep him a few nights, at least: monitor his vitals, that sort of thing. She'd asked her mother if she and Hawthorn should go ahead with their honeymoon because their flight to Paris was only a few hours away, first thing in the morning, or if they should cancel. Her mother told them to go, so they did. Is she supposed to be able to read minds? They landed in Paris, checked in to their hotel, made love. Steve had felt a little awkward when Mary told him this, although what did he think they did the first night of their honeymoon? He tried unsuccessfully not to picture them. Only the next day did she and Hawthorn see the blinking red light on the phone in their room and check the message waiting for them. It was one of Mary's brothers. Her father had had another heart attack, a fatal one this time. That afternoon Mary and Hawthorn were on a flight back home. Adi arrived nine months later, conceived in Paris. Steve asked how they knew it happened that night. No sex for a month after her dad died. Customary mourning period. Maybe that's an adumbration of Adi's life, who knows? Do you believe in reincarnation? Mary had asked Steve. Because maybe her father's soul was reborn in Adi's body. The possibility comforted her.

"What does ordained mean?" Adi hands the phone back to Steve.

"Like, destined to happen."

"Oh." She looks out toward the skateboard ramps, nods.

"What do you think?"

"About what?"

"The poem." Steve shifts his weight again and tucks the phone back in his pocket.

"It's alright. Good, I guess. Except I don't know that word. You should use words people understand."

"Or you can learn new words."

Adi shrugs. "Yeah. True."

"Do you remember Sam reading it to your class now?"

"Nope."

"You don't?"

Adi leans forward, picks up a twig that had been resting by her feet. "She never read it."

Could Sam have lied? Maybe Adi had been absent that day, at home, a fever or cold or something, which would explain why Mary is out of sick days.

Adi is digging around in the ground with the twig.

"Are you sure? I'm pretty sure she did. She told me she did."

"I'm sure." Adi is jabbing at something in the dirt. "I'm the smartest kid in the class."

"You are very smart, that's true." Smartest, though? That's difficult, impossible to say for certain, despite the fact Adi sometimes sounds like a thirty-year-old trapped in a six-year-old's body. Besides Sam is the smartest. In kindergarten Adi and Sam were in the same class so Steve has a good idea how smart all the kids are relative to one another, not that that's very important to him. He's Chinese, yeah, but not that Chinese. Still: there was that one time when Ms. Irwin gave her kindergarten class a problem to solve: everyone had a clear plastic cup filled with water, a paper clip submerged at the bottom, a magnet on their desks. Their mission: to remove the clip without sticking their fingers in the cup and without spilling any water. Sam, Ms. Irwin had told Steve after school that day, the day she'd made the class try the magnet problem, and please call me Katharine she'd added, or Kate if you prefer, was the only one who figured out how to do it with the magnet. Adi, on the other hand, had swallowed the water then stuck out her tongue, proudly producing the clip. Sam was the one who told Steve that bit. Ms. Irwin had only said one of the students drank the water, not naming names. She's a great teacher, though. She asked for Steve, specifically, by name, to volunteer for their field trips to the Burnaby Village Museum, the Gulf of Georgia Cannery, and Lonsdale Quay. When Sam's kindergarten year was over, she gave him a thank you card with a silkscreened print of Bluffwood on the front. You're the most fun, helpful, dedicated parent I've ever had, she'd written in it, which made him inordinately happy even though she'd only been teaching for what, four years? five? how many parents could that even be? a hundred, give or take? Hopefully Daphne will have her when she's in kindergarten.

"There's nothing here." Adi sits up straight and snaps the twig in two, holding one piece in each hand.

"You didn't dig deep enough." An inch at most. "If there's anything down there, you have to work for it."

"I don't feel like it anymore."

"Here. Give it." Steve takes the longer of the two twig pieces and picks up where Adi left off.

If there's one thing he doesn't like, it's quitting in the middle of a thing. Quitting and Vietnamese food. It's not quitters or Vietnamese people he has little to no tolerance for, it's what the quitter does: the action. And what the Vietnamese person cooks: the noodle soup.

Adi stands up, returns to the playground.

Steve digs. If precious stones were on the earth's surface where anyone could find them, they wouldn't be precious, just stones. It's the effort a
person is required to make in uncovering the sardius topaz diamond beryl
onyx the jasper the sapphire emerald carbuncle the gold, that endows them
with more worth than a plain old rock. You don't get gold without work.
Like the one-tenth scale violin Sam is learning to play and not at all enjoy-
ing. She wants to quit, do something easier like the piano, because it's hard
making the instrument sound the way she wants, the way Ms. Cecily makes
it sound. Her fingers have to be curled just right, placed on the correct
string, in the precise spot, and then her bow hand needs to be steady, too,
steady along the Kreisler Highway. On top of all that she has to remember
to smile. Steve has been trying to encourage her to persevere—practice
makes better, he tells her, etc.—but Sam can't see that far into the future
and abstract analogies can only accomplish so much in a six year old. But
here's an idea: the next time she whines about wanting to quit, he can use
this digging he's doing as a tangible illustration of what hard work and per-
sistence can yield. Yes, good idea. It'll work even better if he can whip out a
sparkling geode when he tells her—the fruit of his labor, proof that faithful,
determined resilience pays off, even if he doesn't necessarily believe it himself. Bread is not to the wise. A very good idea. He should write this down
somewhere so he doesn't forget. Thank God for smartphones. A smile starts
to form, then disappears. Is that too irreverent? Is any amount of irrever-
ence too irreverent? Who decides? God, Steve supposes, but is there a line
a person can't cross? His phone is out of his pocket now, in his hand, a note
app open, the twig he'd been digging with next to him.

Tell Sam to dig beauty beneath

He exits the app and tucks the phone back in his pocket, adjusting it
once it's in so it's aligned properly, parallel with his leg. Then he picks up a
pebble by his feet and flings it at the trunk of a small tree. Miss. He picks up
another pebble, flings it, misses again. He picks up the twig.

"Did Sam finish her homework?" Adi is back. The hole she started is a
good five inches deeper now, a little wider, too, but still empty.

"What homework?"

"The fable."

"Which one was that?"

"You know. The fable from your family tradition."

"Rings a bell." It doesn't. Sam almost never tells him anything if he
doesn't ask and even then she doesn't usually give specifics unless it's

something that has impressed her. Very little impresses her. Steve rarely asks Sam about homework because, frankly, he's always too busy. Also he doesn't ask her about homework because she's only in the first grade. But come to think of it, a few weeks ago he'd mentioned something about making up a fable to tell at his sister's wedding, something about bees and plumerias —he better finish that soon—and Sam had said they were learning about fables in class—Connection!—*connection* being a word she'd taken to saying back then, a few weeks ago, when something one person said intersected with something she'd heard in school. Mrs. Canard says it a lot, apparently. Sam hadn't mentioned any homework at the time.

"I didn't finish."

"Your fable?"

Nodding.

"Why not?"

"I don't know how to end it."

"When's it due?"

"Yesterday."

Did Sam do her homework? Steve scratches some more at the bottom of the hole. There's something offering resistance. "I hit something."

"I don't see anything," peering down.

Steve sticks the tips of his right thumb, index, and middle fingers in the dirt, feeling for the object he'd struck with the twig, which he's dropped on the ground now. There's something there alright. He's got it between his fingers, wiggling it free. Ta-da! A stone. It's brown from the dirt, but beneath that is green, neon green almost, and the more dirt Steve wipes off, the greener the stone becomes until most of the dirt is gone and boy is that stone ever green and crystalline.

"Cool," big eyes, big grin. "A shiny."

Steve rubs it between the flats of his fingers. "Pretty neat, right?"

"Can I have it?" looking at him expectantly.

"I'm going to give it to Sam."

"No, you're not."

"I will."

"You're just joking."

"I'm not."

"You're going to give it to me."

"I won't."

"But my chin hurts," sticking it out.

"This rock won't make it feel any better."

"It might. How do you know it won't?"

"Because."

"Because what? Because isn't a reason."

"I'll pray that you'll feel better."

"What's pray?"

"It's asking God for things, sort of." He should be more precise, even with a kid. Especially with a kid, but what more can he say about something he doesn't himself understand? Steve closes his eyes and counts to three in his head. One. Two. Two-and-a-half. Three. He opens his eyes. Adi is still staring at him, still pawing at her scrape.

"Is that pray?" She touches her scrape. "It didn't work."

"The results of prayer are rarely immediate." And sometimes the answer is no. Convenient.

"My chin hurts even more."

"Really," not intoned to sound like a question.

"Can I have the shiny now?" arms outstretched.

He wants to give it to Sam. Sam would really love it. It would reinforce his practice-makes-better speech for sure. But then again he never would have found it, wouldn't have even been there in the park in the first place if it weren't for Adi, so he relents, which, come to think of it, is kind of what it means for a thing to be ordained.

"Fine." He underhand tosses it back in the hole.

"Thanks, Steve." In no time at all she has retrieved it.

"We should get going."

Adi is breathlessly admiring the stone resting in her hand.

"Adi."

"Huh?"

"Time to go now."

"Go where?"

"Starbucks. Breakfast, remember?"

"I'm not hungry."

"If you want to stay and play, give me back the rock."

Adi makes a sort of sneer.

"I'll hold it for you. It's not like you can play while you're holding that."

Adi furrows her brow as if thinking about what Steve has just said, but who knows what's actually going on inside her head? "Alright. We can go. But only because you want to so bad."

"Good." Steve stands up.

Adi follows suit. "Just so you know, though," slipping the green stone into one of her coat pockets, "I have a pocket I can put the shiny in so if I wanted to stay and play here I could and I wouldn't have to give it back to you." She takes it out of her pocket, shows him, then places it back. "But since you did give it to me, I'll go."

"You're very kind."

"I know."

The thing is, Steve needs to pee. He could use the public restroom by the playground, but then he'd have to leave Adi outside, alone. Unwise. Be sober, be vigilant. Roaring lions take on all forms. Sure, there's no one else around right now except the dog walker and sure, she looks harmless and obviously loves animals, how bad could she be? But you never know. Janis loves dogs. It's not that you should always expect the worst in people. Sometimes, though. Besides, in the time it takes him to pee and wash his hands, someone else might turn up. How long does it take him to pee and wash his hands? a minute? less if the sink happens to be broken—nasty—still: whatever length of time it takes—hands rinsed, soaped, dried, or not—is too long. On the other hand if he waits until they get to Starbucks to pee, he'll still have to leave her alone, but at least they'll be indoors and contained, a cloud of witnesses to deter any would-be predators. The baristas, most of whom he knows by name, can help keep an eye on her, too. Is Rachel working today? It's Wednesday, so maybe. Yes, it's definitely safer to wait until they get to Starbucks. Steve has peed at the Starbucks before so he knows the restrooms there aren't the cleanest in the world. It's hard to imagine the playground one isn't many degrees worse.

What a funny word: *pee*. It's the exact word that pops into Steve's head as the urge to do it occurs and the subsequent, almost simultaneous realization that he needs to relieve himself unfolds: *pee*, as opposed to, say, *urinate* or *take a leak* or *piss*. Actually, for the longest time he did think to himself *piss*, and speak it aloud. I need to piss, he'd say, but only when in the company of family. If someone else were present, he'd say he needed to use the restroom, usually, or bathroom if he knew as a matter of fact the restroom he'd be using had a bathtub in it. After Sam was born even his private language changed. You have to, Lola had said, adding, You're wrong, and, I don't care if *piss* is in the King James Bible, even if it's in there eight times; we don't live in 1611: *pee* doesn't sound childish: it doesn't sound immature: it sounds kid-appropriate. Which Steve knew was most likely

true. The truth is, it wasn't that hard to change, because he was already sub-
bing *restroom* for *bathroom* on a regular if not frequent basis anyway. It just
wasn't as comfortable, that's all. It's not as natural to always have to think
before speaking, but it's the only way to break old habits and form new
ones. It is a funny word, though: *pee*. The only word for a bodily discharge
that's also a letter of the alphabet.

Steve adjusts his wedding band, scratches with his thumb the inter-
phylangial space between his ring finger and his middle finger, scratches
with his pinkie the space between his ring finger and said pinkie. With the
thumb and index finger of his other hand he picks at the callus beneath
his wedding band. It's the only callus on either of his hands and he picks
at it all the time; caused by excessive gripping of his car's steering wheel,
most likely. Excessive gripping and friction between the wheel and the
ring. Probably if he wouldn't pick at it so often it would heal, regardless of
what caused it, and his hands would be callus-free. Only he can't resist peel-
ing the thickened skin. He tears a piece of it off, delicately, and drops the
separated skin to the earth, trampling it under foot, and as he does there's a
vibrating in his pocket. Steve takes out his phone.

Pls pick up Rx refill. For me from Kerr pharmacy

Is it bad for his sexual/reproductive/general health that he keeps his
phone in the front pocket of his pants so many hours of the day? Maybe
another pocket would be better. He swipes the screen, enters his password
5-5-5-5 and types: *Refill of what?* She's on too many meds for him to remember what each one does, or is supposed to do. Steve turns his head,
looking back to verify that Adi is still following. She is. She's ten or so feet
behind him, admiring her stone. The phone vibrates again.

Manerix

He stops to compose and send his one-word reply and by the time
he hits send, Adi has caught up and passed him. She's reading the plaque
inscribed on the nearby park bench—

IN FOND MEMORY OF F.O. JOHN MONCKTON RCAF 1919–1943
NAVIGATOR OF WELLINGTON BOMBER,
BROTHER OF SYLVIA & GEORGE
BURIED IN HOLLAND AND GOOD FRIEND
W.O. ALBERT HUNTER 1919–1942
PILOT OF HALIFAX BOMBER LOST IN THE NORTH SEA

Steve is walking again, his pace a little quicker. The urge to pee is
considerably greater now than it was when they left the playground, he

suddenly senses, and he's about to ask Adi if she can walk a bit faster when something strikes him on the top of his head and he wonders if it's bird poo—poo isn't the first word that comes to mind, but he quickly edits himself, internally—and without really thinking about the consequences of touching the top of his head if it is bird poo, he shoves his phone in the back pocket that's free, that's not holding his wallet, whereupon it vibrates again, but rather than check what Lola has written or if it even is Lola, he feels the top of his head, the top of his head which is wet and sticky, and bringing his hand down to see what it is, his initial thought is confirmed: bird shit. And he's got some of the gunge on his raw callus.

"Crap," not quietly enough because Adi has heard him.

"What?"

Without stopping, because all he wants to do now is get to Starbucks ASAP so he can get washed and pee, he shows her his hand. "A bird pooped on me."

"Eww, gross," rumple-faced. "On your hand?"

"On my head and then I rubbed some of it off with my hand."

"Are you okay?"

Steve had expected her to laugh, but her face bears zero trace of a smile. "Good thing I'm bald."

He's not, technically. He has a thin layer of hair you could putt a golf ball from. Every 4-6 weeks he goes to the barber shop to have it shaved, which costs $15 plus tip, so $20. Eulette, who always makes jerk goat for church lunches but hasn't been at St. Joe's the last few weeks, once told him his head resembled a roasted breadfruit. The last time he'd gone to get it shaved was a week ago, a fact for which Steve is grateful now, since it ought to be easier to clean off the bird droppings with less hair on his head than more.

"What are you going to do?"

"I'll clean it when we get to Starbucks. We're almost there."

Starbucks is on the southwest corner of Arbutus and Valley. Steve and Adi have made it to the northeast corner now. Vehicular traffic is moving north- and southbound. With the index finger of his right hand, the hand that hasn't been contaminated by bird guano as far as he knows, Steve pushes the pedestrian call button on the nearest traffic pole, pushes it at least a dozen times in rapid succession. Nothing happens. They're crossing to the south side of Valley Drive. Cars are parked along the road, lots of them poorly, lots of them BMWs. They wait there for the lights to change and traffic to stop. This is a pedestrian-controlled intersection, though the crosswalk buttons don't always seem to work because Steve has had to wait there sometimes as long as two minutes after pushing one, maybe they're placebos, but it's working this day, and by the time they're across Valley, the lights are amber, now red, and cars are slowing to a stop. Steve puts his hand, the one that's clean except for some dirt from the digging that yielded the green stone, on the top of Adi's back, directing her across the street while keeping an eye on the cars on either side of them, making sure the drivers are aware their light is red, that their eyes are on the road and not on their phones or elsewhere. For the second time today he thinks Vancouver drivers are the worst in the country. At least they've made it safely across Arbutus. They walk along the sidewalk behind the bus shelter where a lost-pet flyer clings to the frosted glass by two thin strips of tape. It's a slightly longer route, this route they're taking through the plaza parking lot to Starbucks, than it'd be if they cut diagonally through the gas station, which is what Steve does when he's by himself, but with Adi in tow, safe is the word of the day. It's an extra ten steps maybe. Hardly a burden, and besides, it's additional exercise, that's one way to think about it, and God knows Steve could use it. A white cube van, one of those furniture-moving vehicles, is in the wheelchair parking spot in front of the Starbucks even though there's no wheelchair placard anywhere Steve can see on the dash. He looks for one to no avail as he and Adi walk past the van where an Asian man with a foveated face is sitting on the passenger side, eyes closed. There's no one in the driver's seat. Two moustachioed men are lolling at one of the three outdoor tables, each smoking a cigarette. A dog, blue heeler maybe, is leashed to one of the legs of a chair at another table.

They reach the door.

Adi pulls the handle and holds it open for Steve.

"Thanks," stepping through it, inside.

"Age before beauty."

Strange thing for a kid to say, Steve thinks as he stops next to the creamer station. Daughter's "Youth" has just begun playing over the speakers.

"I need to clean my head." Need to hit it, too, he thinks, but keeps that to himself on account of some things being verboten between a man and any female who isn't an immediate family member.

"I said I need to pee," tugging on Steve's windbreaker. "Are you even listening?"

"Let's go."

There are two public-use restrooms at this Starbucks, neither of which are universals. Maybe there's a staff one in the back, Steve doesn't know, he's never been in the back. He wouldn't be surprised if there was; he wouldn't be surprised if there wasn't. Some coffee shops make their employees use the same restrooms as paying customers. Both public-use ones are locked when Steve tries them: first the men's room, then the women's.

"Occupied."

No sooner than he's said it, comes the unmistakable sound of a lock mechanism unlocking. The men's room door opens. Out steps a gloriously old man, tall, heavy-set, his back hunched, wispy silver hair, wire-framed glasses, an unzipped black vest over half-zipped black jacket. Harmless looking. Agedly avuncular. An oversized nylon messenger bag is slung over his shoulder. He holds the door for Steve who says thanks and presses his palm, the clean one, against it, keeping it ajar.

Steve waits until he's out of earshot before asking Adi to wait for the women's room to free, then meet him where they're currently standing when she's done.

"I need to wash up and make room for tea."

"Tea?"

"Just promise you won't go anywhere else."

"Where would I go? I need to pee."

"Good then, okay."

"Can I use yours, though?" pointing into the single-toilet men's room.

"This is the boys' room," shaking his head, but only briefly because as he shakes it he wonders if the movement of his head is causing any of the guano to splatter.

"I really need to go."

"Just wait." Steve really needs to go, too. "I'm sure the woman in there will be out soon. Besides, the men's room is filthy." He pushes the door open a little wider. "See?"

"It doesn't look that bad."

"Look closer," though he hasn't looked for himself. "Someone's peed all over the toilet." An educated guess.

"Disgusting."

"Wait here, okay?"

"Fine."

Steve walks in, closes and locks the door. He moves to the sink, which has one of those no-handle, touchless faucets that never activate on the first attempt except today it does. First the quick-changing traffic light, now this.

It's his lucky day almost. The soap dispenser is also automatic. He passes a wet hand beneath it a couple of times until a white foam froths onto his palm. He lathers, careful to cover any surface of skin that may have touched the bird excrement on his head. The soap stings a few of his fingers, especially the middle one on his left hand, which is particularly dry and cracked today. Possibly because of the weather. Possibly because he's been using it too much as a shoehorn. Once more he rinses his hands, but sloppily, with little concern for getting all the soap off because he's only going to be washing again in a moment, after he uses the toilet. The only reason he's washing first is because there's no way he's going to reach beneath his boxers until he has. He wipes them more or less dry on his pant legs. From the sink it's a few steps to the toilet. Steve unzips his fly as he walks, extracts his flaccid penis with his still-damp fingers, and after another second getting comfortable with it dangling out in a place that's not his own home, commences evacuation. The seat is up and the rim of the bowl is exactly as he'd described it to Adi. Which must mean that the old man who was in here last, who held the restroom door open, had taken a leak, not a dump. Why didn't he put the seat down when he was finished? Steve watches his urine stream. Could it be that there are no women in his life to rebuke him? Or is it more likely a function of this restroom: a men's room: only frequented by men: which is to say perhaps customary domestic etiquette doesn't apply? Whatever the reason, the guy was polite enough to flush. Then again, what if he'd only been in the restroom to wash his hands and wasn't even at the toilet? Someone flushed, anyway. The water in the bowl is clear. Thanks be to him, whoever he was. Steve shakes out the last few drops, tucks things back in place, zips up. He looks, but can't find a lever to press or a button to push. The toilet flushes on its own. Of course it does. What about the seat? Should he nudge it down with the toe of his shoe or shouldn't he? If he doesn't, the next man in might think him rude, which he's not. If he does, the next man will infer he's taken a dump, which he hasn't. It's conceivable the next man will entertain the possibility that Steve is simply a polite person who raises the toilet seat after peeing, which he is. Conceivable, but unlikely. He leaves the toilet as is and goes again to the sink, waves his hand beneath the tap. It takes another try to get the faucet started this time. When it does, Steve wets his hands, cups them, fills them with water, and pours it over his lowered head. The water is cold. Some excess spills into the sink. Some dribbles onto the counter, onto the floor. He repeats, slowly massaging the top of his head the second time and the third, doing his best to get all the bird droppings out. His Chinese name sounds like the term for bird droppings, he suddenly realizes. Chicken droppings, technically. Streaks of white and yellow mingle with the water. A little gets in his eyes. Puke. He rubs them and his forehead with one of his sleeves. Then he checks the mirror above the sink, trying to verify that all of it is gone. He's bobbobbobbing like that perpetual motion drinking bird physics toy. He can't see the top of his head, though. As hard as he tries, as quickly as he bobs, he doesn't have eyes up there, and what's more, now that he's feeling it more carefully, the top of his head feels a little weird, like bumpy, almost onychorrhexic. Has it always been like that? Is everyone's head that way or is it just his skull that's misshapen? Steve dries his hands on his pants, feels for his phone, remembers it's in a back pocket. He takes it out and readies the camera app, then positions the phone as best he can above his head and snaps a shot. The image isn't clear enough to make out anything that strikes him as unusual. He readies the phone for another photo. Snap. The image looks just like the previous one. He pinches the screen, enlarges. The shadows aren't in exactly the same spots, the angle of the photo is a bit off, but otherwise it's identical. The whole exercise is fruitless. It's probably nothing. It's probably just the natural shape of his head. It must have always been this way and he's only just now noticing. What's the name of that pseudoscience?—Phrenology. He shoves the phone into his left front pocket. What's a little more radiation? Near the sink is a manual paper towel dispenser. Steve grabs hold of a sheet with both hands, pulls a perfect pull, takes another. He uses the two coarse napkins to dry off. Then he uses them to pull the knob of the restroom door open before crumpling them into a ball, tossing it point-guard-like behind his back in the waste bin on his way out. Adi is right where he left her.

The Talking Heads' "Uh-Oh, Love Comes to Town" is playing, nearly over.

"Did you wait a long time for me?"

"I haven't gone yet." Her face is semiotic.

"What do you mean? No one has come out?"

"I can't hold it anymore."

"Maybe I should knock." Steve deliberates a moment before rapping his knuckles three times in rapid succession against the women's room door, hard enough that his hand hurts a little. The last person in the line to order food and drink, which is five people deep and extends near the restrooms, turns her head to see what the commotion is.

Joy Division's "Transmission" starts overhead.

"Someone fell in, I think," for the benefit of whoever is close enough to hear him.

Just then there's the sound of a toilet flushing, and a moment later, not long enough for the woman in there to have cleaned her hands even hastily, the door opens and it's a man.

"Sorry," his head doing something between a nod and a kowtow. "Toilet broken."

"That's the women's room," angrily. "My daughter's friend has been waiting for ten minutes."

"Yes yes sorry."

Steve wants to yell some more, but he's mindful of where he is and who else is around. It's unbecoming of a pastor to yell in public, unfitting, and anyway the guy is almost at the exit by this point.

Adi opens the restroom door, takes a step in. "Disssssssgusting!"

Steve looks, getting a nose full of feculence he doesn't associate with females and their restrooms even though he knows better. Then again, it wasn't a woman who made this mess and smell. The water level in the toilet is rising rising still rising has risen to the point where any more and it's going to spill over and now it has.

Steve forces the door shut. "Wait here."

He takes off, hurrying after the man from the women's room. What if this guy visits the church this week? Be reasonable, calm, Christ-like. Through the front window Steve sees him sitting behind the wheel of the white cube van still brazenly squatting in the wheelchair spot, his finger thrust deep in a nostril, digging upward with reckless abandon. He removes his finger, examines the booger it's extracted, flicks it away indiscriminately.

Steve has the Starbucks door open. He's outside and heading toward the van. The engine is running.

"Hey."

The driver doesn't notice. He begins backing out.

"Hey," again, now realizing he hasn't thought this through. He can feel the two men at the outdoor table puffing on their cigarettes staring at the back of his head.

The van halts. The driver-side window rolls down, coming to a stop once it's half open. "What you want? I say sorry."

"You clogged the toilet." Steve is close enough he could reach in and slap the guy. "Don't do that, man."

"Fuck you."

Why don't you get out of your van and say that to my face, Steve wants to say. Instead he takes a nerve-settling breath. "What?"

"Fuck," slower, louder. "You."

"Why don't you get out of your van and say that to my face?"

The driver bends an arm, makes like he's going to unbuckle his seatbelt. Are they about to fight? Steve hasn't been in an honest-to-God fistfight since high school when he slugged Simon Rabinosomething, who, last he heard, was a professor somewhere with low standards, probably. The man in the passenger seat gesticulates dismissively, the creases on his face evincing his annoyance. The guy behind the wheel, the one who overflowed the women's room toilet, the one Steve is possibly ready to cold-cock the instant both his feet are on the pavement, shakes his head as if he's somehow the better man for his restraint. He slides the van into reverse and resumes backing out.

"Jerk," so loud that the smokers and anyone else nearby can hear him. "He used the girls' room and clogged the toilet." Steve watches as the van trundles safely on to Arbutus, not getting sideswiped or rear-ended, not backing into a tree or over the curb even.

Steve makes his way back toward the Starbucks entrance as the van heads north. He wouldn't have been able to live with himself if he'd just turned the other cheek, but he's also glad it didn't come to blows. He unclenches his fists. The dog is on all fours, still, watching him curiously. Steve thinks about petting it because it's a cute dog and only a benevolent soul with self-control and no anger management issues that need addressing could have the confrontation he's just had and care about demonstrating affection toward a dog. He goes inside instead, pausing by the creamer station. Adi is there.

"Did you see what happened?"

"Where?"

"You didn't see me out there just now?"

"No."

"I yelled at that guy, the one who used your restroom."

"Did he say sorry?"

"He was the opposite of sorry."

"He was mean?"

"Very."

The Velvet Underground's "All Tomorrow's Parties" comes on.

"Why?" She pulls a brown napkin from the dispenser and wipes her hands with it.

"Who knows why? Out of the wellspring of the heart, I guess."

"I guess, too."

"What about you? Don't you need to pee?"

"I went already." Adi drops the crumpled napkin into the creamer station hole meant for garbage.

"How?" Her pants look dry.

"She let me use the one she uses," pointing to one of the three baristas behind the counter.

"She did?" Steve doesn't recognize her. "With the hair?"

A vacant nod.

"There's a restroom back there?"

"Yeah."

"Cool."

"The toilet worked. And there wasn't pee on the seat."

Whatever remnant of rage he harbored after his skirmish with the selfish-parking, toilet-clogging, nose-picking draffsack outside is gone. He can feel the last gasps of tension dematerialize. "Did you wash your hands?"

"Feel," holding out her palms. "Still a bit wet."

"Good," seeing the evidence. "Should we get some food finally?"

"I'm not hungry."

"Something to drink then? Kids' hot chocolate?"

Adi tilts her head, her lips pursed. "Heavy on the whipped cream, please."

It's an optimal time to order. No one is in line, no one is at the register paying. Someone has just pulled into the recently vacated wheelchair spot in the parking lot, probably to come to Starbucks, but it will be a few seconds more before they're parked and the engine is off and they come inside, and anyway Steve and Adi are in front of the two refrigerated display cases with all the foodstuffs already, preparing to order. The barista Adi had pointed out earlier is behind the till. Madeleine, her name is according to the metallic-ink-on-black-badge affixed to her green apron.

"Can I help you?"

"Did you let her use your restroom in the back?"

"I hope that's okay. She looked on the brink of exploding and she said you were outside."

34

"Oh yeah yeah yeah not a problem at all. It was very kind of you. Thanks." Steve pushes his glasses up his nose, not that they were in danger of falling off his face. "There was a guy in the ladies' room and he flooded your toilet. That's why I was outside: to talk to him."

"I saw him." Madeleine makes a face suggesting revulsion. "He flooded the toilet? He didn't even order anything."

"He was parked in the wheelchair spot, too."

"I hate people who do that. What did he say to you?"

"We didn't reach an agreement, let's put it that way."

"Good for you for trying at least," smiling approvingly.

Steve mimics her expression, nodding.

Madeleine brushes some stray hairs from her forehead, tucking them behind an ear. "What can I get for you? Something heroic."

"She'll have a kids' hot chocolate," his hand on Adi's head, "extra whipped cream. I'll have a tall soy unsweetened no-foam green tea latte." Not exactly a Joseph Campbell kind of drink.

"Whipped on yours?"

"Why not?"

Madeleine begins repeating the order. Her partially braided hair is dyed a bright blue and Steve is suddenly conscious of the fact he's staring and also that there's someone in line behind him and Adi.

"Anything else? Something to eat?"

"Maybe later."

"I thought you wanted tea." Adi's arms are crossed over her chest.

"What?"

"You said so before you went to the bathroom."

"You must have misheard me."

Madeleine grabs a paper cup from each of two adjacent stacks, scribbles on the first with a Sharpie, sets it down, scribbles on the second, and passes both of them to Bryan who always seems to be working when Steve is here. She tells him the order. The digital display attached to the register shows how much is owing for the drinks. Madeleine reads the number aloud. Steve takes out his wallet, removes his registered Starbucks card, which he gives to her. She swipes it, then waits to verify that the machine has processed it, and once it has, returns the card to Steve. He puts it back in his wallet, his wallet back in his pocket. "Your drinks will be ready over there," pointing to the pick-up counter to her left.

Steve smiles and thanks her, then turns to Adi. "Let's sit at the bar." He'd prefer to sit on a chair with a back, but all of the tables are taken. Only the bar, which faces the area behind the cash register where the drinks are made and is perpendicular to the counter where their beverages will soon be delivered, has space. There's room for three people because there are three stools—there's another funny word, especially for an object meant for bottoms: *stool*—one of which, the one farthest from the wall, is occupied by the same man who'd been in the men's room before Steve: the old one who may or may not have forgotten to put the toilet seat down. He's reading something on a first-generation iPad. Steve helps Adi up to the middle stool, then sits next to her. Bryan is making her hot chocolate. She's watching him attentively. Probably she wants to make sure he's generous with the whipped cream and chocolate sauce drizzle. There are three people in line now. The woman at the front is possibly the same woman whose paprika-colored Forester is parked in the wheelchair spot. She doesn't look like she needs a wheelchair, but who knows what invisible impairment she might have, what legitimate reason to be parked where she's parked. He can't hear what she's saying to Madeleine; the espresso machine is making too much noise, not to mention the indistinct din of all the other conversations. The air is redolent of freshly ground coffee beans, which is another distraction. The astringent aroma makes Steve a little nauseated. He gags and for a moment feels like vomiting. He hasn't thrown up in more than a year, not since the stomach flu passed from one family member to the other, and the time before that was even further back, one drunken night or another when he was an undergrad and still young. The feeling passes. Madeleine says something to Bryan in an indecipherable verbal code. A drink order, probably. Her face reminds Steve of Sam's Playmobil figures, and one in particular, the one from the mystery pack, with the papoose and baby. Her eyes are exactly where they should be. Her lips are straight with just the hint of an upturn, not one of those perpetual frowns. It's enough to metamorphose her somehow. Which is shallow, he knows, to suggest any kind of transfiguration on the basis of something as superficial as a smile, but it's the only word he can think of. So what if it's shallow?

"Tall soy unsweetened no-foam green tea latte." Bryan places a cup in front of him, Steve's name written in black ink on the corrugated sleeve, encircled by a shape that might be a heart. "And this must be yours," putting a smaller cup in front of Adi. "Kids' hot chocolate, extra whipped cream. I gave you some extra extra."

"Thanks." Adi leans in close, lapping some of it up. She licks the excess off her lips, then goes back for more.

As if on cue, Shonen Knife's "I Am A Cat" comes on the overhead speakers. Steve recognizes it the moment the drums kick in, and instantly he remembers Suzume. God, he hasn't thought about her in it seems like forever: Suzume, who loved *Anne of Green Gables* so much her worst childhood memory was finding out Anne was a fictional character: Suzume, who agreed to go on a date with him because he, like Anne, was from Canada: Suzume, his girlfriend freshman year at Penn; an international student, but her English was as good as her Japanese, which is to say she was fluent in both. Steve started listening to Shonen Knife because they were her favorite band. At one point he had all of their CDs, even a couple of live concert bootlegs. It was entirely out of character. He didn't listen to their style of music, but Suzume was the kind of girl a guy would become someone else for, especially a guy just starting university. It's not like he expected to marry her, though; to move back to Canada after he'd made it on Wall Street, a house on the North Shore, kids, vacation homes in Whistler and on one of the Gulf Islands, retire on a farm where they'd raise goats, make their own cheese, their own Maréchal Foch. He'd hoped. Not Maréchal Foch, though. That's anachronistic. What would it have been at the time? Trappist beer, maybe. She was the third girl he'd ever slept with. Altogether they dated seven months, almost eleven if the summer counts, when Suzume was back in Okayama and he was working in Manhattan having scored a job usually reserved for matriculating seniors. At first they talked every day on the phone, but the time difference was a bummer, and by the beginning of July they spoke only every few days, and then a whole week would pass without a call from either one. Via email they made plans to meet at the Button the day before classes started sophomore year. That's when she told Steve the two of them together was a mistake and she hoped they could stay friends. He agreed, doing his best to play it cool. The first thing he did when he went back to his 8th floor room in High Rise East was throw his Shonen Knife collection down the trash chute. They didn't stay friends either, of course not. Who knows where she is now?

He remembers what it felt like, then, fresh off the break-up, like he was lost in the Milky Way.

The last time he heard this song was probably some time after they'd had sex. It could have been during. She liked listening to music during. Steve doesn't like thinking about those times. It doesn't bring him any joy.

Nostalgia never does. But once a memory forms, good or bad, once it gets going, stopping it is only a little easier than trying to unspill spilled milk.

He and Suzume met in Management 100, the one class required of all Wharton freshmen. The class was divided—randomly? It wasn't by alphabetical order—into four tutorial groups, and they were in the same one. Each was assigned a two-semester-long community service project. Their group was tasked with reimagining and raising funds for the outdoor recess area of an inner-city elementary school. Calling it a playground would be too far a stretch; prison yards have nicer amenities than this school had. He mustered up the courage to ask her out after one of their tutorial sessions. The group had been hanging out one night when Ramin, another international student, wondered about an expression used in a recent episode of *Ally McBeal.*

What's eye candy? he'd asked.

Steve pointed to Suzume, who was sitting between them, and shot him a knowing smile.

Suzume blushed.

That night he walked her back to the off-campus duplex she shared with Hato, a junior she knew from high school in Japan. They arrived to find Hato screaming, standing on a sofa, as a mouse raced across the living room floor. Steve caught it using one of Suzume's sweaters, which she let him keep after. You're my cat, she took to calling him after that. Hato was so grateful she kissed him on the cheek and as she did she whispered that he should ask Suzume out. He called her later that night. Suzume's twin sister Kamome came with them on their first date the next week. She was visiting from Brown and wanted to hear the PSO play Strauss. Suzume arranged to get three student rush tickets. They were supposed to meet before dinner by the Compass on Locust Walk, share a cab downtown, but Steve ran into Kamome earlier that day by the 38th Street bridge.

He called out to her.

When she didn't respond, he repeated himself.

I'm not Suzume, Kamome shot back. She's my sister.

All Steve could think to say was sorry. It was even more awkward later that evening.

This is my sister, Suzume announced when Steve arrived.

He told her they'd met.

Suzume laughed. She already knew.

Suzume, Kamome, Hato: he had no idea where any of them were anymore. Kamome had acting aspirations when she was at Brown. Last he heard she'd landed a recurring role on a major network soap opera. That was years ago. Maybe she's a huge star in Asia now. Hato was an anthropology major.

A new song comes on the speaker—The White Stripes' "Hotel Yorba."

"Earth to Sam's dad."

"Huh?"

"I've been calling you for like forever."

"Sorry. What's up?"

"I'm hungry."

"I thought you didn't want to eat anything."

"That was before."

"Fine." Kids. "What do you want? A cookie? Muffin? Sandwich?"

"Blueberry scone please."

"It's pronounced *scone*."

"You're wrong," head shake. "It's *scone*."

"Ask anyone from Scotland. It's *scone*." A shibboleth.

"My dad is from Wales and he calls it *scone*. That's what I want. A blueberry scone."

"Your dad says *scone*?"

Adi nods. "I love scones."

Steve stretches his legs beneath the bar, wiggles his toes inside his shoes. "Alright then. I guess I was wrong. One blueberry scone coming up." He slides the stool back a half-foot so he can get up, then heads toward the register. It'd be nice just to order from the bar, but 1) he doesn't want to come across as obnoxious, and ordering from the bar might strike some neighboring patrons and the baristas as an obnoxious thing to do; it's what he'd think: an obnoxious thing done by an obnoxious person, and 2) he has to pay anyway, and there's no one in line.

"Something else?" Madeleine is smiling.

"A blueberry scone, please."

"Those are tasty. Have you tried the cranberry one? It's pretty good, if you like cranberries."

"I do. But this isn't for me."

"For your daughter?" looking over at Adi. "She's a cutie."

You're a cutie, Steve in his undergrad days would have blurted out. "She's my daughter's friend, actually. I'm just babysitting for the day." He doesn't want her to think he's a professional manny. Why doesn't he want her to think that? "Her parents are both busy and she's a little sick so I offered."

"Aww. That's so nice of you."

Steve shrugs.

"Does she want it warmed?"

"That's a good question." Steve turns toward Adi. "Do you want it warmed?"

Adi looks up, whirls both pupils to the same side, deliberates for a moment, nods.

"I think that's a yes."

"I'll bring it over to her."

"That'd be great," feeling for his wallet. "How much do I owe you?"

"Don't worry about it."

"Are you sure?" his voice rising a little.

"I'm not going to charge Babysitting Dad of the Year for his babysittee's scone." She pronounces it just like he does. "I couldn't." Was that a wink?

Steve thanks her again and shoves his hands in his pockets as he passes the Mastrena espresso machine, heading back to his stool. He navigates the narrow space between the bar where Adi is seated next to the man from the restroom, and the other bar, the one parallel to it, facing outdoors. There's a young boy seated at this other bar, with his mom it looks like. The Weepies' "Not Your Year" begins playing. The boy and this woman have the same rumpled hair, like a sheep in need of shearing. He looks to be about Sam's age or older. Why isn't he at school? He must be sick. But he doesn't look sick. But neither does Adi. Maybe he's cutting class. He might be home-schooled. His mom doesn't look like the homeschooling type.

"All done." Adi slams her cup down next to the lid she must have re-moved at some point earlier without Steve noticing.

"Already?" Steve is back on his stool now, comfortable. "That was fast. Want another?"

"Nah," scratching the corner of her mouth. "Where's my scone? Did you forget it?"

"It's warming, remember? Madeleine is going to bring it for you when it's ready."

"Who is?"

"The girl who took you to the restroom," angling his head in her direction.

"That's nice of her."

"It is."

"Or maybe it's just part of her job."

"I don't think so. But maybe." Girl—is that right? Should he have said woman? She looks to be about twenty, give or take. Definitely under 25. Young woman then? He rubs a finger over his callus. It's not a trivial distinction. Words are so important; he should be more careful. He's a Minister of Word and Sacrament, after all. It's his job. The young woman who took you to the restroom, he should have said. Or: The person who. That's even better. Who or that? The person who. The person that. He feels his callus again. He should mention his callused palm in his Good Friday sermon, which is in need of some illustrations. Something to do with gripping the steering wheel, holding on to things too tightly, good things that become enslaving things, we hold them clutch them cling to them and before long they reverse the hold, they grasp us, and squeeze. That might preach.

"Steve?"

"Yeah."

"Did you use the toilet paper when you went to the bathroom?"

"I did not. Didn't need to. Why?"

"The one in the bathroom I used was really asperous."

"Asperous?"

"It means—"

"I know what it means. I've never heard a kid use it before." Or an adult, for that matter.

"Like when my eczema flares up."

"That's not surprising."

"Why don't they stock something softer?"

"Soft TP is expensive," scratching his elbow. "If there was something to be gained from the extra expense, like if more people would buy their coffee and their scones, or if people would buy more of them, because the toilet paper was nicer, I'm sure they'd bear the extra cost. But nobody chooses which coffee shop to go to on the basis of how good the toilet paper there is."

"I would." Adi crinkles her nose and squeezes her eyes shut a full second. "If I was a grown-up, that's exactly what I'd do. The drinks all taste about the same."

"I don't know about that. Most grown-ups avoid using the restroom when they're out of the house. But rough toilet paper is pretty awful."

"My mom buys the one with the bear."

"That's the brand we use at my church." He uses it once or twice a week, always in the morning after he's had his first cup of coffee, drop of cream, dash of sugar, splash of Redbreast 12.

"It's soft."

"It is." He's not an alcoholic, though.

"It's better than the one here."

"I get it for home when it's on sale at Safeway." He's not a walking cliché, not a trope—the drunkard pastor.

Madeleine has got the scone out of the oven now, on a porcelain plate, and she's bringing it over.

Steve picks up his latte, takes a sip. The whiskey is just an eye-opener, that's all.

"Your blueberry scone." Madeleine sets it in front of Adi.

Steve puts his cup down, folds his arms and rests them on the bar. There aren't enough fictional pastors in literature, on TV, the movies, for the inebriated minister to have become a trope. Elmer Gantry—

"Why does everyone pronounce it wrong? It's *scone*." Adi touches the top of hers.

"My manager says it your way."

"She's smart."

"She is." Madeleine takes a quick look over each of her shoulders. Only Bryan, who is not a manager, is within earshot.

"Say thank you." Steve picks up his cup again.

"Thanks," obligingly.

"You're very welcome," a purr almost. She looks at Steve. "Can I get you anything else?"

He shakes his head. "This is great. Thanks again."

"I like your hair."

"Aww." Madeleine purses her lips, the bottom lip a little over the top one, her cheeks slightly puffed. Craig Cardiff's cover of "Time After Time" begins playing. "I think yours is pretty great, too."

Adi is expressionless.

Madeleine returns to some busy work, tossing an unfolded towel beneath the counter, dropping a whisk and a spoon into the sink. The utensils clang with something else already in there. A mixing bowl maybe. Steve's view is partially obstructed by some blenders. It could be a mixing bowl.

Madeleine glides past Bryan, who's crouched down behind the food display case, taking an inventory of sandwiches and wraps.

Adi feels the top of her pastry again.

"Are you going to try it?"

"Later. It's too hot still."

"Have you had the blueberry scones here before?"

"Lots of times."

"What about the cranberry? Madeleine said the cranberry ones are good."

"I don't like cranberries."

"What's not to like?"

"Only if it's in sauce form with turkey at Thanksgiving."

"Jellied. With ring marks."

"Except I don't eat turkey anymore. I'm a vegetarian now."

"You are?" That explains the recent Hot Dog Days.

"Speaking of fowl, did you clean the bird poo off the top of your head? Connection!"

"All of it I hope. You want to check?"

"Sure," with a declension of something like existential ennui in her eyes. It could be pensiveness.

Steve tilts his head until his chin touches his clavicle, which probably gives him a double or triple chin. Adi isn't feeling his hair with her hands, just looking, which he's happy about. "Next year I'm going to have something called Tofurky." Not happy—relieved. He can tell she's checking, though. He can sense her head close to his.

"Did I miss anything?"

"You have a weird bumpy thing kind of right in the middle of your scalp."

"I felt it earlier. I'm not sure what that is. Any bird poo, though?"

"I don't see any."

He raises his head. "Good." He'll have to wash it properly tonight, with some extra heavy duty shampoo, the one that gives off a scent that makes Lola sick even though it's not an offensive smell, it's actually quite pleasant, a faint licorice, but she says her meds have done a number on her olfactory glands despite the fact nausea isn't a listed side effect anywhere, and if anything, her sense of smell ought to be dulled not heightened, at least according to the medical web sites. "Want to know a secret?"

"Always."

"It's not the first time I've been pooped on."

"You got pooed on before?"

"Shh." He presses his finger to his lips. "Twice. Have you ever been to Tacoma?"

Adi shakes her head.

"It's next to Seattle."

"I know."

"There's this nice zoo in Tacoma. The Point Defiance Zoo and Aquarium it's called. Mrs. Canard told Sam about it. Sam told me."

"I've been to the zoo in Seattle."

"Woodland Park," nodding. "We've been there, too. I love the hippo and the tiny deer."

"It's called a pudú."

"That's right. Pudú. A woman from my church once saw one in the wild."

"In Vancouver?"

Steve chuckles. "In Chile."

"Is that where she was born?"

"She was born in Singapore, I think. I'm not sure when she was in Chile. Vacation, probably? Do you know where Singapore is?"

"Captain Obvi."

"You know where Chile is, too?"

"Duh."

"I didn't know where Chile was when I was your age. Or Singapore."

"Most kids don't."

"Anyway, that's where she saw the pudú. In Chile. In the Andes."

"They're so cute."

"Yeah."

"Is that what pooed on you?" Adi smirks. "Did a pudú poo on you?"

"A bird," rolling his eyes.

"In Tacoma?"

"At the Point Defiance Zoo and Aquarium," nodding again. "A few years ago. Before Gillian was born. This woman with an expensive purse was walking a bit in front of us with her friends, and out of nowhere she starts to shriek, like Ahh! Ahh!" flailing his arms, "and before she could tell her friends what happened, I saw it: this streak of gunky guano all over her purse and on her jacket and in her hair."

"Barf."

"I empathized because a bird pooped on me when I was in high school—that was the first time it happened to me—so I knew what it felt like, physically and psychologically, but once she went to the restroom to get cleaned off, I laughed, and a lot, and for a long time."

"That's mean."

"A couple hours later I look down at the left sleeve of my favorite Kelly green hoodie and there's this massive blob of fresh bird poo on it." Ingrid Michaelson's "End of the World" begins playing. Steve forms a ring with the thumb and middle finger of his right hand. "Massive."

"Burn."

"Do you believe in karma?"

"That has something to do with reincarnation, right?"

"They're kind of intertwined, yeah. Or they intersect."

Adi rucks up her chin. "Do you believe in it?"

"In reincarnation?" Should he tell her her mother asked him the same question once? Is that a kind of déjà vu? "Not really. YOLO, right?"

"I might believe in it."

"*Man lebt nur einmal.*"

"Huh?"

"Karma, though. There's some plausibility. I laughed at that poor woman, then the same thing that happened to her happened to me." You reap what you sow. That's biblical.

Adi picks up the lid to her cup, twirls it around her fingers. She sets it back down on the bar. "Who decides about the karma?"

"What do you mean?"

"Who makes up the rules? Is it a grown-up? Like, what if you've done something bad? How do you know? And can you have a re-test?"

"I don't know."

"It wouldn't be fair if you can't. And how are you supposed to know what you should do and what you shouldn't? Is there a book?"

"I really don't know. My aunt teaches at a Buddhist college in Taiwan. She'd know. Your gut is supposed to tell you what to do and what not to do, I guess. There are books, though. They probably say more."

"Who discovered it?"

"Buddha maybe. You'd have to talk to an expert. Or an adherent."

Adi picks up the plastic lid again, squeezing tight enough that a visible crease forms and remains when she releases her grip and sets it down. "It doesn't really matter if you believe in it or not, right? You don't believe in karma, but you still got bird poo on your hoodie. Your disbelief didn't prevent it from happening."

"That's an astute observation."

Adi gazes at the porcelain plate, or else the scone resting on it, or both. "But your story isn't really even an example of karma because what happened to you isn't the same thing that happened to the woman you made fun of. You only had poo on your shirt, right? Not on your hair or an expensive purse. Just an old hoodie."

"It was my favorite hoodie, though."

"Wait a minute." Adi's posture straightens, her palms flat on the bar top. "Is it that hoodie you wear every day?"

"I don't wear it every day. I'm not wearing it now." The hoodie he's got on now beneath his windbreaker is a slate gray, some would call it a shade of blue, the color of the distant mountains seen on the return ferry ride from Long Harbour to Tsawwassen if it's close to sundown. "But yeah, that one. It's basically a jacket."

"My dad would have thrown it away."

"Sam's mom suggested the same, but like I said, it's my favorite hoodie. If anything, I made out worse than that woman did."

"Did she throw her stuff away?"

"I doubt it. It was a Louis Vuitton or something. You don't just throw a purse like that in the trash, not unless a whole colony of gulls pooped inside it."

"I think she threw it away. Girls are weird about poo."

"That's true," waggling his head. "Girls and women are strange birds."

"She could've asked her boyfriend to buy her a new one."

"If she had a boyfriend." Steve takes a long drink of his latte, savoring its inoffensive sweetness. It's still warm. "How's the scone?"

Adi's face is a moue.

"It's not good?"

"It's fine."

"Why aren't you eating? I thought you were hungry."

"I kind of lost my appetite."

"Sorry."

"That's okay. I like hearing your stories."

"That's good because I like telling them."

"What about the first time you got poo on you? You said you were in high school."

"I was with my church youth group on a retreat, which is kind of like a summer camp. We were all having lunch beneath this big leafy tree and all of a sudden—plop—I feel something wet on the top of my head," patting it. "This kid called Myles notices, and he starts to laugh and soon everyone is laughing."

"The church kids laughed at you?"

Steve nods.

"Shouldn't church kids be nicer?"

"I guess. But church or not, teenagers can't help being teenagers." He'd been one, he ought to know. "Anyway, some people think it's lucky when a bird poops on you."

John Mayer's "Stop This Train" starts.

"Sounds like something someone who got pooed on would make up to not look bad."

"It does, doesn't it?"

"Did anything lucky happen to you after?"

"Actually, the first time, back when I was in high school, a girl who once in a while went to the youth group I went to, who I was crushing on, Patricia, she helped me clean it off. I was already keeping my head shaved so all she had to do was pour bottled water on it while I wiped with some paper towels." The Chinese for *shaved off* sounds like the car model your mom drives, Steve thinks about saying. "If it wasn't for the bird poo, I'd have never worked up the courage to talk to her."

"Did she become your girlfriend?"

"No." They hooked up once, but that doesn't seem like a thing he should share.

Adi looks unimpressed. "What about the other time?"

"The other time?" Steve thinks for a moment. Was there anything lucky about the second time? What happened that day? "We saw the octopus. I suppose if it wasn't for the five minutes I had to spend cleaning off the poop, we would have gone to its tank earlier and missed what we got to see by being there later." He pauses for rhetorical effect. "You've been to the aquarium in Stanley Park before?"

Adi nods.

"You know how the octopus is always hiding in a cave somewhere? All octopuses do that. The octopus at the zoo in Tacoma was doing that when we first got to its tank. It was curled up in a corner so all we could see were a few suckers on one of its tentacles. But then for no particular reason it uncoiled and started swimming around, almost like dancing, and not just dancing, but balletic, like a Paganini concerto was being piped into its tank from some underwater stereo that only it could hear. If it wasn't for the bird poo, I guess we'd have been there earlier and might have missed the performance? It's the only time I've ever seen an octopus really move."

Adi still looks unimpressed. "What about this time?"

"The day's still young." Steve glances at the plate in front of Adi. "And we've already got a free scone."

"If bird poo is lucky, you should stand under a street wire when there's a bunch of pigeons perched on it."

"A kit."

"Huh?"

"Never mind. The point isn't that I believe it's lucky. I'm just saying someone could make a case it is, that's all."

"It still doesn't seem very lucky to me."

"Me either." *Neither*? He straightens his back. "How is your scone by the way? It must have cooled down by now. Is your appetite back?"

Adi shrugs, glances at her pastry, picks it up, tears off a piece from one end. "It's fine." She takes a bite, chews.

The mother and son sitting at the counter behind them are talking about something that's got the mother upset. She's shrieking—You used what to make those?—Shears. S-H- . . . E- . . . shears.—Don't do that again. It doesn't look good. Next time your father gets you jeans, tell me and I'll do it for you.—But mom.—Hey. Look it. You're lucky you've got a mom with style. Lots of parents wouldn't let their kids rip up their expensive jeans.—I know.—There are a lot of cheap parents.

Definitely not homeschooled, Steve thinks. He shifts to get a better look at the mother, hoping she'll make eye contact. Why he wants her to make eye contact he's not sure. She doesn't. She's examining the homemade cuts in her son's pants. Steve is still staring from his stool when he feels his phone vibrating. An instant later the *Parks and Recreation* theme song sounds. It's the ringtone he assigned a few months ago to his church office, hoping against all hope it'd give him a psychic uplift whenever he got a call from Janis. Helpful to be in that condition preceding a conversation with her. Used to be each time he heard it he thought about Gillian who, when she hears it playing on the TV, starts to dance in that involuntary self-forgetful manner possessed only by infants and toddlers and some others. Steve lets the call go to voicemail. She'll call back if it's urgent.

No she won't.

She could text.

She won't do that either.

She'd have to use her cell phone to text. Her personal phone. No way she'd call him during business hours for business reasons on her personal phone. Emergency or not, she's tried once, just now, to reach him. That's sufficient. That's all her job requires and heaven forbid she do any more than the bare-naked minimum. If she did more than that, people would start taking advantage of her. They used to. Christ—God forgive her tongue, the same tongue she uses to bless for chrissake, but Christ—people used to come up to her on Sunday mornings before service and ask if she could get them such-and-such a form from the office or if she knew how so-and-so was doing following his surgery. Sunday morning, her time to worship, can you believe that? Well. She'd had enough, put her foot down, had to. Wasn't pretty, but there was no other way. That's not her job. She's not paid to work on the Lord's Day. The Lord's Day is for her and her Lord. They want information, they could have asked any time Monday through Friday, nine to noon, her office hours. But did they ask at any of the appropriate days and times? Did they? No, they didn't. So she told them. She didn't want to, but she did. Now if anyone needs anything, they ask her during the week while she's in the office. Now nobody bothers her on her day to commune with her True Boss. The Boom Boom's "Dry Your Tears" is playing. Now people know better.

Steve takes his phone out of his pocket. Missed call, it says on the screen, from St. Joseph's, and a new voicemail. He should listen to it in case it's an emergency. He should listen to it even if it's not an emergency. He's the pastor for Pete's sake. It might have something to do with the foot washing logistics for tomorrow night or the Good Friday service. If she's calling about one of those two events, he should definitely listen to his voicemail. It's 10:38. The voicemail can wait. Even if it can't, it will. He'll check at noon and call back if Janis has left a message asking him to. Sure, there's a certain logic to not putting off until later what you can do now; there's also an argument to be made for not doing now what you can put off until later. It takes a certain kind of wisdom to know whether the time and circumstance calls for action or inaction. Cf. Proverbs 26:4–5. He swipes the screen, clearing the alert, and puts his phone next to his latte, screen side up. He'll call at 12:01. No. He'll call at 12:05 to be safe. Janis will have left by then.

More than half of Adi's scone is gone. Crumbs fill the space between the plate and the edge of the counter. There's a smattering on the front of her coat.

"You've got crumbs all over you."

Adi sees them, wipes them off with one hand, her other holding the last bit of her scone. Some crumbs land on her lap, some on the floor. A few remain on her coat. "I want to save the rest." There are two bites of it left, maybe three.

"Up to you."

She shoves the leftovers in her coat pocket.

"I can wrap that up in a napkin."

"I'm bored." She's playing with the lid of her cup again. "What time is it?"

"A little after 10:38."

"What time is it exactly?"

Steve hits the home button on his phone. "It's 10:39. Recess time."

"Can we go now?"

"Back to school?"

"Somewhere fun."

"Right after I finish my drink." Steve jiggles his almost finished latte. "You've still got some crumbs on you."

Adi sees the ones she missed and shrugs. "Maybe a bird will land on me and eat them."

"If it did, it might poop on you."

She smiles. "You must not like birds very much."

"No, I do. For the longest time I hated them. After that time I was pooped on in high school some of the kids in the youth group got me a Gary Larson card as a gag. On the cover was a bird on a branch looking down at three people: a man, a woman, and a kid, I think, each of them with a bull's-eye on the top of their heads. The caption said something like, How a bird sees the world."

"You said a strong word."

"What?"

"You said the H word."

"Hate?" feeling his chin. "It's warranted. I hated birds."

"Because they pooed on you?"

"Pretty good reason, no?"

"But now you like them?"

"I love them now."

"Why?"

He sips his drink. The truth is, Sam got a bird feeder for her last birthday, one of those ones you have to paint and assemble yourself, which she did. Steve set it up on their back patio, and lo! birds started coming and going, different species—red-breasted nuthatches, brown creepers, northern mockingbirds, cedar waxwings, orange-crowned warblers, even a few black-billed magpies and western scrub-jays. He read about these birds, listened to their singing, beholding and considering them until his affections were changed. It was a surprise, as love always is. "Because they're beautiful and they can fly."

"Butterflies are beautiful and can fly. Do you love butterflies?"

"Sure."

"I like blue-footed booby birds."

"Sam has a Playmobil one."

"I like flamingos, too."

"Flamingos are cool."

"Fast Car" by Tracy Chapman starts playing from the speakers.

"Do you know why they stand on one leg?"

Steve presses an index finger to his chin, for show. "To keep warm?"

"How did you know?"

"Sam told me. I think she learned it from Mrs. Canard."

"She did. I knew from before."

"When I was in university I went one summer to a city in Switzerland called St. Gallen for this student business symposium thing. The next-door neighbors of the house I stayed in had a big pen in their front yard with something like a million flamingos in it."

"You're lying."

"Not literally. Somewhere between, like, sixteen to twenty. Twenty-four, maybe. In that range. Real live flamingos, though, not the plastic ones."

"Are you lying?"

Steve shakes his head. "Honest to God."

"Did you feed them?"

"This was back when I still hated birds, so no."

"What a waste."

"If I could get a do-over."

"Isn't it too cold for flamingos in Switzerland?"

"I guess not."

"Can someone have flamingos in Vancouver?"

"I don't think so, but maybe. I've never seen any here."

"I wish I lived in Switzerland."

"It's alright." Most of his two weeks there he spent chatting up girls, mostly from Thailand—Chulalongkorn and Thammasat students—but also from China. Girls who saw his Wharton credentials as a meal ticket, probably, not that that bugged him. Everyone wore badges with their universities clearly labeled for a reason. The most memorable thing about St. Gallen was going up the Alps with a girl from Beijing, Bessie, whose name couldn't have been less suited to her appearance. "I like Vancouver more."

"Can you hurry and finish your drink?"

"It's still half full."

"Still? You've been drinking it for an hour."

"There's no rush." He has to meet with Marcel later, that's the only firm commitment, and that's not until noon. At which time he has to remember to check his voicemail. Should he give Marcel a heads-up, let him know Adi will be joining them? But chances are Marcel isn't going to show anyway. He flaked on their last, what is it, five meetings? Steve has lost count it's been so many times. The last time he didn't even bother to call to say he wasn't coming. Steve waited at Café D'Lite on West Broadway for nearly ninety minutes. He didn't order food, either, because he didn't want Marcel to come in while he was mid-meal. That would have been rude. He takes another sip of his latte.

"Do you know who that was?" Bryan is standing across from them on the other side of the bar.

"Who?"

"The guy who was sitting next to you." He rests his forearms on the bar top, leans forward. There's a deck of cards tattooed on his bicep.

"He kind of looked familiar, but I wasn't really paying attention."

"Dude."

"What?"

"That was Alfred fucking Bester."

"Hey." Steve shoots him a look, his head tilted in Adi's direction.

"Oh," his teeth gritted through open lips. "Sorry."

Steve exhales, nods. "He's got the same last name as my all-time favorite hockey player. Who is he?"

"Big-time science fiction author. *The Demolished Man*?"

"The Wesley Snipes movie?"

"Who? No, dude. *The Stars My Destination*?"

Steve shakes his head. "The guy who was sitting over here?" indicating the now vacant stool.

"You were a foot away from a living legend, man."

"The old guy? He looked like he was a hundred." He looked like a handful of the oldest parishioners at St. Joe's. Older even.

"He's a frickin oracle. A frickin Nostradamus."

"Hmm," nodding, trying to place the name. Was he the guy who wrote that dog-eared paperback Tariq used to carry around with him in seventh or eighth grade, telling anyone who'd listen how mind-blowing it was? Steve can almost picture the cover. The guy who wrote the screenplay to *Johnny Mnemonic*, which he saw in the theater with Melanie, the girl he was dating at the time? "Yeah. Okay. The cyberspace guy?"

"Nah. You're thinking of William Gibson. That's a totally different dude, dude. No. Bester. Alfred Bester."

"Never mind then." Steve clears his throat. "Does he come in often?"

"About as often as you," straightening his posture. "I'm surprised you haven't noticed him before."

"If he's here all the time, I've probably seen him around and he just didn't register."

"He's not exactly what you'd call nondescript, though," snickering. "You're just not that attentive."

Adi angles her body and looks out the front window.

Steve does likewise. Bester is at the far end of the parking lot, moving slowly, his hands in his pockets. "Do people recognize him?"

"I've only ever seen one guy ask for his autograph. This real fanboy nerd."

"Yeah?"

"Kind of looked like you."

"Ha."

"He had an armful of books." Bryan looks like he's holding an invisible pumpkin.

"Did you know who he was?"

"The kid? Not his name. He comes in here once in a while. Usually sits over there," pointing to one of the vinyl-cushioned benches.

"Not him. This Bester guy. Did you know who he was before that kid asked for his autograph?"

"Hell no. Do I look like I read science fiction to you?"

"You never know. Don't judge a book."

"Nah," looking over toward the register, checking for new customers, probably. There aren't any. "I had no idea who he was until the kid with all the books started going, Omigod omigod, like a girl at a One Direction concert." Bryan laughs. "He showed me one of the books he got signed. You know the page in the front where they print the title and author's name?"

Steve nods once.

"He'd put one of those triangle things without the bottom line, like an *accent circonflexe*, between Alfred and Bester, and wrote Good Better. Better with an E, not an O. Alfred Good Better Bester. That's how I remember his name."

Steve has his phone out and Safari open. "His Wikipedia page says he died in 1987. Which means if he were alive today, he'd be 99."

"You said yourself he looked like he was a hundred."

"The photo here is from a long time ago." Steve turns it around, showing Bryan.

Shakira's "She Wolf" starts playing.

"Search for more recent images."

Steve taps back to the previous screen, taps again, scrolls through the results, and shows Bryan the phone. "What do you think?"

"Could be him. There's a resemblance. He might've faked his death and become a recluse in his old age."

There is some resemblance, true. Steve is trying to form a thoughtful-sounding explanation when Adi interrupts. "Let's see where he's going."

"He's gone already," looking out the window. Bester is nowhere to be seen. "He's probably in his car headed who knows where." A couple of Steve's parishioners who lived past a hundred drove into their late nineties so it's not that far-fetched.

"He didn't go in a car. He walked. I saw him turn over there," pointing southeast to the place where their view of the street is cut off.

"I'm sure you'll see him here again if he doesn't croak first." Bryan leaves to greet and take the order of a returning patron, a medium-built Asian guy with glasses who's been sitting alone at one of the round tables with a laptop plugged in to a wall socket. He's got a short cup in his hand.

"Please can we follow him? I'm so bored."

"What do you want to follow him for?"

"Because."

"You don't even know who he is."

"Yes I do. Your friend said he's an oracle."

Steve looks outside again. Some cars are headed north on Arbutus, others south. A few people are in the parking lot, coming, going. The same two guys are still sitting at the outdoor table, still smoking. The dog is gone.

"I don't see him anywhere."

"I'm telling you he went that way," pointing again, with her other hand. "If we go now, we'll see him. Hurry."

Steve takes a long sip of his green tea latte, which is thicker, more syrupy now than when he took his first sip. He checks his phone—10:47—10:48. He needs to do something with Adi until noon, kill the time somehow. God, he hates that expression.

Shakira is howling overhead, something about being a disciple of the moon.

"Fine. Why not?"

Steve slides off his stool, helps Adi down from hers, holding it steady by the top of the backrest while she lifts herself off the seat and drops to the floor. He pulls his jacket zipper part way up, stopping at where his pectoral muscles would be if he had any pectoral muscles, then slips his phone in his pocket, grabs his unfinished latte, and removes the lid, keeping it in his right hand. With his left he pours the contents of the cup down his throat, not swallowing until his mouth is full and the cup is empty. There's a drop or two left at the bottom so it's not technically empty, but empty enough that throwing it in the trash isn't going to fill the plastic garbage bag with an excessive volume of liquid. A drop or two is hardly an unreasonable amount to dispose of. He should have brought his own tumbler, though, so there wouldn't be anything to dispose of at all. Next time. He collects Adi's cup, pinching its rim between his ring finger and pinky, sweeps up all the other detritus on the bar top including a crumpled brown pastry bag that Bester left behind. That's another thing Steve doesn't like. He doesn't like it when people leave their waste on tables and counter surfaces at Starbucks for the baristas to throw away. Is it really that hard to put it in the garbage yourself? Then again if everyone cleaned up after themselves, maybe there'd be less need to keep as many baristas employed. Someone might be laid off or have their hours reduced because the store was always so clean. Maybe being thoughtless indirectly enables the people who need these jobs to keep them. Lots of them are students, after all, and those that aren't, are old, not as old as Bester, but old still, or recent immigrants. He should be more sympathetic. Bester could've left his garbage deliberately for precisely that reason: an economic stimulant, a social service, an act of mercy. Next time that's what Steve will do. This time he tosses all of the things he's gathered into the trash bin on his way to the door. No, next time he'll bring his own tumbler, remember? Adi is by his side, at his right hand.

Outside, he lets the wind wash over him as he closes then opens his eyes, re-familiarizing himself to the sunlight. Adi has moved two feet ahead and to his right, slightly, raring to get a move on, but cautious about stepping off the strip mall sidewalk and entering the parking lot proper without him next to her. He thinks about holding her hand or her forearm between her wrist and her elbow or guiding her by the shoulder or the back of the head. He settles for sticking close. It isn't safe for a four-foot-tall kid to walk unattended while near heavy motor vehicles. He must tell Sam this every time they're in a parking lot together. You repeat a thing often enough and something is bound to stick. Stay close—you're short—the drivers can't see you—don't assume they can see you—make eye contact—make sure they're not moving—always be alert—never let your guard down. It's dangerous and irresponsible for an adult to stand by and let a kid skedaddle blindly through a parking lot. Yet every other week it seems like there's a story on the news about a pedestrian being struck and killed through no fault of their own: because of a distracted driver, usually. Sometimes it's at a crosswalk; just as many times it's a parking lot. Half the time the victim is a kid.

They're heading south now, toward Kerrisdale. Bester is some distance ahead of them, nearly at 33rd where the traffic light has just turned green. He's ambling, hands at his side, arms barely swinging. His movement is almost all legs, his shoulders only lightly waggling with each step like a buoy in tranquil waters, disturbed by the occasional passing fish, otherwise floating lazily. At their current pace they're liable to overtake him before long. Which raises the question: should they continue at this speed or slow down? And what is it they're doing exactly? What are they going to do if Bester turns around and sees them? We're on a walk, Steve could say. He doesn't like lying. He's good at it, though. He hates that he's good at it. But it's not like they can tell Bester the truth: We recognized you back at Starbucks, remember us? We were sitting next to you, you had the breakfast sandwich, we had the scone, you left, left your sandwich bag on the counter, was that on purpose to keep the baristas employed? We wanted to see where you were going so we left, too. Not sure why exactly, but we aren't stalkers, honest to God, we're not, we definitely aren't stalking you, are you Alfred Bester? Yes? Aren't you supposed to be dead?

Their pace has picked up. Steve's legs are moving in lock step with Adi's.

                                               Right.

Left.

                                               Right.

Left.

                                               Right.

Bester has crossed the intersection up ahead. He doesn't appear to be in a hurry. If anything, he's moving slower. Is it because he's old he's going so slow? That would make sense. Whether the guy is really Bester or his doppelgänger, he's old. There's no question about that. Then again, some old people are pretty spritely. E.g., the first time Steve went up the Grouse Grind he was passed by a quartet of seniors. One of them held an oxygen tank in her hand. Bester—or whoever it is they're following; it can't really be a guy Wikipedia says died in 1987, can it? hiding out, alive, in Vancouver the last twenty-five years?—isn't using a cane or a walker, not holding an O2 tank. He's in good shape, in other words. He's not limping, i.e., he doesn't have an apparent leg injury, so the reason he's moving like molasses must be something else. Maybe it's just a function of Vancouver life. Steve used to think the reason everyone walked so slowly here was because the city was more laid back compared to Manhattan or Philly or even Toronto. Then he went out east one winter and everyone in Charlottetown was in just as much of a hurry as people living and working in the epicenter of urban sprawl, which he hadn't expected, and it was then he realized it's not a city's pace of life that correlates to walking speed. It's the weather. Too hot, too cold: move fast. In Taipei people are constantly on the fly, always trying to get out of the heat.

In Vancouver—

what's

the

rush

?

It's always nice in Vancouver. Even in the spring and fall. There's an effulgence to the rain.

"Can you go faster?"

"We're good where we are," making sure she's far enough from the side of the road. "This is a safe distance. Any closer and he might make us."

"Make us what?"

"He might notice us tailing him."

"He's so far away."

"But look how slow he's going. We'll catch up in no time."

"Where do you think he's going?"

"No clue."

"I think he's going to get a Slurpee."

Effulgent.

Not that days like today, days where it seems the very idea of rain doesn't exist, aren't welcome. Days like this are great: ideal for walking, for thinking. It's just that people are always ragging on Vancouver because it rains here a full third of the year, when the truth is, folks who live here love it. It seeps into you. So why all the complaints? Steve's theory is that Vancouverites complain about the rain to non-Vancouverites because there are enough people here already, real estate prices are obscene enough already, without even more demand driving already unaffordable prices even further up. Locals don't want more eastern and central Canadians moving west. They certainly don't want Americans relocating here. Definitely not more Chinese immigrants. It's Hongcouver enough as it is.

Vancouverites is an odd-sounding demonym.

Or maybe the weather has nothing to do with why Bester is walking slowly. It might just be what writers do: walk slowly in service of deliberate thinking. His age might be a factor, too, not because of any physical limitations that exist, but because he has a heightened awareness of the roses he didn't stop to smell when he was younger, a thing virtually every middle-aged and older person at St. Joe's has told Steve at one point or another they wish they'd been more attuned to when they were his age. When you think about it that way, walking slowly is an effort to resist the enfeebling of human experience, that sort of thing. It must be good, this flânerie life, the writer's life. Nowhere to rush to, no deadlines to meet, not always thinking ahead to next Sunday.

Steve and Adi have reached the corner of 33rd and Arbutus. They're crossing the street. Bester is nearing the top of the bend, two, maybe three hundred meters ahead. Approximating distances isn't easy without two reference points, X and Y, the actual distance between which is known.

"*Survivor* is on today."

"The reality show?"

"The TV show," looking up at him, puzzled.

"I didn't know that was still running."

"Who do you think will get voted off?"

"I don't know. I haven't seen it since the first season."

"You know what it is, though?"

"Of course."

"I think the girls should join together and get rid of the boys."

"That would be smart."

"They probably won't, though."

"Do you watch it with your parents?"

Adi hesitates, staring ahead blankly. "Only my mom. She says I shouldn't tell anyone."

Steve laughs. "I won't tell her you told. Her secret is safe with me."

"The tribes merged last week."

"What do you like about the show?"

Adi looks off to the side, as if giving the question some thought. "Watching it with my mom."

"That's sweet."

"She's so funny when it's on."

"What do you mean?"

"She's always talking back to the TV. Sometimes she yells."

"Your mom gets that into it?"

"Last week there was this challenge and they split into two teams, orange and blue. And the orange team, I think, or was it the blue team? No, the orange team. Right? Yeah. Anyway, let's just say it was orange. It might have been blue, but I can't exactly remember, so just assume it was orange. They were definitely orange and blue, I'm sure, because those are my mom's favorite colors. One of the teams got off to a big lead. Let's say it was the orange team. I think it was orange. Anyway, they got off to a big lead, like huge," stretching her arms as far as they'll go. "And my mom was yelling at the other team to hurry up because she liked this chef guy on that team, Jonas. And then they did. They caught up."

"The team with the chef?"

"And my mom was so excited, but then the orange team still won in the end. And then they voted off Jonas."

"Sounds dramatic."

"Also, if you watch the show, a lot of times when teams are behind, they come back and win, so it's almost like you were expecting it when the blue team caught up. Like, that's what the people who edit the show want you to think will happen. I really thought they were going to win. But then they lost."

"It's the tortoise and the hare remixed."

"When the blue team started coming back, my mom kept on saying, It's not how you start, it's how you finish."

"Both are important."

"That's what I told her. Finishing is fine, but getting off to a good start is just as important. If the blue team had started faster, they would have won. They didn't start fast enough. My dad is always talking about first-mover advantage."

"Sometimes being quick to act means first-mover advantage, which is good."

"My dad is a genius."

"But sometimes you end up like Protesilaus."

"Not Proto whatever. His name was Jonas. There's no one called Proto whatever you said."

"Never mind."

"Jonas."

"Why did your mom like him?" Was he particularly good looking?

"Does."

"What?"

"Why *does* she like him. You said *did*, but she still likes him. You should have said *does*. Present tense."

"Sorry. Why *does* she like him?" Is he particularly good looking?

Adi shrugs. "She watches a lot of cooking shows."

"Was he on one?"

"I don't think so. She just watches a lot of cooking shows."

"Like what?"

"My mom loves *Top Chef*. Do you watch that?"

"No, but I was on it."

"You weren't."

"I was."

"You're lying."

"I wasn't competing. I was in one episode, though. In the background."

Adi looks at him disbelievingly. She takes the blueberry scone scraps from her coat pocket and shoves them in her mouth with no discretion at all.

"They were filming in January on Granville Island, at the Public Market. I was buying smoked salmon and vegetables."

"Seriously?"

"Cross my heart," crossing it. "You can see me briefly in one scene where the cheftestants are running around, picking up groceries. One of the producers, or it might've been a camera man, said it was the finale."

"Cool. I'm going to tell my mom. She'll be really impressed." Her voice is the voice of someone entirely serious, but is she?

Steve is trying to remember the mental list of conversation topics he conjured earlier.

Weather.

Canucks.

Walking to school.

What else?

Vietnamese food.

Places he's been.

Places she's been.

Books she's read.

Music.

Extracurriculars.

And?

Friends.

Boys.

Church.

No, not church.

"Have you been to the burger place there?"

"Is that the one near the windows facing the water? Across from the French onion soup pot pie place?"

"That's the one."

"I haven't."

"They make my favorite burger in the city."

"Do they have veggie burgers?"

"Probably. If I had the car today, we could've gone."

"That's alright. I'm not really a burger fan."

What else was on his list of conversation topics? Disgusting culinary. Connection!

"They eat gross things on *Survivor* don't they?"

"They don't eat very much. Everyone loses weight by the time they go home."

"Would you ever want to be on *Survivor*?"

"I'd rather be on *Top Chef*."

"Oh yeah?"

"Mm-hmm."

"How come?"

"You don't need to have accomplished anything to be on *Survivor*. But for *Top Chef* you have to know how to cook. Not just cook. You have to be good at it. Also, I like food. And art."

Crossing the 35th Street cul-de-sac, Adi sees a notice taped to the stop sign pole, beneath the No Exit sign. There's a picture of three dirty-white chickens roosting on some grass. Roosting? Standing? Above the photo: MISSING CHICKENS, all-caps, in a large serif typeface. Beneath it: some more text, smaller, and a phone number.

"Someone lost his chickens." Adi reaches up and touches the poster.

"Probably to a coyote." Neither of them pauses long enough to read the short paragraph below the photo of the chickens. Does anyone stop to read a lost-pet flyer? Even so, he says a quick silent prayer that the guy who has lost them will find them or have them returned. Does he believe his prayer will be answered? Not in the affirmative. Not this time. Not unless the guy who has lost his chickens goes and finds them himself. Life is life, that's how Sam would put it.

"He's looking at us." Adi stops.

Steve bumps into her. Up ahead, Bester is facing them. A forest green RAV4 passes southbound, moving, it appears, faster than the speed limit. Bester cranes, tilts and readjusts the slant of his head to see the car zipping past him as if he's trying to make out the identity of the person driving. It doesn't stop. He resumes walking.

"I don't think he was looking at us. He was distracted by that SUV."

"He was staring right at me," pointing at her chest.

"It looked like he was staring at the car."

"He's getting away."

"You still want to follow?"

Adi takes off running.

Steve doesn't. It's not just that there's something resembling weakness to a grown man running when it's not for exercise—to catch a bus, say, or because he's trying to catch up to someone, or for any other non-health-related reason. There's a certain indignity to it. But he picks up his pace a little so that Adi doesn't get too far away. Just a little. It's not a terribly steep hill. But still. No sense in exhausting himself.

"He's going into the 7/11."

She might be right. There's some kind of hobby store next to it so he might be going there. Steve can't tell from where they are, here beyond the laneway, coming up on 36th.

"Don't cross the street. Wait for me."

Adi is waiting. "Hurry up."

Steve does. There's a twinge of an ache in his knees that flares with each step—a childhood injury suffered when he fell off his bike, over a bridge, into a shallow brook.

"There's no cars. Come on," and she's off again, in a sprint, Steve speed-walking beside her, his head on a swivel because the lanes here aren't that wide and a car could come barreling out of nowhere.

They pass a basil-colored lamppost on which is taped another missing chickens poster. Steve seriously needs to get back in shape. He's not moving that fast at all and his breathing is already growing labored. On top of his aching knees. He's thirty-four, but has the cardiovascular fitness level of someone much older. Embarrassing. It's not like this stretch of Arbutus has anywhere near the elevation of the Grouse Grind either. It's understand-able, huffing and puffing, doing the Grind. Walking up a small hill? Not so much. He'd better get in shape. Too unhealthy for too long and who knows. Run a little faster you fat—

"Come on already." Adi has stopped on the sidewalk by the parking lot shared by the 7/11 and the hobby store.

Steve pretends like he's not tired, like going this distance, up this gradual incline, hasn't made him the least bit dizzy and winded. "Did you see where he went?"

Adi nods vigorously. "Right there. The 7/11 just like I said."

Steve can't see him from where they're standing: in the cover of some shrubbery, some seven steps off the main sidewalk, near Magic Box Hob-bies, in front of which is parked the only car, an unoccupied gold Corolla, in the otherwise empty lot.

"Are we going in or do you want to stay out here all day?"

"I don't know."

The thing is, Steve's not sure he wants to go into the 7/11 either. Go in and they're bound to talk to Bester. There would be no avoiding it if they were to follow him in, and Steve still hasn't figured out what he's going to say if they have a face-to-face. All things considered, it'd be significantly easier to carry on walking. Maybe pick up the prescription refill from the pharmacy. Though picking it up now would mean having to carry a bottle of pills around the rest of the day. Unless he were to drop it off at home, but Lola wouldn't like it, having one of Sam's friends over while she's there, not to mention the place is a mess, as if someone broke in and trashed it, looking for something valuable to steal. Jewels. Which they wouldn't find because all of the jewelry she owns is at the bank, in a safe deposit box. Really did a number on it, is how the cops would undoubtedly describe the scene of the crime. The computer, though, with all the kids' photos. That's valuable. He needs to get an external hard drive to back everything up. Plus, he and Adi have already passed his home. Another thing he could do is he could leave the meds at his office, but who knows when or even if they're going to be at the church. He's got to get the script filled eventually, though, and today. There is one other alternative he hasn't thought of until now: they could stay here and wait for Bester to come out, then resume whatever it is they've been doing the last fifteen minutes or so. Whatever it is, it's not stalking. Stalking is a crime, he's pretty sure, and following a guy from Starbucks to 7/11 down the street because they're curious about him, that doesn't rise to the level of a criminal code violation. It's nothing more than innocent curiosity. So that's what they could do: postpone any sort of confrontation until Steve has thought it through some more, at least until he has his opening line down. Mr. Bester? Hi, sorry to bother you, we recognized you at the Starbucks earlier and my young friend wanted to say hello. My young friend? My daughter's friend? We were a little shy, which is why we waited till now. We were a little shy? She was? Absurd. Something along those lines, though. Or maybe they should pretend like they hadn't been following him, but had recognized him earlier, like, Hey, aren't you famous science fiction novelist Alfred Bester? And weren't you sitting next to us at Starbucks? We wanted to say something, but were too shy. We thought you were dead. Can he say that? It's ridiculous he's being so diffident about the matter. Bester is just another human being. A man-pleasing, man-fearing man, made of blood and bone and fear and sin. He has to use the restroom just like anyone else. Unless he's a ghost. Ghosts don't open doors, though. What's got Steve so cowed? He's never intimidated by people, even celebrities, and Bester barely qualifies as a celebrity. Steve doesn't know him, didn't recognize him, has never read him. Then again, it's not exactly true that he's never intimidated by people. Most of the time; not never. There was that time sophomore year at Penn when he and some buddies had gone to see what turned out to be Gretzky's last game against the Flyers before he retired later that spring—99 in '99. He'd recorded two assists. After the game Steve and his friends hung around outside the Spectrum, hoping to catch a glimpse of the Great One on his way to the team bus. Steve was pessimistic about their chances of meeting him.

He should've had more faith because sure enough, there he was, coming out the security guard-guarded door. Hey fellas, Gretzky had said when one of Steve's friends, Ramin, Steve thinks it was, Ramin, who didn't know what eye candy meant and had never seen a hockey game in person until that evening, called out, Wayne! Wayne! Gretzky came right up to them, close enough they could see and feel his spittle when he spoke, it was awesome. He shook all their hands. Steve stuck his out like a raging idiot. A mute, raging idiot. Afterward he thought about all the things he ought to have said, things he maybe would have said if he'd been prepared. If, say, he'd thought of a few opening lines ahead of time, he could have told Gretzky how when he was a kid, the first time he heard that Gretzky was taking the Lady Byng home with him, Steve thought she was a real live woman and wow, he really is the Great One, not realizing until the next morning when the sports pages ran a photo of Gretzky with the trophies he'd won the night before above a caption identifying said trophies, one of which was the Lady Byng, that the Lady Byng was a piece of hardware. Named after a real woman who'd once been alive, sure, but just a silver cup on a wooden base. Probably not even real silver. Not as cool as an actual lady, Steve had thought, but then again, still cool. Everyone loves trophies. Gretzky might've found that funny and maybe they'd be fast friends today. He might even drop by St. Joe's for service once in a while when he's in town. Steve had three trophies of his own for winning three different speech contests at Saturday morning Chinese school, over three consecutive years, 1987–89. Stacked one above the other, they wouldn't have reached half the height of the Lady Byng. He could have told that story, or some portion thereof, to Gretzky outside the Spectrum, instead of making no sound whatsoever as they shook hands. He hadn't so much shaken Gretzky's hand either, as had his own limp hand shaken by the Great One. Whatever the opposite of a firm grasp is, that's what Steve had offered up. It was the opposite of the handshake they teach you at Wharton.

It's like 1999 all over again.

Steve is determined to have none of it.

It's not 1999. It's 2012. He's a father now and a pastor and a man.

"Let's go in. You want to talk to him, right?"

Adi shrugs emphatically.

"We followed him for a reason. Might as well say hello. There's no reason to be shy. Be strong and courageous."

"How do I?"

Steve puts a hand on Adi's shoulder and they begin walking toward the 7/11, cutting through the parking lot. "He's been in there a long time it feels like."

Adi doesn't answer.

Steve runs his other hand, the one that's not on Adi's shoulder, through what little fuzz of hair he has, back to front, then back, then feeling the bumps on the top of his head with the tips of his fingers. Four ridges. It doesn't hurt to touch them. What if he pushes down on them, hard? That doesn't hurt either. He traces around the rest of his scalp, searching by touch for additional bumps. Nothing. What does hurt a little are his knees, still.

Steve pulls open the glass door, holding it for Adi, who walks inside. He's never been to this 7/11 before. All these years in the neighborhood, and this is his first time here. Then again he hasn't been inside a lot of the stores in Kerrisdale. The last time he was at a 7/11, any 7/11, was when? The only times he can remember are from his trips back to Taiwan, when, having grown tired of the local food, he'd duck into a random 7/11 on a street corner somewhere to grab a sandwich with the crust cut off, usually ham, egg, and tomato, and a sarsaparilla soda.

"Do you see him?"

Adi shifts her head around like a periscope with a bolt loose, her eyes darting from one section of the store to another. "Where is he?"

The cashier looks up from an open psychology textbook. "Can I help you with something?"

"No, thanks." Steve has seen her before somewhere. The condo? Studying at Starbucks? She has a tiny mole between her eyebrows. "Actually, there is something. We thought we saw someone we recognize."

"No one here but me."

"Tall?" bringing a hand a few inches above his own head. "Really old white guy, glasses?"

"Someone looking like that was here a few minutes ago," nodding, "but he left."

"He's not here?"

"I don't think so," doing a quick scan.

"Is there a restroom he could've gone to?"

"It's staff only," pointing at her chest. "He asked about a brand of cigarettes that we don't carry. Then he left."

"There isn't a back door he could have gone out?"

"Not that he could've used."

Where is he then? If he's not in the restroom and he didn't leave out the back, he must have gone through the front, which means he must have left while Steve and Adi weren't paying attention. People don't just vanish into thin air. There are certain immutable laws that time- and space-bound material beings are incapable of violating, try as they might, pray though they may. Comic book characters, sure. Mythological creatures, fine. One of Bester's own invented heroes or villains, if he's that kind of science fiction writer, no problem. Fiction isn't subject to the properties of the natural world. But real three-dimensional men don't disappear. If this were a dream, that'd be one thing. Steve pinches some flesh on the top of his hand. But could both he and Adi have been distracted for so long they missed Bester altogether? That's equally preposterous. What must have happened is Bester must have ducked out the back without the cashier noticing. Her face had been deep in her textbook when they came in. Cramming for an exam, probably. A UBC student, probably. Why would Bester have wanted to leave without being noticed? That's obvious. He'd spotted Steve and Adi tailing him, didn't want to be recognized, who knows what he thought, but the point is he didn't want to talk to them so he squirreled away.

"I have a feeling we'll bump into him again," holding the door open for Adi.

She steps outside.

Steve follows.

"But where did he go?"

"I bet he's one of those antisocial authors who doesn't like to talk to people. He might have staged his own death for that very reason. He must've figured we recognized him, saw us following him, and thought we were going to ask him about being dead, or for a selfie, so he hid. He probably snuck out the back."

"What back?"

"All stores like this have back entrances for deliveries."

"Do you think he's there?"

"I doubt it. He could be anywhere by now."

"We should check just to be sure," earnestly.

"We can." They head toward 37th. "Why do you want to talk to him anyway?"

"He's an oracle."

"Bryan wasn't being literal, you know? Oracles aren't real. No one knows the future."

"As long as he can talk to spirits."

"Looks like the back entrance is actually the side entrance." There's a narrow passage between the store's exterior and the adjacent house, but it's not exactly traversable. "We have to go back, then around," gesturing with his hand the route they're going to take. "And you're thinking of something else, another word," which escapes him at the moment. "An oracle is someone who knows the future, not who communicates with the dead."

"Someone who knows the future is a prophet."

"They're synonyms. Do you know what that means?"

Adi gives him a look evincing her aggravation: half eye-roll, brows raised. "I know oracles are real. My dad plays a game on the computer called the stock market and he's always talking about this guy, Walter Buffett, the Oracle of Omaha, which is a city in Nebraska, but not the capital. The capital of Nebraska is Lincoln, named after Abraham Lincoln, the sixteenth president of the United States. I've never been to Nebraska before, have you?"

"Warren."

"My dad's name is Hawthorn."

"Warren Buffett, not Walter."

"How do you know? Do you know him?"

"I met him once." Steve kicks a chunk of broken glass off the sidewalk, farther away from the road, leaving the smaller fragments of translucent green shards where they are. "What's funny is when I was in university I dated a girl whose father was called the Warren Buffett of Japan. I'm not talking about Masayoshi Son, in case you've heard the moniker attached to him."

Adi's face doesn't give anything away.

"Masayoshi Son might have a daughter, he might not. The girl I dated was the daughter of another man who some people also called the Oracle of Okayama. I did meet the real Warren Buffett once, though, like I said. He was giving a lecture at my school."

"Did he talk to spirits?"

"It wasn't a séance," shaking his head. "But everyone wanted to hear him and seating in the auditorium where he was speaking was limited so my school had a lottery to distribute tickets and I won a pair. The girl I brought called him her hero."

"Was she the Japanese Warren Buffett's daughter?"

"This was another girl."

"How many girlfriends did you have?"

"In university?"

"Ever."

"Not that many."

"Nineteen?"

"Not that many."

"Nine?"

"Somewhere between nine and nineteen, I guess. I haven't kept count."

Liar.

"So Warren Buffett isn't really an oracle?"

"He's not," and it comes to him now. "The word you're thinking of is a medium."

"Like small medium large, medium?"

"Same spelling, different meaning."

"A homograph."

"This medium is a psychic intermediary who can communicate with the dead. A high priest of purgatory."

"What?"

Steve smiles, pleased with himself. "He's not an oracle, no."

"But the guy we were following might be."

"Whoever he is, whether he's really Alfred Bester or not, I promise you he's not an oracle or a medium."

"How do you know he's not?"

"Mediums aren't real either. Anyone claiming to be one is a charlatan."

Adi's face is a slough of despond.

"Doesn't look like he's here." A couple of dumpsters and a few corrugated boxes, some flattened, some not, and other refuse dot the space behind, or rather, beside the 7/11, but no Bester. The alleyway is every bit as empty. Trash containers and recycling bins not properly put away are strewn on the unpaved lane. A porta-potty here, construction materials there. Zero people.

"Where did he go?"

"If you want enough not to be found, you find a way to hide."

"Do you think he knew we were going to follow him to the 7/11 and then look for him back here? Because he's an oracle?"

"Impossible."

"You can't know that for sure."

"It's as impossible as wiggling an earlobe."

"That's not impossible. I can do it." She does: she makes her left ear-lobe twitch, then her right, without any other part of her face moving, not a muscle, at least not visibly. "So that means oracles might be real and he might really be one. So maybe mediums aren't not real, too."

"All it means is I chose a bad example."

"But how do you know they don't exist? You don't know everything. Maybe one of the things you don't know is that there really are people who know the future and other people who can talk to spirits. There are probably a million things you don't know about."

"More than a million for sure."

"So he could be an oracle and there could be mediums."

"If not impossible, highly improbable." Though there is the medium of En-dor, the necromancer. "But if he is, that's going to make it a lot harder to find him. If he knows we're looking."

"But just because he can predict the future does that mean he knows everything about the future or just some things?"

"You're the expert. You tell me."

"Just some things."

"Then there's hope. But we aren't going to get anything done just standing here." Steve looks around. The alley is still empty. "Let's go to the pharmacy. I need to get something for Sam's mom. Maybe we'll bump into Bester on the way."

"He has to be in this neighborhood somewhere."

"Right?"

"He might be an oracle, but he can't teleport."

They're on the move again.

"Actually, maybe if you believe in oracles and mediums, you should believe in the possibility of teleportation." Steve feels a self-rebuke coming on. "Once you open one supernatural door, all manner of things could come out of it. Teleportation doesn't even properly belong to the supernatural realm. It's quantum mechanics."

"What?"

"Just talking to myself."

Some people at St. Joe's think it's odd and possibly unbefitting for a pastor to be so skeptical about the miraculous happening here on earth, here today. After all, the central tenets of the Christian faith hinge on the historicity of miracles like the incarnation. And perhaps they're right. But at least teleportation has some scientific theory to commend it. Which isn't to suggest that faith is irrational. Faith has its reasons and ought to be reasonable. But skepticism is almost always a healthy thing to have in some quantity. No pastor, no matter how devout, is entirely devoid of doubt that his prayers are little more than self-talk. Lord, I believe; help thou my unbelief. Doesn't make a guy a lesser Christian. And anyway, Steve doesn't believe improbable things—things some would term miracles—never happen, or can't. He's not so naïve as to be an out-and-out cessationist, no sir, not if you start with the *a priori* assumption that God exists. Nor does he make his own experience, or lack thereof, of unexplainable phenomena, universally normative. Faith and doubt aren't binary categories. In fact, there was one time he raised a Fortean interpretation from the pulpit; not the wisest decision, granted, but it was Transfiguration Sunday, he was preaching from the Lukan account of the scene, describing the history of interpretation: how could Moses and Elijah, both long since deceased, appear in bodily form on the mountain with Jesus? He hadn't been speaking anything like *ex cathedra*; merely offering one of a handful of suggestions and saying only that there was something he found wonderful about the one he, himself, favored—wonderful as in full of wonder, awe, that sort of thing, a thoroughly biblical sensation on par with joy and hope—and after service that morning no small number of congregants confronted him about it, including Merab who once, immediately after telling him over coffee that he was doing well, generally speaking, as their new minister even if he could never measure up to his predecessor the Very Reverend Indeed Pastor Barnabas, proceeded to pull out of her handbag a half-dozen sheets of foolscap on which she'd written in her sorry shoddy penmanship all the specific things he wasn't doing well. Normally Merab waits until her Monday morning meetings with Steve, the ones she insisted he maintain when he started because Pastor Barney was religious in seeing her, she was second only to God to Pastor Barney, normally she waits until then to voice her critiques, but after Steve's Transfiguration sermon, she pulled him aside to tell him what she thought about the way he'd tried to explain the passage: she'd thought all that time-travel, teleportation hoo-ha was fairy tale talk, and there's no place for fairy stories from the pulpit. Teach the Bible, Pastor. He should be more mindful of the words he uses, she'd said; words can be dangerous. Yes or they can be delightful, depends on how they're being wielded, and who's wielding them. Yes it does, she'd said, giving him her version of the stink-eye. Steve can summon the look in an instant. His week isn't complete without seeing it at least once. Despite the pushback, he maintains there's much to his reading of the text worth further exploration. If he had more time and the inclination, he would put it all down on paper, send it off to a peer-reviewed theology journal. Then maybe someone else would see it, maybe cite it, maybe have it inform the monograph they're working on, which might get read by another academic who's writing a commentary, which might get read by a pastor, and maybe work its way down to a congregation somewhere. Consider the essentials: 1) God appeared to Moses in the burning bush on Mount Horeb; 2) God appeared to Elijah, after an earthquake and a fire, also on Mount Horeb; 3) the Mount of Transfiguration is none other than Mount Horeb, which is disputed, yes, but there's reason to suggest they're one and the same; 4) what if, rather than being three discrete moments in history, all three events occurred at and in the same space-time? The stuff of make-believe? An overactive imagination? Or an uncommon yet no less orthodox outworking of faith? Maybe pastors ought to consult speculative fiction by writers like Bester, instead of those technical commentaries churned out by tenured and tenure-track professors. Steve adds him to the top of a mental list of novelists he's planning to read someday when he has more time. Maybe he can ask Bester about it if they run into him later. Maybe oracles and mediums aren't so implausible. Given his worldview they can't be excluded out of hand. He should be more consistent.

"Where are we going again?"

"The pharmacy. It's just up ahead."

"I'm hungry."

"We can have lunch after I get Sam's mom's medicine."

"Is she sick?"

"She is."

"With what?"

How does he answer that? He doesn't really understand her illness, how could Adi? "I'm not really sure."

"Are you a good husband?"

"That's a funny question."

"My mom thinks you must be a good husband."

"When did she say that?"

Adi shrugs.

"Was it recently?"

"And she thinks you're a good dad."

"That's nice of her." Steve tries to hide his smile as he adds Adi's words to his collection of compliments. Ms. Chelsea started calling him Super Dance Dad last year, after that day he applied Sam's make-up and put her hair in a bun for her ballet recital at the Gateway Theatre. He'd been heavy-handed with the blush, chose the wrong color so her face looked like one big bruise, but the bun wasn't bad and he was the only dad backstage, which he felt awkward about because he could read the mothers' minds, but if they'd known why Lola couldn't be there, couldn't leave their home, that a walk to the foyer to pick up the mail was a big step, they wouldn't have judged him for being a man, not that he blamed them. Other fairly recent additions to his collection: Husseyn, who'd been in Sam's kindergarten class but has Mr. Poppelwell for first grade, told Sam her dad was awesome. This was after he'd helped supervise the field trip to the pumpkin patch. One of the perks of a pastor's schedule is Steve can do those sorts of things more often than not. He has to remind himself of this every few days. And Thomas, who left Bluffwood for either West Point Grey or Saints, Steve had known once, but doesn't remember because private schools are all the same, had boasted to his own father and in front of half of Ms. Irwin's class, that Sam's dad was the coolest. Sam had been so proud when she recounted those stories to him at pick-up. Every day after school when Steve asks how her day was, she says fine, never any more, never any other word. When he asks what she learned, she says nothing. But on the days Husseyn and Thomas had said those things about him, she'd conveyed their praise before Steve had asked her a thing. Which means she must be proud to have him for a dad, right?

"What time is it?"

Steve reaches for his phone, blindly pressing the home button as he takes it out of his pocket. "It's 11:24." He holds the screen in front of Adi so she can verify it. Then he puts the phone back in his pocket and opens the door to the pharmacy.

It's mostly empty inside. Steve can't see the entirety of the store from the entrance, but the feeling of people's absence is unmistakable; a sensitivity pastors acquire over time.

Three customers are in line to drop off or pick up their prescriptions. The elderly couple at the front is in the process of being helped. There's a woman a few feet behind them, in front of Steve and Adi, awaiting her turn. Her knee-length, chain-print, pleated skirt exposes bare calves thicker than Steve remembers them being, as is the whole of her figure, really. Even so, and even from behind, he recognizes her instantly. The way her head is tilted: the mien of a sensitive listener; her hands around her waist like a Magritte painting, the one of the naked woman who's part flesh, part wood. She's got a bit of familiar skin visible, too, between the bottom of her blouse and the top of her skirt. His gaze lingers there. A memory begins to form. Eyes up, Steve. Eyes above her shoulders, on the back of her head. He wills them there. Should he say something? Call out her name? If he doesn't, she'll probably notice him on her way out, at which point they'll end up exchanging phatic pleasantries, that's all the time they'll have before she heads out and he walks up to the counter. Though it's possible she walks right past him without so much as an initial glance. Would he regret his silence if that happened? She might get a phone call or a text and be so distracted she misses him completely. Would that be so bad?

"Veronica," doing his best to sound disinterested. He's not sure whether to smile or not.

"Who's Veronica?" Adi is tugging on the sleeve of Steve's coat.

Veronica turns around.

Steve's face is a Potemkin village.

"Hey." There's a trace of what sounds like excitement in her voice. It might be feigned. It might be masking ambivalence or worse.

"Hey," trying to match her level of enthusiasm.

"I said, Who's Veronica?"

"Hi there." Veronica shifts her gaze to Adi. "What's your name?"

Steve sees now the cause of her thickness. "This is Veronica."

"Your tummy is round."

"It is," rubbing her stomach.

"You're pregnant."

"I hope that's what this is," still rubbing. "What about you?" nodding in Adi's direction. "Is she yours?"

"This is Adi," bringing his hand to rest on Adi's shoulder. "My oldest."

"Hi Adi."

"Hello."

"I thought your oldest's name was Sam."

Steve shakes his head slowly, furrowing his brow for good measure as if he has no idea what she's talking about.

"I must have you mixed up with another friend."

"Hmm." Is that what she thinks they are to one another? And how does she know about Sam? They've never met. There were no birth announcements, and even if there had been, Veronica would have been the

81

last person in the world to get one. The last time Steve and Veronica saw each other was how long ago? How long has it been since they broke up? There was a time he knew the exact length of time in days.

"She kind of looks mixed, doesn't she?"

"We get that sometimes."

The couple at the counter is finished with their business. The pharmacist calls for the next person in line.

"Sorry." Veronica spins around, her skirt twirling like in the movies. She approaches the desk and hands over a prescription she must have been clutching the whole time she was talking to Steve, though he hadn't noticed her holding anything. Why had he lied about Adi? Why hadn't he told her the truth? There's nothing embarrassing about babysitting one of Sam's slightly sick friends for the day. Nothing embarrassing in helping a busy mother. It's actually pretty generous of him, she might think. She might be impressed. There's nothing impressive about a dad taking his daughter to the drug store. Plenty of dads do that with their kids. Adi tugs on Steve's sleeve again. He presses his index finger to his lips and gives her a furtive look before turning back toward Veronica. She used to insist she was never going to have kids, which isn't the only reason they broke up, but it didn't help. Steve wanted a big family—four kids at least; six being the dream: three boys, three girls, two fully stocked curling teams. Sometimes he thinks he still wants this. Veronica said she didn't want kids because she'd love them too much and the most loving thing a person can do for their kids is not to have them in the first place because life is sorrow heaped upon sorrow, world without end.

That's the way she is—or the way she was, to be more precise, because who knows? she might be different now; must be different, in fact—always with the hackneyed pseudo-philosophizing. She used to think his trite observations were utter genius. Steve had never understood her depression when they were together. Now she's pregnant, last trimester clearly, getting some kind of mother's tea prescription filled, probably, as her accouchement nears. Meanwhile he's picking up Lola's Manerix refill. The irony isn't lost on him. Lots of things are lost on him, but not this. When did she even get married? Is she married? If one of their mutual friends had told him she got married, he would remember. If the wedding had been local, he would have gone, invited or not. He would have worn his best suit, the bespoke one from Harry Rosen he wore at his own wedding. He would have driven up to the church or wherever the ceremony was being held, parked on the other side of the street, a pair of binoculars at the ready or just the zoom lens on his phone's camera. He would have waited until her limo pulled up, and of course it would be a limo, though maybe a vintage Rolls Royce if someone like the Queen or another member of the royal family had once been a passenger because she loved the monarchy, was fascinated by Charles and his sons and even the Queen's husband, and he would have watched as her bridesmaids helped her out of the car and up the church steps and through the probably wooden doors, and he would have followed her in, but at a safe distance, far enough back that she wouldn't have spotted him. Not as far back as he and Adi were when they trailed Bester, but far enough. He would have watched from the corner of a back pew as she exchanged vows and rings and kissed the man that could have been him.

He doesn't see a ring on her finger.

"Next." The pharmacist is calling.

"One second," smiling weakly.

"I'd better get going." Veronica is a foot away. "I still have a bunch more errands to run before baby arrives."

When are you due? he wants to ask. Is it a boy or a girl? is this your first? how has the pregnancy been? morning sickness? what hospital? which doctor? or maybe not a doctor; a midwife? "You're going to be a great mom."

"Thanks. I hope so."

He extends his arm to shake her hand.

"Give me a hug."

He does, feeling her belly against his, breathing deep her bergamot and vanilla-scented perfume before letting go, stepping back, putting a hand on Adi's shoulder again. He hated the smell of vanilla before he met Veronica. "It was good to bump into you."

"You, too."

He smiles. She hadn't caught the pun.

"Oh," turning, "I don't know if Lola told you, but I ran into her not that long ago."

"Where?" And when? It's been a while since she's been outside.

"In your condo. I was visiting a friend on the second floor and saw her in the lobby."

"She didn't mention it."

"We didn't really get a chance to talk. I think she was getting the mail? Tell her I said hi."

"Sure." He gives a casual wave and watches as she heads toward the door. He can't take his eyes off her.

At last he and Adi approach the pharmacist.

"Daddy," her voice dripping with alacrity. "Can you buy me some candy?"

"I'm picking up a prescription."

"What's the last name?"

Steve answers, spells it out letter by letter because sometimes people get it wrong on account of mishearing him. The pharmacist finds the record on his computer, asks if he has the correct first name, and after Steve nods, turns to the wall of alphabetically arranged plastic containers, goes to one, and rummages. A moment later he's found it. Another moment and he's in front of Steve, handing him a pill bottle.

"She's used this before?"

"She has."

"Okay then, that's it."

"There's no charge?"

"It's all covered by her insurance. We have it on file unless you've moved?"

"Nope." Steve would like to move, though, to someplace with more space.

"Then that's it. Can I help you with anything else?"

"No, thanks." Steve shoves the medicine in an empty pocket and turns, heading toward the entrance/exit.

"I thought you were going to get me candy."

"Later maybe. We're in a rush. We weren't before, but we're running a little late now."

"Your friend is long gone by now you know."

"Veronica?"

"She's definitely gone."

"I'm not looking for her."

"Yes you are."

"Why would you think that?"

"You were looking at her all goofy and your voice was different. But for sure she's gone. I saw her get in a car and drive off."

They step outside. Steve looks down 40th, then up and down West Boulevard. Veronica isn't anywhere. "What do you mean my voice was different?"

"You sounded not your normal voice. You sounded like my mom, kind of."

"I don't sound anything like her."

"When you were talking to that lady you did."

"That's crazy."

"You were all like, You're going to be a great mom," high-pitched, blinking her eyes rapidly.

"I didn't do that."

Adi's face is dry as granola. "Can we eat now?"

Steve checks his phone figuring five minutes have passed since he last checked. It's been more than eight. Is this what time flies means? "Sure. Let's get lunch."

They head south.

"Why did you tell her I was Sam?"

"I don't know."

"Did she used to be your girlfriend or something?"

"We almost got married."

"To her?"

"I almost proposed."

"My dad took me to a baseball game in Seattle once where a guy pro-posed on the big screen." She traces a giant rectangle in the air with her fingers.

"Did the person say yes?"

"He kissed him."

"That's cool."

"Why do people propose at sporting events? Wouldn't it be kind of awkward if the person says no?"

"Nobody says no when there's that much peer pressure."

Adi swings her arms like she's holding a baseball bat. "What do you think is the best sporting event to propose at?"

None is what he thinks, but if he had to choose? "A tennis match maybe? Or Ultimate? I have no idea. Not golf."

"Why not?"

"Golf is terrible."

"My dad golfs."

"Definitely not a college sport either."

"Why?"

"I was at a college football game where the guy proposed and the girl said yes and then they got pelted with toast."

"That's mean."

"I guess."

"But also sort of funny."

"True."

"Was it garlic toast at least?"

"I'm pretty sure it was plain and dry."

They cross the alley next to the barbershop where Steve last got his hair shaved a week ago. The door is open, two chairs occupied.

"Why before did you say *Survivor* is like the tortoise and the hare?" scratching her cheek.

He's trying unsuccessfully to remember.

"That's a fable, by the way."

"It is." He still can't remember what point he was trying to make.

"I get that the orange tribe got off to a big lead, like the hare did. But they didn't lose in the end. They still won. The hare lost."

"I honestly don't remember what I meant."

"The tortoise and the hare doesn't even make sense if you think about it."

"How do you mean?"

"Everyone says it's better to be the tortoise. Slow and steady wins the race, right?"

"Go on."

"But the hare was a close second."

"He lost by a hair, you might say."

"Lame."

Steve shrugs, smiling.

"He lost, fine. But he got to nap, watch TV, have carrot cake. The tortoise walked non-stop, and for what? Do you know what the prize they were racing for was?"

"I don't."

"Nobody does. There was no prize. What's the point of winning? At least in *Survivor*, the winning team gets a reward. The tortoise got nothing. It would have been better for him to relax a bit, take a few breaks, have some snacks, watch some TV. Even if he finished second, so what? He wouldn't have been any worse off."

"The race is not to the swift."

"Slow and steady is fine, but not because you want to win a race. Just if that's the way you'd rather live."

"We're almost there."

"Where are we having lunch? Papa John's?" sounding hopeful.

"We're going there," pointing at a white food truck diagonal from the northwest corner of 41st and West Boulevard where they're standing, waiting for the traffic light to change so they can cross the street. Six or seven years ago, before Sam was born, Steve was standing at this very spot when a gold Sienna turning west was momentarily stopped at the intersection, waiting for pedestrians to clear out of the way, and who was in the passenger seat, but none other than Arthur Erickson in the flesh. Steve waved at him. He waved back. Then the minivan drove off. How many more times in his life will Steve remember that day?

The light changes.

"What is that?" stepping onto the street.

"I'm meeting a guy from my church here at noon."

"At a food truck?"

"Do your mom or dad ever have lunch meetings with people from their work?"

"No," hesitating. "I don't know."

"A big part of my job is talking with people," waiting for the next set of lights to change, "and lots of times that happens over food."

"What kind of food truck is it?"

"It's called Potstikkr. Do you like potstickers? These are the best in the city."

The east-west lights change, but oncoming traffic has an advance green. Steve and Adi wait a little longer, watching as an Alaska green Jetta turns left, followed by a mud-caked maroon Outback, no more cars after that, but the arrow signal remains. Maybe it's the color of the traffic lights or maybe it's the Jetta, but whatever it is, Steve suddenly remembers he has no money in his wallet and Potstikkr, unless they've changed since the last time he was there, doesn't accept credit or debit cards. Normally he avoids places like that, but he makes the occasional exception.

"Shoot. We have to go to the bank first." He turns, puts a hand on Adi's shoulder, who turns, too, and they're walking again.

"Why?"

"What do people go to banks for?"

"Money."

Steve taps the tip of his nose, twice.

"Why did you tap your nose like that?"

He lowers his arm. "It means you're right. People go to banks for money."

"I thought we were going to eat. I'm starving."

"Food costs money."

"Don't you have any?"

"I do not."

"So we're going to the bank so you can get money so we can get food?"

"Exactly." The nose tap again.

"Why don't you have any money in your wallet? Is it because you're poor?"

"In a manner of speaking." Riches are not to men of understanding.

"My mom says you must be rich."

"In a manner of speaking."

"She says pastors make lots of money."

"Sometimes. None of the pastors I know, though. But enough not to have to worry about daily bread."

"Huh?"

"Never mind."

"My mom can let you borrow her money." She rubs her nose and sniffles twice. "But only some. Not all of it."

"That would be nice of her, but unnecessary. I'm not that poor."

"You know if you don't have that much money, you shouldn't eat at food trucks or restaurants. You should cook your own food at home."

"I do, usually. How many times have you been over for dinner?"

"A few."

"And don't I usually cook?"

"I guess," shrugging.

"See?"

"Sometimes it's just frozen from a box, though."

"No it's not."

"I've been there before," pointing at the Nestings Kids furniture store.

"For what?"

"What do people go to kids' furniture stores for?"

"I mean, what specifically?"

"I have a toy piano from there. Also my loft bed."

"I think I bought Sam a jacket there. A checkered one."

"Kind of tartan style? Different greens and purples and light blues?"

"Those are her favorite colors."

"I like that jacket."

"Actually, it might be from there," motioning at the Gap Kids to their left. He gazes through the storefront window as they pass it. There's no one he recognizes inside.

"I have some tartans. They're from my dad's clan."

"I thought your dad was from Wales."

"He is." Adi has a bemused look on her face.

Steve is too embarrassed to ask. It seems like something he should know: that of course Welsh people have tartans and clans; did he think they were only a Scottish thing? It's just that he's never given it any thought before. Why would he? He won't ask. He'll look it up later. Because he cares even what a six-year-old girl who's not his daughter thinks about him. Pathetic. He goes on walking, hands in his pockets, trying to look cool, trying to look smart, worldly. So pathetic. It's entirely possible he used to know about the Welsh and tartans. In high school, when he was one of four members of his national championship-winning *Reach for the Top* team, he might have known. He knew a great many things back then. But if he had, he's since forgotten.

"I wish we could have pizza instead."

"Papa John's, though."

"I love Papa John's."

"You should ask your parents to get you Timothy's at Oak and 16th. They make some good pies. Besides, a potsticker is kind of like a pizza."

"How is it?"

"When it's done right, you've got the perfect dough-to-non-dough ratio."

"It's nothing like a pizza."

"Food definitions are pretty fluid. Think about it: what makes a pizza a pizza?"

"The dough." She looks annoyed. "The dough is what makes pizza pizza. A potsticker is more like a pierogi."

"That's actually probably technically true."

"I'd still rather have an actual pizza."

"Trust me. Potstikkr is otherworldly."

Steve puts a hand on the back of Adi's head and guides her the first few steps across Yew, toward the Royal Bank.

"You're exaggerating."

"Only slightly."

Adi bites her lower lip and squeezes her eyes shut a second, then opens them. "Fine. We can go. But if they're bad, can I have Papa John's?"

A gray-haired man steps out of the bank as the two of them arrive at the door. He holds it open, expressionless.

Steve thanks him as he steps inside, Adi beside him. "Sure. Papa John's if you don't like the postickers."

He has his wallet out again, searching for his debit card. Once, by accident, he used his credit card at the ATM. The fees were outrageous. Ever since, he's been extra careful to make sure he's using the proper card, including right now, and he is, he's double-checked. He inserts it chip first, into the slot with the blinking green light.

Please Wait / We are retrieving your card information

The message appears in French, too, but Steve doesn't read it.

Please enter your PIN then press OK

Adi is looking out the window. Steve enters his four-digit code and hits the green OK button.

Another *Please Wait* screen appears, followed by an option menu.

Steve taps the button next to the *Withdrawal no receipt* prompt. How much does he need today?

$20

$40

$100

$200

This machine only dispenses $20 and $50 bills.

One hundred, why not?

From his chequing account.

Your request is being processed

It shouldn't take long. It should just be another moment now.

The completed transaction screen appears.

He would not like to do another transaction, no.

Please remove your card

It ejects on cue. Steve pulls it out, and there's the cash, a bunch of twenties, as opposed to two fifties. He takes the bills, counts them to make sure there are five altogether, there are, then puts the money and his debit card back in his wallet, his wallet in his back pocket.

"All done. Let's eat."

"Finally."

Steve is first to the door. He steps outside, holding it for Adi. They're back on West Boulevard. A part of him wants to cross the street to avoid taking the same route they'd taken to the bank. There's no fun retracing your own steps so soon after you've taken them. If they're going to do it, cross to the north side of 41st, now's the time, at the traffic lights, cars stopped. But crossing here would only necessitate having to cross back again, up ahead. The fewer times crossing the street, the safer; the safer, the better. If he was by himself, sure, he'd already be on the north side in all likelihood. He'd grab another coffee at the Starbucks here, which isn't as nice as the one by Valley Drive on account of it being so much busier, noisier here, but the coffee is the same, in theory. Then, coffee in hand, he'd window-shop while making his way to the intersection. Some shops he'd actually go in and browse. At Hill's, where he got his *Ulysses* tee. At the stationery store, whose name he always gets wrong; not Buchanan's, but something like Buchanan's. At the kids' toy store where one of Sam's friends had a pottery painting birthday party last year. Who was it?

"Did you have a pottery painting birthday party last year?"

"What?"

Steve repeats himself and points at the toy store across the street.

"That was two birthdays ago, when I turned five."

"But that was you?"

Adi's face is unreadable.

"Sam was there, right?"

"I invited all the girls from my class and Sam was in my class, so yes."

"I remember."

"We painted piggy banks, but not all of them were pigs."

That's right, okay, Sam did an owl. "Was yours a pig?"

"An owl."

"Do you still have it?"

"It's empty right now. Once I lose my first tooth, I'm going to put in it what the tooth fairy brings me."

Sam's owl is on the mantel over the fireplace, kept warm by a thick blanket of dust, having never been used the way it was meant to be. Steve had a piggy bank that wasn't a pig when he was around their age, or a little older; when he was old enough he could bike on his own around the neighborhood. It wasn't a pig or an owl, but a yellow duck, and not ceramic, plastic; and not a trademarked duck from one of the large animation studios, a knock-off. His parents had had a garage sale and the money from each item they sold they deposited in the slit at the top of the duck bank, or maybe the slit was in its beak. The point is, they put the money in the duck at the POS. Stupid. Some teenager, who must have seen one or more transactions take place, waited until the right moment, garage sale over, the duck bank inexplicably left in the garage, the garage even more inexplicably left open, and made off with all the money they'd made, weaseling away on his POS BMX. Steve was the one who saw it all go down. He'd been in the living room and happened to look out the window at just the right time. First thing he did was run outside, get on his own bike, a POS BMX knock-off, and take off after the teenage thief, pedaling as fast as his little legs would move, which was not very. His parents were righteously peeved he hadn't told them right away. If he had, well. His dad would've tracked down the thief, definitely, in his sparkly black S-series Saturn.

Around the same time, folks on his street were waking up to find roadkill, dead squirrels usually, left in their mailboxes. Probably that same teenage menace, his parents believed, wrongly.

"It's another missing chickens sign." Adi stops momentarily to point at the notice taped to a streetlight.

Steve gives it a cursory glance. "Why did the chicken cross the road?"

She stares at him, straight-faced, like she's waiting for him to answer.

"To get to the other side."

"That's even less funny than the satisfactory one," grimacing. "Why would a chicken want to go to a mattress store?" She's looking at the Sleep Country shop across from them.

Steve bought Daphne's twin Tempur-Pedic there. "It's funny because it's so straightforward. It's the obvious answer, which makes it unexpected, which makes it funny. It's probably the most famous joke in the world."

"I bet an adult made it up. It sounds like the kind of joke only an adult would find funny."

A westbound silver Audi SUV accelerates through the intersection, turning south in front of Steve and Adi, tires screeching. Audi drivers are worse even than BMW ones.

"Can I ask you something about the food truck place?"

"What's up?"

"Is it vegan?"

Steve puts both hands in his pockets. "It's not. But they have a veggie potsticker on their menu, I think."

"What's in it?"

"What's in the veggie potsticker?" It should be safe to cross now. Steve checks to his left, then behind for right-turning cars because you can never be too safe. The coast is clear. "Vegetables?"

"I know that," exasperated-like. "What kind?"

"Cabbage, green onions, mushrooms, water chestnut, carrots, herbs, parsley sage rosemary thyme, bamboo? Turnip? I'm just making this up. I have no idea. But probably some variety of cabbage."

"Bamboo isn't a vegetable."

"Sure it is."

"It's a Chinese tree."

"Trees are basically vegetables."

They're across the traffic median over which the discontinued railroad tracks are laid, crossing from West Boulevard to East. There's a sermon illustration here.

"That's a lot of people," an arm outstretched, finger pointing.

She's not wrong. At least fifteen people, most of them high school students from the look of it, PW students, most likely, are crowded around the side of the truck where orders are placed.

"It's not that bad. The lines are sometimes forty-five minutes long."

"I've never seen this food truck before. I've seen the grilled cheese truck and the pupusa truck and the Korean truck, which is more like a cart than a truck. Not this one, though."

"I think they're only here once a week. Most of the time they're parked beneath the Arthur Laing bridge."

"Where the buses go?"

"Right by the terminal, yeah. The next time you're in Richmond with your parents and you're coming back to Vancouver via the Oak Street bridge, ask them once they're over it to turn on Marine Drive and head up Granville. That'll take you beneath the Arthur Laing. There's a cement beam there with a graffiti tag: THE MEANING OF LIFE IS LOVE, it says. Right behind that beam is usually parked a junk removal truck with a website printed on its side: THATSRUBBISH dot CA. So you're driving along, you see a sign that says the meaning of life is love, and the very next thing you see is another sign that says that's rubbish. The Potstikkr truck is normally there, behind the rubbish one."

"Is that their logo?" nodding toward the side of the truck.

"It is."

"That's not how you spell potsticker," her face creased. "Is it?"

"They've stylized it. It should be S-T-I-C-K-E-R."

"It's not very easy to read either."

"Their graphic designer decided to use that stereotypical Chinese-takeout-box typeface, for whatever reason. To be intentionally cheeky, hopefully."

"Why is there a leaf instead of a letter O?"

"It looks cool?"

Adi shakes her head, unconvinced. "I think because they want to be patriotic. Only that doesn't look like a maple leaf at all."

"It doesn't," nodding. They're potstickers not maplestickers.

"What a terrible design."

"I like it."

Adi gives him a look like he must be joking.

He isn't. He's not being deliberately difficult.

"Is your friend here yet? I'm starving."

"Doesn't look like it," a cursory scan of the nearby faces. He would have seen Marcel by now, or vice versa.

"Do we need to wait? Let's order first."

"We can do that." Chances are Marcel is going to cancel last minute again. Why bother waiting? "Let's line up."

He thinks about counting how many people are in front of them, but it's not worth even the minimal effort. If it were three or four, he wouldn't have to count. He'd just see and know. No, no counting. When it's their turn to order, it'll be their turn. Knowing the exact number of people they have to wait for isn't going to change the fact they have to wait. This is how patience is learned: by having opportunities to practice it. Steve has been praying for more patience—with his family, with the lack of visible growth at church, with a handful of obstinate elders he has to deal with and can't get removed from their position because of the church's antiquated by-laws. Here's a chance to exercise some, grow some. It's not like they're likely to wait long anyway. The one time he waited forty-five minutes was at the other location beneath the Arthur Laing, when the line had extended up Granville past Park, as far as 49th, almost. That had been soon after Potstikkr's grand opening, though, and how many years ago was that? The line today is a fraction of a fraction of what it was then. Two, four, six, eight, nine, ten, eleven. There are only eleven more people in front of them and some of them must be together. Already they've moved up a few feet.

"How many do you want?"

"How many are you getting?"

"Two orders, I think. Sixteen potstickers in total."

"That means one order has eight."

"Good math."

"I'll have two orders, too."

"Seriously? You think you can eat as much as me?"

"I told you I'm starving."

"They're pretty big." Steve motions to one of the teenagers ten feet to their right, holding an oyster pail in one hand, a fork in the other. At the end of the fork is a plump, partially eaten pan-fried dumpling, golden brown on the bottom. "That kid is doing it all wrong, though. He has no dipping sauce." Unless he's poured it directly into the takeout box.

"I can eat more than eight of those."

"Sixteen, though?"

"Leftovers."

She has a point, but—"I don't want to have to carry around that box the rest of the day."

"I can carry it."

"But will you?" He means it to be rhetorical.

"I guess not," smiling. "But you can."

"That's the point. I'm not going to want to. My arms are already tired thinking about it."

"Well," pressing the tip of an index finger to her chin, "you wouldn't need to hold it the whole rest of the day. I'm probably going to be hungry again in an hour. You only need to hold it until then. An hour isn't that long. The time will fly by. Didn't you say before that time flies?"

Had he said that aloud?

She has a point, anyway. They're a few feet closer to placing their orders.

"Fine. I'll get you two."

"Make sure they're veggie."

"Of course."

"What are you getting?" looking at the handwritten menu affixed to the side of the truck. "Pork or veggie?"

"Pork."

"What does it mean when it says *with* and *without*."

The girl directly in front of them turns to look at Steve, then Adi. She looks like a girl Steve went to high school with.

"They have, like, how would you describe it? A special sort of spice thing that you can get in your potstickers if you want. With the spice or without it. That's what it means."

"I like spices."

"This one isn't for kids."

"That's not fair. Grown-ups are always bossing kids around. It would be fairer if we could eat the same things."

"It would be way fairer," nodding. "But it has nothing to do with bossing you around. Some foods are good for kids, some aren't. That's all it is."

"You're just like Ms. Fernandes."

"How?"

Adi nods. "Once I was in the library to borrow some books and she said that I shouldn't only read werewolf books, I should read books with gold or silver medals on the cover, so I borrowed one and it was boring and when I asked her later who decided to give the book a medal, kids or grown-ups, she said grown-ups, but I knew that already because if it was kids, that book would never have gotten a medal."

"What was the book?"

"Unless it was a medal for badness."

"What was the name of the book?"

"She called it a classic."

"Classics are good."

"Werewolf books are better. Have you read any?"

"I haven't."

"Then how would you know what's better?"

"You don't need to read everything to know one book is better than another."

"Sure you do. That's another reason medals for books are stupid. Have the grown-ups who decide what book gets the medal, have they read all the books? It's impossible. So how can they judge?"

"That's a fair observation I guess."

"Best is subjective."

"Maybe when it comes to books." The line waddles forward a few more feet. "The potstickers here are the best, though, and that's a fact."

"Are you getting yours with or without?"

"I haven't decided."

"It's not fair if you can get it with the spices and I can't."

"Fine. I'll get them without." The better tasting ones are the ones with, but she's right. It's not exactly fair. Sam is allergic to kiwis so Steve hasn't had one in over six years for this precise reason. He used to love kiwis.

He scratches the top of his head. One of the by-products of keeping it shaved is it itches more than it would if he had a full head of hair. It doesn't matter how recently he's washed and shampooed it, and it may not be universal, i.e., other people with similar hairstyles, if the absence of hair can be called a hairstyle, may have no problems with itchiness up there. Steve does. He never did when he kept his hair long, unless he hadn't washed it in too long, which for him is anything more than twenty-four hours. Now the itchiness comes and goes with seemingly no correlation to how recently he's showered.

The bumpiness is still there and feels somehow denser, larger, like cartilage. Maybe it's his imagination?

"Did you ever hear the story of the first time I shaved my head?"

Adi's face is autumnal.

"I was telling someone's mom. Hailey's, I think."

"It wasn't me."

"Do you want to hear it?"

"There's still so many people in front of us, might as well."

"I'll tell you the story and before you know it, we'll be at the front of the line."

"Don't keep on telling me you're going to tell me. Just tell the story already."

"It was the summer before I started high school. My hair was down to here," his hand indicating the top of his shoulder. "And it looked really good, but it was the summer and it was one of the hottest summers ever so having long hair made it even more intolerable. No A/C anywhere except the mall. I tried flipping it up and shaving off all the hair beneath," rubbing the back of his head, above the neck, "thinking it would keep me a bit cooler. It didn't. It'd taken me more than a year to grow it out so I really didn't want to cut it. Not to mention having a regular kid's haircut was decidedly unappealing. Regular kid's haircuts are so boring, so one-note. But what choice did I have? The heat was unbearable. So I went to the hairdresser and asked for one of those ugly regular kid cuts where my hair in the front would be parted to one side like a doofus. Anyway, after forty minutes, which is a long time for a guy's haircut, she was done and it was the worst looking haircut in the history of the universe. So much worse than I'd imagined it would be. That's when I told her just to shave the whole thing. She was so mad, and was like, If you wanted to shave it, why didn't you tell me that to begin with? Why did you waste my time? And I was like, Well, I didn't know you'd make it look so awful. Ever since then I've kept it shaved. And look, see? We're almost up."

There are two more people in front of them, a couple, which means only one order, effectively. Unless they pay separately. But the boy is ordering for the both of them. He's asking the girl what she wants or to confirm what she's already told him she wants. Now he's taking a twenty from his wallet, a brown wallet, fat, stuffed with old receipts. The girl has her hands in her coat pockets, not reaching for any money of her own.

"Alright then. Two orders of veggie potstickers, without?"

"Sure." Adi's eyes are fixed on the girl's jeans, which look like regular jeans.

The boy in front of them is getting his change, all coins. He and the girl with him move toward the storefronts, and now Steve and Adi are at the order window.

"Two veggie, without. Two pork." He clears his throat. "One without, one with."

"Hey." Adi is staring up at him, pouting, forehead a scrunch, the space between her eyebrows narrowed.

The Chinese woman inside the truck repeats Steve's order. "Is that all?" She speaks with no trace of a foreign accent.

"Do you want anything to drink?"

Adi shakes her head, still pouting.

"That's it."

"We have a special on today." She points to a sign on the metal counter. "With, with salvia. No extra charge."

"Salvia?"

"It enhances the flavor and all-around experience. Limited time only. It's part of *hanshi jie*."

"What's that?"

"Cold Food Festival. It's ancient. Nobody celebrates it anymore except us. Want to try?"

"Why not?"

"So two veggie without. One pork without. One special."

"Sounds good."

"Thirty-three sixty."

"How did she do that so fast?" peering up at Steve.

"Practice and experience." Steve has his wallet open. He takes out two twenties, checks to make sure he's only got two and not three, then hands them to the woman inside the truck, his fingers and hers touching, no sparks, as they make the exchange.

She drops the bills in an open cash box too far inside the truck for someone standing outside to reach in and steal, or steal from. What his folks should have done with the duck bank. Now she's rummaging for change, finds a five, lays it in front of her, then a loonie, followed by an assortment of small silver-colored coins.

They clang as she drops them casually in front of her.

"Six-forty, your change." She pushes the mess toward Steve. "And a sticker for the girl."

He picks up the bill, sweeps the rest of the money into the same hand that's got the fiver, and stuffs all of it into one of his front pockets, including the sticker. He'll put the paper money into his wallet later. He's confident he'll remember to do it, but he isn't entirely doubt-free because it's happened before, more than once, where he left a bill of some kind in his pants, forgot it there, washed the pants, dried them, then found the vestiges of what used to be money the next time he shoved his hands in his pockets. Who hasn't done that? Once it had been a fifty.

He takes the five-dollar bill from his pocket. "Look."

"What am I looking at?"

"The beginning of *The Hockey Sweater*," holding it up to her face. "Remember we were talking about it before?"

"Not really."

"I told you how my old teacher gave me a copy, and how my mom got me the one from the book? When we were walking from school to the park."

"Right. You wanted a Canucks sweater, but she got you a Bruins one."

"Something like that." He grabs and unfolds his wallet, slides the five-dollar bill in front of his remaining twenties. "That was the first line of the book."

"Can I see it?"

"I just showed you."

"You were talking so I was listening and not looking at the money."

"I'll show you later if you remind me. It's probably better not to touch it now, right before we're about to eat."

"Why?"

"Because germs. Do you know how many people must have handled that bill? Hundreds, at least, probably thousands. Assuming not all of them had clean hands, that's a lot of germs."

"You touched it."

"I had to. Adults have more immunity to the kinds of communicable diseases that can be spread from touching germ-riddled paper currency."

"I have a little Purell in my jacket." She unzips an external chest pocket, reaches in, then holds out her palm, revealing a travel-size hand sanitizer.

"That's good. Why don't you use some now? Our food should be ready soon. I'll show you the money after we eat, if you remind me."

He should think about getting one of those miniature Purell bottles for Sam. No, not think about, there's nothing to think about, he should get her one. They probably sell them at the pharmacy. Shoot. He could have bought one when they were there. He should get more than one. He should get two. One for Sam to bring to school, one to keep at home, a back-up, for when she loses the first one. If she doesn't lose the first one, she can use the second one when the first one runs out. Do hand sanitizers have expiration dates? Probably not. He should get three of them, come to think of it. One for Sam to bring to school. One to keep at home. One for him to use. He should get four. How much can one of them cost? A couple dollars? Three? Costco probably sells them in bulk, but Steve doesn't have a membership. Maybe he can ask someone from church to get him a gift card. He'd pay for it, of course. That way he won't need to go with someone who is a Costco member. He can go by himself. One of his church members would do that for him, wouldn't they? It's not one of the vows they make in their covenant with the church. What would people think if he made a joke about it the next time someone becomes a member? Probably they'd think it too ir-reverent. Or maybe they wouldn't. Which could be worse. Maybe they'd think it's a stupid joke and not funny. Which would be worse. Becoming a member of Costco is a matter of small consequence, unlike becoming a member of the church. Steve will have to become a member of Costco one day, probably. Once his girls hit puberty he'll be there every month for sup-plies. The first time he went alone to buy these products was in high school, for Melanie. She'd written down exactly what she wanted him to get, but wrote it on some scrap paper, it could have been an old movie ticket stub, it could have been the stub for *Johnny Mnemonic*, and he later mistakenly discarded it because he hadn't looked carefully at the handwriting. So when he was at the store, rifling through his backpack for her instructions, he couldn't find it and because this was before he had a cell phone, he couldn't call her to ask. Instead he asked a woman in the aisle what he ought to buy and when she looked at him all confused, he asked her which one was her favorite, thinking he would just get that, it was better than him guessing blindly, but she wouldn't answer him, she only stared. Of course he bought the wrong ones. Why did you get wingless? Melanie had asked.

"Your order."

Steve looks over to the food truck window.

The woman who took his order is smiling at him and nodding.

"That's us." He leaves Adi on the sidewalk in front of the store where they'd been waiting, then turns back to check she's staying put, which she is. He grabs the two paper bags off the counter, unfolds the top of one, opening it. A medium-size container is inside. A letter V is written on the top of the box in bright green ink. A pair of chopsticks and some napkins are crammed to the side. "It's all here?"

"Two veggie without. One pork without. One pork special."

"Are the two pork ones just mixed together?"

"You can tell which is which. It's obvious."

"Dipping sauces?"

"Inside."

"Great." Steve spins around, looking for Adi. It's a dollar store she's in front of. He's never noticed it before. How can a dollar store afford to stay open in Kerrisdale? Maybe it's a front for something sinister. "Food's ready," raising his right arm, elevating the bag he's clutching by its thrice-folded top. "Where do you want to eat?"

"There's nowhere to sit."

"We could go to the school across the street and sit by the playground," pointing beyond McDonald's on the north side of 41st. Except the elementary school students will be outside soon. "Or there are some outdoor benches even closer, just behind us a little ways. The only thing is, people like to smoke there."

"What about your friend?"

Steve pulls his phone from his pocket. It's 12:03. "He's late," showing Adi the time. "Do you want to wait for him?"

"He's your friend. Do you?"

Friend isn't the word that comes to Steve's mind anymore when he thinks of Marcel. "You're hungry, right?"

"Starving."

"Our food isn't going to keep warm very long. We ordered. Might as well eat."

"Can we just eat here?"

"Standing?"

"You said there were benches?"

"Just behind the liquor store," pointing. "Near the walk-in medical clinic. We can eat there if no one is smoking."

"It's better than staying here talking about what to do."

They navigate the crowd gathered on the sidewalk. Some people are eating, some are studying the menu, which is so sparse, vegetarian/pork, it's not so much studying as it is looking at. The crowd has grown since Steve last considered its size. It's a veritable horde now. A small one, anyway. What is it going to be like at 12:30 or whenever it's busiest? There have been times when he's gone to Potstikkr's other location, mid-afternoon, on his way up from Richmond, where he'd spent an hour walking in Finn Slough or Steveston Village, heading to get Sam from school, and he'd stopped beneath the Arthur Laing for a snack and they were all sold out of the pork. On each of those days he'd settled for the vegetarian option, without, because they're better than nothing, which isn't even true, they're delicious in their own right. But the point is, they shouldn't sell out of any of their menu items so early in the day. They probably don't have anyone dedicated to sales analytics. They should. They could be selling, what? hundreds more potstickers a day? thousands? tens of thousands? Hundreds, at least. No food-and-beverage industry operation wants to be left with unsold inventory that needs composting at the end of the day, so maybe selling out of food most evenings is unavoidable, but the margins could be so much stronger. They should also consider franchising.

Just beyond the liquor store they hang a right and head beneath a cement archway abutting the street-level storefronts, toward the open courtyard in front of them where, hopefully, some unoccupied and smoker-free benches await. It's a good thing the weather is so fair today. It doesn't rain that often the first week of April, maybe one or two days in seven, and even that seems like more than experience suggests. It does rain, though. It could have rained today. If it had, they wouldn't be here and they wouldn't be about to eat outside. In fact, if it had rained today, Sam would have been genuinely late for school, what with the umbrellas they would have both been carrying, and the boots that would have slowed her pace.

"Watch for cars."

Adi looks both ways at the back alley crosswalk and, seeing no approaching vehicles, crosses, Steve two feet behind her.

His new, go-anywhere, pocket-sized Davek umbrella arrived at TSB Shipping in Point Roberts last week. They'd emailed, letting him know a package had been delivered and he had three weeks—two now—to pick it up, before they started applying extra storage charges.

"This is one of my favorite sushi places," pointing as they pass Ajisai, trying to remember when he was last there.

"It's tiny."

"The best restaurants are."

The extra charge at the Point Roberts receiving service is only three or four dollars a week. There's no need to stress about getting there in the next two, in other words.

"Let's take the last bench," meaning the one closest to 42nd.

It'd be difficult to get to Point Bob in the next two weeks.

Adi sits.

Steve gives her one of the brown bags he's holding, guessing for no particular reason it's the one containing her order. He sits next to her.

She begins to open it: unfolding the top, sliding one hand inside, grabbing the takeout box. It's shorter and wider than the ones TV sitcom characters eat from. She unhinges the lid. Inside are sixteen perfectly pan-fried potstickers, arranged four by four. They're definitely the vegetarian ones. Through their translucent wrappers, more flecks of green and orange are visible than what Steve would expect to see in the meat version. A small clear plastic container with dipping sauce is also inside the box. Adi reaches back inside the bag and hands Steve her chopsticks.

"I don't want to get a splinter."

She removes the lid to the dipping sauce while Steve grabs hold of one chopstick in each hand and pulls, successfully splitting them down the middle. He rubs the two sticks together, filing down any stray bits of wood, and gives them back to Adi.

"Here you go."

With ease and better technique than Steve has, she holds the chopsticks loosely and picks up a potsticker, rotating her wrist to examine it from multiple angles. She dips one end of it in the sauce, the takeout box resting in her lap, then takes a cautious bite.

Chewing.

"How is it?"

Adi nods her head energetically and baptizes the rest of the potsticker in the sauce, then puts it in her mouth.

Steve usually takes two bites each, too. Some people stick a whole one in their mouth. He prefers to savor them. Three bites is too many, though: the individual mouthfuls falling short of the ideal filling-to-wrapper ratio. Three bites and usually what you end up with is one bite has too much meat, another too much dough, and the last not enough of either.

Adi is halfway through her second potsticker.

"Don't eat too fast."

"I'm not eating fast, you're eating slow. You're not eating at all."

Steve unfolds and opens the top of his brown bag, letting the savory aroma of pork mingled with weed waft up and out, breathing it in. There's nothing in the world like the smell of freshly cooked potstickers. He knows not everyone agrees. When he was in the third grade, his mother would sometimes pack him her homemade potstickers for lunch. She would have made them more often, but they took the better part of two consecutive afternoons to prepare. Though they were room temperature, they were still delicious by the time he ate them, sitting in the cafeteria next to and sur-rounded by white kids, mostly, who didn't appreciate the distinctive smell. Didn't or couldn't? Unrefined palates, whatever the case. Steve understands now it wasn't their fault they found it unpleasant. But they didn't have to tease, laugh at, mock, humiliate him, tell him his food was farts, or flip his bento box and all its contents, potstickers and sauce, on the lunchroom table, on his clothes, on the floor, which they did on multiple occasions. Especially considering what most of them packed for lunch. Sandwiches. Two slices of usually soggy white bread with some fractionally edible mon-strosity smeared between them.

Peanut butter, smooth not even crunchy, and without jelly.

Tuna salad.

Egg salad.

Baloney.

No person in his right mind, even a kid with zero palate, ought rather have a sandwich over a potsticker. So it's not the kid who's to blame, it's his mind, or her parents. Not even grilled cheese, the only good sandwich, ought to be preferred to potstickers. He should have pitied them, really: pitied their lack of worldliness: their lack of culinary sophistication. Instead, after about the tenth time, he insisted to his mother that she not pack him any more potstickers for lunch. He'd told her the truth: all the other kids teased him about their odor. She didn't believe it was literally all of the other kids. All the ones that count, though. All the cool kids: the white boys who played hockey on actual peewee club teams—ice hockey, in skates—who didn't have to be constantly moving nets from the middle of the road with their Pakistani neighbors while dodging honking Oldsmobiles; those boys—them, and the cute Jewish girls. Times have changed. Things have changed. Sam isn't even a minority at her school. Most of the kids probably bring potstickers some day of the week. Now it's probably the white kids with the white bread, sulfurous-smelling egg salad sandwiches that get teased. To his mother's credit, she stopped packing him potstickers for lunch as soon as he'd asked. She also confronted his teacher about the bullies, but Ms. Losgen was the worst of all, so of course she dismissed it as boys being boys. She never excused him to use the restroom in the middle of class after that, even that time he raised his hand and shook it violently in the air above his head because he really needed to go. Not even when he begged. You're lying, just like you lied about being bullied, she'd said right before he pissed—yes, pissed—his pants. He showed her. His mother had still made potstickers, too, with just as much frequency as when he was bringing the leftovers to school for lunch. The only thing that changed was the ones he didn't finish at dinner, he had the next day, at home, an after-school snack. He'd eat those cold, straight from the fridge because no one was around to tell him otherwise. He'd let himself and his sister in using the house key he wore on a red string around his neck, drop his coat and backpack at the door, kick off his shoes, and head directly for the kitchen. Some days Emily would want to eat, too, and like a good big brother, he always shared when she asked. She and Matt will be married soon. He'd better finish writing his thing for their wedding. It's a couple of weeks yet, but the time is going to pass like that.

"Why did you snap your fingers?"

Steve smiles.

Maybe he can say something about his mother's potstickers. Maybe have that be a recurring image in his two-minute wedding speech. How many times can he mention potstickers in a hundred and twenty seconds without it being overkill? A good marriage is like a good potsticker. Too cheesy.

Now there's an idea: potsticker with cheese. Cheese does have the miraculous property of making most foods taste 50-percent better, at minimum.

Sprinkled on lomo saltado.

In a butifarras.

Cubed and served poutine-style with olloquito con charqui.

As a filling in palacsinta.

On ramen.

In jjajangmyeon.

Over pad Thai.

With fried rice.

With Hainanese chicken rice.

Mixed into dol sot bi bim bap.

And mee goreng.

In all manner of sushi, including Spam musubi.

With sesame oil and salt on a pan-fried mantou, the only variety of sandwich worth eating, non-grilled-cheese division.

Grated, over yangnyeom tongdak.

Grated, over ojiya.

As a coating for karaage.

As a sauce for dipping lo bak go in.

Stuffed inside onigri.

Stuffed inside manapua.

Stuffed inside lihapiirakka.

Generously sprinkled over goulash.

Or töltött káposzta.

Tossed into soondubu jiggae.

Baked and melted over tom kha gai.

Or saimin.

Or bulla cake.

In rocoto relleno.

In dipping sauce form for samsa.

Rolled into a cōng yóu bing cigar.

There's not one dish he enjoys that wouldn't be improved with the presence of cheese, or in the case of those traditionally served with cheese, with more. Who says it doesn't go with Asian food? Why not as a potsticker filling?

Pork and cabbage and cheese.

Vegetables and cheese.

Weed and cheese.

Instant nouveau classics.

Actually, the cheese and veggie option might not work, not at Potstikkr anyway. He's not sure if vegetarians eat cheese, not unless it was vegan cheese, which doesn't make anything taste better.

"Can I have your last two?"

Steve looks at the open oyster pail on his lap, then at the one on Adi's. "I can't believe you ate all of yours."

"I told you I was starving."

Steve is only about 75-percent full.

"Can I have them?" her hand suspended above his container.

"Hey," tapping her knuckles.

Adi clenches and unclenches her hand, keeping it over the last remaining potstickers, moving it, in fact, an inch closer.

Will two additional dumplings get him to 100-percent? Does he want to be 100-percent, or is something closer to three-quarters full more desirable? Of course it is, but stopping at 75-percent is easier in theory than in practice, which is another reason he's packed on some pounds. A pastor ought to have more self-control; more love, too, and joy and peace, long-suffering, kindness, goodness, faithfulness, meekness; but especially self-control, which used to be called temperance. No one trusts a fat preacher, nor should they, self-induced girth and hypocrisy being proportionally related. There's a joke there, somewhere: something to do with gut feelings.

Adi has one of his potstickers in her hand. She's bringing it to her mouth.

"You can have that one."

"Thanks." She bites.

"Wait," remembering. "There's pork in there."

Her jaw stops moving and for a moment it looks she's going to expel what's in her mouth, but she doesn't. The muscles in her neck contract the way neck muscles do when swallowing.

"There's no such thing as reincarnation you said, right?"

Steve doesn't know what to say.

Adi sticks the rest of the partially eaten potsticker in her mouth and chews.

It occurs to him now that not only is there pork in it, which is trivial, really, because reincarnation is hokum, the relevant concern is the one she's eating and has now, from the looks of it, finished, might be the special.

Steve eyes her carefully. "How is it?"

Adi shrugs. "Not as good as mine."

"It's pork, though."

"I don't want to think about it." She looks at the pavement beneath her feet, possibly at the long crack running through it.

Cheese inside Jamaican patties.

Melted over coco bread.

Coating roti prata.

Paneer samosas. Is that already a thing?

Steve looks up, drawn by the sound of a bus barreling westward on 41st. He shifts in his seat to reach and take out his phone.

12:15.

"I should call your mom and let her know you're having lunch."

Adi nods.

"Or do you think I should text her?"

"Anything is fine."

Steve swipes the phone's screen, enters his password, clicks the camera app. "Look here."

Adi does as instructed.

"Show your mom your empty box."

She does.

Steve takes the photo and shows Adi. "I'll send this to her." He taps at the screen a few times, bringing up a New Message composition box, then scrolls through his contacts, looking for Mary under her last name, slowing down once he's mostly through the Bs. She's the fifth C, after Desmond Cai, whoever that is. He taps the number listed for Mary, attaches the photo to the message, and types with his thumbs: *Just finished lunch. Potstikkr on 41st. Yum!*

He rereads it: *Just finished lunch. Potstikkr on 41st. Yum!*

Maybe he ought to specify that Potstikkr is a food truck.

He presses his index finger on the screen, sliding the cursor to the appropriate spot, and adds: *food truck.*

Just finished lunch. Potstikkr food truck on 41st. Yum!

Once more he repositions the blinking blue text cursor, this time at the end of the message: *Adi had 16 veggie ones.*

He heard somewhere that young people don't end texts with a period because ending texts with a period, while grammatically proper, is a sure sign the message sender is angry with you. It's kind of harsh, Robin, one of the teens at St. Joe's had told him. There's probably also an element of anti-establishment rebelliousness, too: the creation of a new rule as a way of saying shove it to the old rule, and especially the old rule makers.

He deletes the period: *Adi had 16 veggie ones*

On its own that wouldn't look so weird, but coming as it does after a string of syntactically proper clauses including two periods and one exclamation mark, there's something odd about the way it looks, just sort of naked, unclothed. And what if Mary hasn't heard about this rule, which she most likely hasn't? Will she think he's grammatically lazy? Or worse: that he's trying to be hip? Why does he care so much what she thinks of him?

He replaces the period and reads over the whole message: *Just finished lunch. Potstikkr food truck on 41st. Yum! Adi had 16 veggie ones.*

Should he end it with an exclamation mark instead or would that be too emphatic? But doesn't eating that many potstickers deserve emphasis?

Just finished lunch. Potstikkr food truck on 41st. Yum! Adi had 16 veggie ones!

Maybe it deserves more emphasis. Maybe it calls for a reverse interrobang.

Just finished lunch. Potstikkr food truck on 41st. Yum! Adi had 16 veggie ones!?

That looks awkward. He deletes the question mark.

Should he mention the seventeenth? What if Adi tells her later? What about that *Yum!*? Does that come across as juvenile? Or is it cute and sweet? Unable to decide, Steve hits send, a digital swoosh tone sounds almost immediately. There's no undoing it now. He's about to slide the phone back in his pocket when it dings. That was fast. But as he checks the screen, it's not Mary who's written back, it's Marcel.

Where are you bro?

Another ding.

I'm in front of the truck. The line is so long.

Ding!

Thanks again for taking care of her, Steve. You're the best!

Steve taps Mary's message and replies: *Anytime!!!*

Then he answers Marcel: *I'm around the corner at bench by walk in clinic*—send.

Swoosh.

Silence.

Ding.

Be right ther

So it's really going to happen, and imminently. All those months of no-shows and finally Steve is about to see him. What might Marcel have wanted to meet about? At one of their meetings, whether it was shortly after he'd started attending the church or a while later, Steve can't remember, but it happened in the church, in his office with the door wide open, Marcel had asked Steve how to convince his wife to give him a blowjob. Umpteen years of marriage and she'd only ever done it once and even then she'd barely done it at all, not more than five seconds before she'd stopped, disgusted. She didn't want his pomegranate juice, is what he told Steve she'd said. Could he have come today to talk about his sex life? It wouldn't be surprising. He has almost no shame, this guy. The open mic Q and A they did after every sermon that one summer: Marcel smiling, speculating out loud about Abraham's wrinkled body and is it even possible, physiologically speaking, for a man that old, he was what? ninety-nine? to have an erection? and ejaculate? He'd used those words, too; they came out of his lips like a teenage boy unable to keep it in. As if they were in a bar and not a sanctuary. He's the reason they discontinued Q and A. Still, Steve has a soft spot for him. It's hardened somewhat, become a bit calloused like the physical one on his palm, which he's rubbing, but he hasn't stopped caring entirely. For one thing, Marcel babysat Sam and Daphne a few times before Gillian was born. He's also the only congregant who's ever asked him out for a beer. Usually people suggest coffee, or if they're going to be eating together, a White Spot somewhere or, once in a rare while, Burgoo. Never beer. But that's Marcel, and now he's crossing the alley, waving.

Steve stays seated and waves back. Should he stand up? Maybe he should. And then what? Stay standing until Marcel is directly in front of him? Which will be how long from now, another twenty-plus seconds? That's a long time to be standing, waiting like a doofus for an approaching friend. No, not friend. What are they to each other now? Not pastor-parishioner and not friends either. Friends spend time with each other and get invited to spend time with each other's other friends. Acquaintances? Not enemies, at least.

"Pastor Steve." He's smiling like they're brothers.

Steve stands. "Marcel," extending his hand.

Marcel bats the hand away and hugs him, squeezing too tight, too long.

Don't hold on to me, Steve wants to say, like Jesus said to Mary Magdalene outside the tomb. Marcel releases his hold.

"And who are you?" He drops to one knee, a grin on his face. "Is this Sam?"

"You look like Santa's son."

"Are you calling me fat?"

"Kind of."

"You can't be Sam," still smiling. He stands. "Sam is polite."

"I can be polite or I can be honest."

"This is Sam's friend Adi. I'm babysitting for the day."

"Not babysitting," a pout. "I'm not a baby."

"It was last-minute. I would have called you, but honestly I didn't think you'd show up."

"No worries, bro. I deserve that. But I called the church and talked to Janis. She was supposed to let you know I was coming."

The call he didn't answer. The voicemail he hadn't checked. "I haven't spoken to her."

"She must've forgotten. She's always so busy, that lady."

"Like a beaver."

Marcel nods and sees the empty takeout containers and crumpled brown bags. "You ate already?"

"Sorry," looking down at the oily residue on the bottom of his box.

"That's okay, bro. I'm not hungry anyway. I had a huge breakfast. Three eggs, six sausage links, buttered toast, juice, hash browns." He pats his stomach.

Steve forces a smile, struggling to come up with something to say. "You wanted to meet?"

"Right here?" He's looking at Adi, who's watching as diners file into the sushi restaurant.

"There's a community center nearby. We could go there."

"Sure, man."

"Did you drive?

"Bus," shaking his head. "Emperatriz drives the car to work."

Steve had forgotten her name. "Shall we go then?" He taps Adi on the shoulder.

"What about the garbage?"

"I got it," Marcel reaching.

Adi hands him her trash. Steve does the same.

Marcel turns around, his neck twisting left, then right, before spotting a nearby waste bin. He steps toward it, the garbage all in one hand.

"That's your friend?"

"He used to be a member of my church." Steve is no longer account-able to God for Marcel's soul.

"Doesn't he look like Santa with a brown beard? Like a young Santa, but not that young."

"Shh," a finger to his lips.

"That's why I said Santa's son."

Marcel is coming back, step step step step step, and now he's here.

"*Lai ho ma*," a bastardized accent.

"What?" squinting her eyes.

"Don't you understand Chinese?"

"Was that what that was?"

"You said a word palindrome."

"*Lai ho ma*," correcting his pronunciation. "It's Cantonese, not French."

Why do people pretend like they're linguists when their knowledge, such as it is, of a foreign language consists of nothing more than a handful of phrases and dim sum menu items? Why is Steve so judgmental?

Adi is looking up at him—for help?

"Marcel's wife is Chinese so he knows a few words."

"More than a few. I took two years' worth of classes."

"You should ask for a refund," deliberately widening her eyes.

"It's true," giving Adi a playful scowl. "And Molly is actually my ex-wife now, officially. The divorce was finalized last week."

"Hmm." What else is there to say? He could ask him how he's handling it; ask about the kids; how Emperatriz is doing. Should he ask that? Are they still living together? They're probably still living together; she took the car to work he said, which implies they're living together. Is marriage in the cards for the two of them? But Steve doesn't care about the answers to any of those questions. Should he change the subject? And talk about what? Sports? The Canucks? "The weather's nice today, isn't it?"

"Beautiful."

"Have you seen all the cherry blossoms?"

"God's creation is awesome."

"Hmm," nodding as he tries to come up with something wise to say, or witty. "Should we go?"

"The community center?"

"It's close."

"Sounds good."

Adi stands as Steve and Marcel step away from the bench.

They're heading toward 42nd.

Steve smiles at her. "There's a playground outside the community center where you can play while Marcel and I talk."

"What are you going to talk about?" She slides between the two of them.

"Grown-up stuff."

"Can I listen?"

"Definitely not."

There's no telling what might come out of Marcel's mouth. An armchair shrink might spend four minutes with him and promptly diagnose whatever frontal lobe disorder makes a person unable to discern what's appropriate to say out loud, what's not, and she might be right. Steve thinks Marcel sometimes doesn't think enough before he speaks, or he does think, but has glaring social blind spots; i.e., maybe he thinks as far as his intellectual limits will allow, which doesn't extend to polite conversation, and can you really blame a guy for that? Everyone is finite. No one can think of everything. Then again there are some things that should be obvious.

"You smell like my dad."

Without breaking stride Marcel elevates his elbow a couple of degrees and tilts his head, sniffing his armpit. "He must be a good-smelling man."

"Like cigarettes."

"You have a sharp nose."

It doesn't take a highly refined sense of smell, Steve wants to say as he inhales.

Adi points to a spot on the front of Marcel's raincoat. "There's food on your jacket."

He dabs at it with a finger and examines the evidence. "That's not food, it's birdshhhhhhhhhiiiiiwhat's that word? Scat? No. Wait. Is that it? Scat? Scut?"

"You said a bad word."

"Mental constipation." He laughs like he's pleased with himself. "Ironic. Get it? Constipation?"

"You're weird."

"Feces."

Adi smirks.

"It's feces," looking at his finger. "Definitely feces."

Her expression sours.

Marcel puts the tip of his finger in his mouth and sucks. "No, you're right. It's food." He licks his lips. "Sausage," wiping at his jacket for any residual meat.

"Gross."

"Who are you again?"

"Who are you?"

"I thought I was Santa's son."

"You don't know who you are?"

"Santa's son. You said it."

"I said you look like Santa's son. Look like. Santa isn't real, so he can't have a son, so you definitely can't be Santa's son."

"Who told you Santa isn't real?"

"My dad."

Marcel shakes his head. "Kids should believe in Santa. Mine are believers. He brings them gifts every Christmas. Maybe you don't believe in him because you haven't been nice enough and that's why he doesn't bring you anything. Have you thought about that?"

"My dad says the Santa myth is stupid. How nice do you have to be to get a present? How many times are you allowed to be naughty before you get nothing or a lump of coal? What is coal even? Besides, Roger brought this iPad to class one day for show and tell and he said Santa gave it to him for Christmas and Roger is the worst kid in the school so obviously it wasn't Santa. It was his parents. Or at least his mom. His dad lives in China. If Roger got an iPad from Santa, that's proof Santa isn't real."

The three of them cross the train tracks parallel to East and West Boulevard.

"Or it's proof Santa got him nothing so his mom had to pretend so his feelings wouldn't be hurt."

"You shouldn't lie to your kids. You should tell them the truth. Otherwise they won't believe anything you tell them when they're teenagers."

"I would never lie to my kids."

"You tell them Santa's real."

"That's not a lie."

"Sure it is."

"Tell her, Pastor Steve. Tell her about Saint Nick."

Steve shrugs. "I have no dog in this fight."

How long ago was it that he'd asked Marcel to consider singing in the choir? He said he was flattered, honored, humbled, and would pray about it, then dropped off the face of the earth: him, Molly, and their kids. His phone number stopped working. He didn't reply to email. Neither did Molly. No one ever answered their front door. In all likelihood Steve would still have no idea what had happened were it not for Marcel's parents telling him through tears that he'd left his family and was shacking up with a slut someplace, their words, who knows where, not them, they didn't know, they'd severed all ties with him after he refused their ultimatum: return to your family, to your wife and kids, or else. Would Molly have taken him back if he'd asked? Steve hasn't seen her or their kids since that day he'd asked Marcel about the choir. She was too humiliated to go back to church, Marcel's folks had relayed. Maybe it was inevitable their relationship would fall apart. Not necessarily like this, but dissolve in some way. Shortly after they began attending St. Joe's, they'd told him they had their first child before they were married. They'd walked into his office mid-week, no appointment, having decided to make St. Joe's their home church, and they wanted to tell their pastor everything up front, no secrets. Steve hadn't thought it was worth them mentioning that their first kid was born out of wedlock, it didn't matter to him, but everyone has different hang-ups.

Steve has never told his church any of his own secrets. People tell him theirs all the time. He could write a book.

The three of them are going west on 43rd now, down the south side of the community center. Steve turns his head to the left, his pace slowing slightly as he sees the Pacific Spirit building he knows too well from visits for baby weighings, pediatric flu shots, speech therapists. No one is coming in, no one coming out, no one parked outside in either of the two available spots by the curb. A rarity. Why can't it be like this when he needs a space to park?

"Can I run to the playground?"

"Go," a quick flick of his head. "Be careful."

Adi takes off running.

A black squirrel darts up a tree. It roosts on a branch, surveying the territory beneath it.

"Tell me again why that girl is with you, bro?"

"I ran into her and her mom when I dropped Sam off this morning. She was feeling sick and her mom couldn't take another day off work and the teacher didn't want her to stay. You know how it is. Might get the other kids sick. They were in a bind so I offered to watch her."

"You're too nice, brother."

"Nah."

"Seriously, Pastor Steve. Who else would do that?"

"Plenty of people. If they didn't have work obligations, most people I think."

"She doesn't look sick to me."

Up ahead Adi has slowed to a jog. Did she run to get away from Marcel, who really does reek of smoke? Steve will have to ask her later when he's gone. When will that be? He's not going to have to talk to him for an hour, is he? He slips his phone out of his pocket, holding it inconspicuously near his waist. 12:29. Is that it? He needs to be somewhere at one, that's what he should tell Marcel, which means he has to leave at quarter-to, which gives them only about twenty more minutes, but is that too little? Why does he even care? If it's not enough time to talk, tough, that's what he should be thinking. Where does he need to be at one, though? Something vague yet plausible. A parishioner's. For what? Something important, because what if Marcel asks if it can wait? There's only a small window of time where she's available. She or he? How is he going to explain the lie to Adi, assuming she overhears? There's no way to guarantee she won't. He shouldn't lie anyway. He's so bad at it.

"Over here?" pointing to a wooden bench under the cover of some trees near the sidewalk.

"Sure."

Adi is climbing the playground equipment.

Steve and Marcel sit.

Three birds chirp from a branch overhead, which reminds him of that Corinne Bailey Rae song he used to hear on the radio when they were living in Montreal, before Daphne was born. There was a time he heard it almost every day on his way to the daycare, Guarderie something, someone's name, Rose or Rosa or Rosie, something like that, after first dropping Lola off at the Royal Vic, sometimes the General. Sometimes he'd hear it again after dropping Sam off at the daycare, which was east of the city, but inexpensive, so worth the commute. One time at drop-off he realized he'd forgotten to bring Sam's mittens and had to drive back to their condo on Île des Sœurs, pick them up, and drive back to the daycare. He found the kids outside, six to a multi-toddler stroller, Sam gloveless, wearing a black toque. She smiled so big when she saw him, surely thinking Daddy was going to bring her home. It had only been forty minutes, but they must have felt like forty days to her. He placed the mitts over her numb pink hands, kissed her on the cheek. Why hadn't the daycare staff given her a pair? It was about then that she realized she wasn't leaving with him and started crying. Not loud, not audibly at all, in fact, which made it worse. Just a few teardrops rolling halfway down her cheek until they froze in place; and her expression: a look of resignation and disappointment that Steve will never forget, in part because he'd snapped a photo of her with his phone. A Nokia? It was a sorry excuse of a camera phone by today's standards, whatever brand it was, but it did the job, and Steve still sees that picture every now and then when he's browsing old photos on his desktop. He really needs to get a dedicated external hard drive. He's been meaning to. Something about the devil and good intentions. He ought to know his idioms better. If anything happened to that computer: the photos that'd be lost forever: the memories. One of the spotted towhees on the branch above the bench where he and Marcel are sitting takes off, then another flies away.

"So." Steve crosses his right leg over his left. "What did you want to chat about?"

"I'm sorry I missed the last couple of times we'd agreed to meet. Things came up, out of my control, you know?"

"That's okay."

Marcel crosses his legs, left over right.

Their knees touch.

Steve uncrosses his legs and sets his feet on the ground.

"What have you been up to, bro?"

"Same old," then pointing at Adi, who's making her way across an eight-inch-high balance beam. "And babysitting."

"The family?"

"Everyone's good," slow rhythmic nodding, deciding what generic phrase to add. "What about you?"

"Emperatriz and I are doing well." He pauses, his lips slightly parted, looking like he's waiting for Steve to respond, but Steve can't think of what to say. "Her dad has been sick," Marcel continues, "so we've been at St. Paul's a lot. I haven't seen Lola, though."

"She's been working at another hospital lately."

"Must be nice having a doctor for a wife. You know, the elevators at St. Paul's are so confusing."

"Are they?"

"It's been a crazy time with her dad there. Plus we just moved."

"Where were you living before?"

"Her place. Behind the BC Dive and Kayak store on West 4th. You know the one with the big koi mural?"

"Sure."

"We just bought our first place together."

How could they afford to buy? "Housing is expensive."

"It's tiny, but it's ours. Right by Grimmett Park."

Congratulations? "Hmm."

"You would love Emperatriz if you got to know her, bro. She's a big animal lover. Actually, that's why we decided to move. She had a dog at her old place. It died. Eaten, can you believe that? We think it must have been a coyote."

"That's horrible."

"We woke up one morning and normally the dog is barking, but that day, nothing. Then she found him in the yard, just bits of his body." Marcel shakes his head, diverting his eyes from Steve's. "It was terrible."

"Terrible."

"Which is why she wanted to move."

"Understandable."

"He was a cute dog, too. His farts smelled like KFC."

"How often do you see your kids?" Steve can't remember their names.

"Every other weekend. Some holidays."

"That must be tough."

"You know, bro, it's better this way. Honestly. When me and Molly were together we were fighting all the time. I swear, she was worse when I was around. I was terrible, too. I'm not blaming her. It was both of us. It wasn't a good environment for the kids, you know what I mean? Toxic."

"Hmm."

"So toxic, Pastor Steve," shaking his head, his eyes not looking any-where in particular expect possibly the past. "She used to yell at me in front of the kids for no reason. Like scream. If she got really mad, sometimes she'd hit me, punch, kick. She took a kitchen knife out this one time and waved it around like she was going to kill me. Because I hadn't done the dishes when I said I would. I stayed with her all that time because of the kids, but I'm not going back."

Over in the playground Adi is climbing the chain link rope ladder. The sound of metal striking metal reassures Steve she's not hurt.

"I'm sorry that happened to you. I didn't know."

"It's behind me."

"The two of you are officially divorced you said?"

"That's right. There was no reason staying separated." He rests his right hand on the top of his head. "Neither of us wanted to get back together. We both moved on."

"How many years were you married before you split up?"

"Seventeen, bro," bringing his hand back to his lap. "Almost two decades. We tried. I tried hard to make it work for the kids' sake, but I was so unhappy all the time. I know you would see me at church, this happy smiling Marcel on the outside, but on the inside I was miserable." He moves his right arm to the top of the bench. "Ever since we broke up everything has been so much better."

"It must be hard for the kids."

"You know though, I think they're good. Like I said, the home environment really wasn't healthy. Chester is going off to university in September so he's got his own life now. Harvey and Ellen have friends. They're really good. And you know what, Pastor Steve? A lot of their friends from school have parents that are divorced, or the dad lives in another country, so I think that's made it easier for them to accept."

"And Molly? Do you two talk?"

"We get along better than we ever have. It's really amazing. We're civil with each other. No more yelling. No more abuse. We'll never be best friends, but she'll always be the mother of my kids."

"There's no love there anymore?"

Marcel smiles. "There never was, Pastor Steve. That's the point."

"You loved each other enough to get married."

"No, Pastor Steve. You know how we got together, right?"

"I know you were high school sweethearts and had Chester before you were married."

"That's it?"

"As far as I remember."

Marcel opens his mouth wide, keeps it in that shape a moment, then starts to speak. "That's why you don't get it. You don't know the whole story."

Steve waits for him to tell it.

"We weren't really high school sweethearts. We dated a bit. I was in my last year, she was one grade below me. Nothing serious, just having fun. Molly was so pretty when she was a teenager. That's why I'm going to be really worried when Ellen gets older. Really have to watch out for the boys she dates, you know? She looks so much like her mom."

"I've got three girls. I know the feeling."

"We're going to have it hard in a few years, bro."

"I should tell you before you go on, I can't stay too much longer."

"Oh okay sure sure sure, I don't want to keep you. I really just wanted to catch up and apologize for all our missed meetings."

"I've got another fifteen minutes or so." It's probably closer to twenty, but whatever.

"Alright, so you want to hear about how we got married? I think it will help you understand the situation better."

"Go ahead."

"What happened is, I graduated, went away to university, and we lost touch. The summer after my freshman year, I was back home with my parents, helping out with their business."

"This was up north?"

"Prince George, yeah. And one day Molly shows up at my door, holding a baby. I hadn't seen her since high school graduation. She tells me it's mine. Can you believe it?"

"I knew you had him before you were married, but not the details."

"We told people we were high school sweethearts because it was easier than telling the truth. Some of our family members knew and they were so judgmental. You'd think Christians would show more grace."

"Hmm."

"We only had sex a few times. Always with protection or I'd pull out. We didn't even date a year. I was going with another girl when Molly came to my door holding the baby. I was just a kid myself, but I was raised well, bro. I didn't hide it from my parents. My dad was so angry. My mom said I had to do the right thing, you know? So I broke up with Mandy, and me and Molly got married that same summer."

Steve wants to say something thoughtful. Nothing comes to mind. "That must have been a shock."

"There was never any love between us. We were only kids."

"You did an honorable thing to marry her," though the moment after the words come out of his mouth Steve's not sure he actually believes them.

"And I stayed married to her for seventeen years. It's not like I gave up without trying. It just got to be too much." He clears his throat. "I married the wrong person. Molly did, too."

Hauerwas says you always marry the wrong person.

"Hmm."

"I know I sinned when I left my marriage, Pastor Steve, and I know I'm living in sin now, but I don't care. I'm happy. I just wish the rest of my family could forgive me." He looks like he's about to cry.

Steve feels a little sorry for him and also a little for himself.

"That's the real reason I wanted to meet," a sniffle. "I know my family isn't going to St. Joe's anymore, but I was hoping you could reach out to them," another sniffle. "Did you know they cut me off?"

"What do you mean?"

"None of them will talk to me. I email, phone. No replies. I'm the least in my father's house."

"I didn't know."

"I haven't spoken to my parents or my brother in more than a year," and now he's crying. He doesn't wipe the tears. "The only one who's talked to me is Louise, and it was only once," wiping at last, with his left sleeve. "She didn't want to stop communicating with me, but I bet my dad found out and made her."

"That doesn't sound like him."

"My dad is the biggest Pharisee. He goes, I'm no longer his son unless I get back together with Molly, but bro, I'm doing the same thing he did to my mom a thousand times. You probably didn't know that either, did you? They seem like such quiet, humble people, but my dad broke my mom's heart so many times. So many times. Sleeping around. Every time she took him back. So I don't feel bad, bro. When I think about it now, all those years trying to make the marriage work, what a waste. If I'd been more brave, I would have left a long time ago. But I was so scared. I didn't know what the future would look like if Molly and I weren't together. All my life I thought I'd have a traditional family and what if I didn't, you know? But I finally decided if I want my kids to turn out to be brave, I had to set an example for them to follow. That's what a dad's for, isn't it? A good dad, a good example.

Not to fail at marriage, of course that's not what I mean. You understand. But brave enough to follow their own hearts."

"And you think if I speak to your family it'll help?"

"It can't hurt."

"What do you want me to say to them?"

"To forgive me."

"It doesn't sound like they're going to do that unless you're repentant."

"That's pretty sub-Christian. If it was anyone else they knew, they wouldn't be so intolerant. They'd just forgive."

"I haven't talked to your family in a long time."

"That's okay. My parents love you, man. They were always saying such nice things about you. I'll say that for them. When they said they prayed for you, they did. Not like those people who, when they say they'll pray for you, are saying it only as a, what do you call it?" He blinks both eyes twice, keeping them shut slightly longer the second time. "A token gesture."

"I've always thought very highly of them, too."

"They can be so nice to other people, just not to each other."

"Hmm."

"So will you reach out to them for me?"

"I'd rather not get involved, to be honest."

Marcel looks surprised by the answer. "You're on their side." He sinks into the bench.

I'm not on anyone's side, Steve wants to say, but isn't he? And shouldn't he be? "I suppose I am."

"Even you're against me."

Steve sighs. "You cheated on your wife, man," voice steady. "You have three kids who don't get to live with both their parents, so yeah, I guess I'm not rooting for your new life to work out."

"That really hurts me that you'd say that."

"That I'd say it or that I'd think it? Because I could lie to you. I could keep my true feelings to myself."

"Why are you saying these things, Pastor Steve?"

"Look," measuring what he'll say next. "I'm not your pastor anymore. Even if I were, I'd feel the same way. The only difference is maybe I wouldn't tell you to your face."

"I told you all my secrets." He stands, making his chest appear broader than it is.

Should Steve stand, too?

Adi has somehow got herself into one of the toddler swings.

Marcel's palms are open, at his side.

"I'm not going to tell anyone the things you've told me," still on the bench. "Your secrets are safe. I'd never say anything scurrilous." He pats his chest once, in the spot he thinks his heart is, and keeps his hand there.

"You won't use me as a sermon illustration?"

"Of course not." To illustrate what? What would he say? He once had a parishioner who confessed to masturbating while watching women's long track speed skating on TV? Hardly moral paradeigma. "Sit down. Relax."

"I don't believe you."

Marcel turns away from the playground, toward the community center. He takes two steps that way, turns back and faces Steve. "You always bring up old church members in your sermons."

"Name one time."

"All the time. And it doesn't matter what you say. The way you feel now, I know you won't tell anyone today or this week. But your feelings will change or you just won't be able to help yourself. Trust me, I know. Marriage vows are exactly the same. You mean one thing the day you make them, but as far as a promise of future fidelity? Come on. In some moment from the pulpit, you'll do it. You'll use me as an object lesson. You won't mean to. You won't plan it. It might be extemporaneous. But you're gonna do it. Remember Marcel? you'll say, and then God knows what."

"You'll just have to trust me."

Marcel lets out a loud sigh, as if he's standing at a ten-items-or-fewer express check-out line and the person in front of him has a dozen things but doesn't think all of it should count because three of the items are identical cartons of almond milk, which means only one needs to be scanned, which makes it basically ten items, not twelve, and he doesn't want to say anything, that would be rude and confrontational so instead he sighs because then maybe the rude person will hear and turn around and apologize and rationalize the three cartons of almond milk being only a single thing even though she has to pay for all three of them, since they are, in fact, three separate items. "You're not going to talk to my family for me?"

"I don't think so. No."

"I thought you were my friend."

"I was your pastor. But I haven't been that for a long time."

"We were never friends?"

"How many friends do you call mister, the way you call me pastor?"

"I babysat your kids."

"You did, and I appreciated it, but you were also already cheating on Molly." It goes to character, doesn't it?

"I'm so disappointed," He takes a few small steps in place, then turns three-hundred-and-sixty degrees. "Not just disappointed. I'm pissed, bro."

Steve stands up, which he knows he probably shouldn't. "That's your prerogative. Your family is pretty pissed, too. And maybe I don't have a right to be, but I'm also a little upset."

"If you weren't my pastor, I'd —" hesitating, as if either trying to complete the thought in his head or deciding whether or not to complete it. "I'd knock your block off."

Steve takes a moment to settle his nerves. "Let's just shake hands and go our separate ways."

"But you aren't my pastor, are you?" He clenches his fist. "You're the one who keeps insisting you're not anymore."

"Maybe we should pray."

Marcel swings.

Steve bends his knees, ducks, the punch grazes the top of his head. Instinctively, he jabs, short, quick, putting as much force as he can into the blow, which has caught Marcel square on the nose and thrown him back, one step, two, three, he's staggering, trying to regain his balance, and down he goes, a barely visible tuft of dirt rising from where his rear hits the ground.

"You hit me." He covers his face with his hand, then holds it back out in front of his face. "I'm bleeding. You broke my fucking nose."

Steve takes a step back.

Marcel, a trickle of blood coming out of each nostril, leans his elbow on the ground, maneuvers to a knee, and slowly gets back to his feet, straightening his back. On top of everything, he's crying again.

"I'm sorry," approaching Marcel, offering him a hand. "I didn't mean to. It was instinct."

"Fuck that," slapping Steve's hand away.

"Beat that sword into plowshares, man." He really is sorry, though. Which is why he's apologizing, and also Marcel could file assault charges, but maybe he won't if he knows how genuinely apologetic Steve is, but if he does, it was self-defense.

"I take back everything good I ever said about you. You're a terrible pastor."

"You threw the first punch. I was just reacting."

"What happened to turning the other cheek?"

"I think we should call it a day. You're bleeding pretty bad."

Marcel wipes his upper lip, then his eyes. He grimaces.

"They might have some first aid supplies at the community center." The parking spots in front of the building are occupied now. "Bandages, cloths, that sort of thing."

"I need to get to the hospital. My nose is broken, man. I know what a broken nose feels like and it's definitely broke."

"Are you sure?" It doesn't look bent out of shape. "I didn't punch you that hard."

"Yeah, I'm sure. Are you going to drive me?"

"Come again?"

"How else am I going to get there?"

"I don't have the car today. Otherwise I would." Would he though?

Marcel sits on the bench.

Steve is about to sit next to him when Adi shouts his name. She's in the toddler swing, squirming. "I want to get out of here."

"I'll be right back," then to Adi, raising his voice, "Coming. Hold on."

He hadn't hit Marcel that hard, though not for lack of trying; he's just not that strong. How much force does it take to break a guy's nose? And shouldn't his knuckles hurt if he really broke it? On television people are always icing their knuckles after slugging a guy in the jaw. Steve looks at his, clenches and unclenches, moves his fingers like he's Lang Lang warming up before a concert. There's no pain whatsoever.

He's got Adi by her armpits and lifts while she twists and struggles to free her legs and feet from the swing without losing a shoe. He sets her on the ground. His hand doesn't hurt in the least. Maybe he's stronger than he looks.

"There's something [garbled] on the top of your head."

"What?" Did she say weird or there?

"It's red and bumpy looking."

Steve feels the top of his head with the same hand he'd knocked Marcel down with, his right. It does feel bumpy, more knobby than it did when they were at Starbucks, and bigger almost. Had Marcel struck him? Steve didn't think he made that much contact, but maybe he did. Maybe the adrenaline kept him from feeling anything. He rubs the area again, feeling several distinct fleshy protuberances each about a half-inch tall. "Is it bloody?"

"Bend down or lift me up so I can see."

He gets on both knees. The playground pebbles are a bit of a nuisance. Adi is touching the top of his head.

"What do you see?"

"Gross," still touching. "It's definitely reddish, maybe pink. But not blood. One, two, three, four. Four of them."

"Of what?"

"Pointy tips. Like spikes. Like barbs. It kind of feels like bone, but kind of not. Like really tough skin, but not exactly."

"Let me try and take a photo," and he readies his phone, steadying it over his head."

"Can I take it?"

Steve hands it to Adi. "Tap the big button."

"Don't move or it'll be blurry."

Click.

"Did it turn out?"

"Here," handing the phone back to Steve, who takes it from her, his fingers brushing against hers, and stands back up, gingerly again because of his knees. That's what happens when you have a near-catastrophic bicycle accident at age thirteen.

Pebbles brushed off his pants, he pulls up the photo Adi has just taken and it's exactly as she described. He zooms in, rotates, zooms out. "You know what it looks like? It kind of looks like a cock's comb," feeling the top of his head again.

"You mean a rooster's crown?"

"Doesn't it?"

"Let me see again."

Steve bends over, lowering his head so Adi can inspect it.

"It does," nodding. "Why do you have a rooster's crown growing on the top of your head? Is it because you've been eating a lot of poultry? Like, you are what you eat sort of thing?"

"Could be," though he doesn't actually eat much poultry at all. Swiss Chalet on his birthday may have been the last time. When he was single he used to do a generic-brand version of Shake 'n Bake every couple of weeks or so. Every fortnight—fortnight: a word he learned when he was eight or nine, watching Wimbledon on TV. He could have gone to Wimbledon when he was in London on his layover from Mumbai, this also pre-marriage, pre-kids; could have caught a train there, caught Federer in action.

What had he done instead? Something far less memorable whatever it was. In middle school one summer, after they'd moved to Vancouver, he went with his family back to Toronto to visit relatives. One of them took him to watch the semis of the tennis tournament hosted at York University, the one where the women are there one year, the men the next. Somehow, in between matches, he stood close enough he could have reached out his hand just a bit and squeezed Steffi Graf as she was on her way to or from the court. Someone had passed an oversized tennis ball through the throng of fans huddled around the walkway the players were taking to and from the court, and he was one of the last people to handle it. He could have been the last, could have been the one to put the ball in her hands, talked to her, heard her lovely, lilting voice speak back to him, if not for the middle-aged pervert who snatched it out of his hands to give to Steffi himself.

"Where'd your friend go?"

Marcel isn't on the bench where Steve left him, and in fact, he doesn't appear to be anywhere in the playground area anymore.

"He might've gone to the restroom."

"Should we wait for him?"

"We don't need to," shrugging. "I said goodbye."

"I'm thirsty. You didn't get me a drink."

"We can get one now. What do you want?"

"Just something. My throat is parched."

Where should they go? Not to one of the vending machines inside the community center. Marcel might really have gone to the restroom there. And not back to Potstikkr. They'd have to wait too long in line and the drinks are too expensive. You can get the same thing at London Drugs for half the price.

"Let's go to London Drugs."

Maybe not half the price, but less then full. Two dollars instead of two-fifty. Four-fifths then.

"What about the rooster's crown?" stepping out of the playground enclosure, to the sidewalk.

"Just leave it," feeling it again. Is it just him or has it grown?

"It's your head," as opposed to hers, she means, i.e., if it were her head, she'd be concerned.

It is his head, though, and he sees no sense worrying about things outside his control. The human body undergoes a million changes in a person's lifetime, most so minute as to be unnoticeable day-to-day, only discernible at a temporal distance, like changes in height, for instance. Genuine trans-figurations, you can count on one hand: birth, death; for a girl, her first period, probably. Three daughters means Steve will experience three first periods, albeit second-hand. That Costco membership. But that's far away. Costco might not even be around by the time his girls start menstruating, it's that far away.

If only.

It's not far at all. Objects in mirror are closer than they appear. In a book, time can be suspended. Stories can be retold, relived. A seconds-long escalator ride can be stretched to a hundred-plus pages. Fictional time can be manipulated. Fictional time is artificial. Real time flies. He has, what? six more years? Once Sam turns twelve, seventh grade, what's going to happen? She's not going to be his little girl anymore. It might even happen when she's eleven. Mightn't it? Or ten? That's a transformation he hadn't thought of before: from single- to double-digits. Parents, when their first kid is a baby, think they'll have her until she's eighteen, until she moves out of the house, starts life as an undergrad. They forgot what they, themselves, were like as kids, as teens. Steve was an idiot. By age thirteen if not sooner, an imperious, indolent, inimical, insouciant—can he think of any other I-words?—imbecile. He hung out with other like-minded, like-mannered kids, too. Not all of his friends, but enough of them. Some days some of them would come over after school. Some days during, instead of. Which is why he has sympathy for teens. They're just tyros at life. Six more years with Sam before it all starts unraveling. Six, tops. By reason of strength, maybe seven, but that's it, seven, tops.

"I asked if that's an iris?"

"Sorry, I was thinking about something. An iris?"

Adi points at a flower sprouting through a crack in the sidewalk.

"I think that's a weed."

"There was a question about irises on *Jeopardy!* yesterday."

"You watch *Jeopardy!*?"

Nodding.

"With your parents?"

"By myself. Sometimes Freesia will watch with me, but she's too young to understand."

"Aren't you too young?" He knows she's not.

A shrug. "Mrs. Canard sometimes shows us old *Jeopardy!* clips on YouTube."

"She does?"

"That's how I started watching. There was a question yesterday about irises. I thought that looked like one," glancing back at the pavement behind them.

"It might've been. I'm no expert on flora."

"The man said rose, but he was wrong. One of the women got it right, but not the woman who won, that was another woman."

"*Reach for the Top* is kind of like *Jeopardy!*"

"What's *Reach for the Top*?"

"Weren't we talking about it earlier?"

"No."

"Hmm," certain he'd at least thought about it, but was that all he'd done? Hadn't he said something out loud? Or had he imagined it? Or is he conflating a memory from yesterday, from another day, another conversation with another person? "Whatever. It's not important."

"I want to know."

Steve, his hands in his pockets, feels the contours of his phone, pausing at an unfamiliar dent. His other hand grips then releases the medicine bottle from the pharmacy. "If you really want to know, it's like *Jeopardy!* except with teams and for high school students. I did it when I was in high school. For one year."

"Were you good?"

"We were national champions."

"But were *you* good? Not your team."

"I was so-so. I used to love game shows when I was younger."

"I want to do *Reach for the Top*."

"You should. It's fun."

"Do you still play?"

"*Reach* is just for high school kids. Before Sam was born I would sometimes go to the bar for trivia nights. Other than that, no, nothing anymore."

"Trivia in bars?" mimicking a drinking motion

"It's a thing."

"That's silly," a giggle, almost.

"I agree, but it's fun still."

"Why would someone go to a bar to do trivia? You go to a bar to drink beer, right?"

"And other stuff."

What was the name of the bar he and Marcel would go to? The one on Lulu Island where they watched the floatplanes come and go as they ate on the open-air patio, back in ignorantly blissful days? The last time they'd gone Steve had a blue cheese burger and whatever was on tap. Marcel had the fish and chips, his usual, and a Molson.

Technically speaking, a burger is a kind of sandwich.

Grilled cheese, mantou, burger.

What would a fifty-fifty beef-pork patty, smothered in cheese, dressed with kimchi or just a gochujang-based sauce, in a mantou bun taste like? A pan-fried mantou bun? With some thinly shaved pickled turnips?

"I'm kind of hungry again."

Adi contorts her lips, deliberating something. His statement? Her response? "I am, too."

"We can get a snack after we get you your drink."

"What do you want to eat?"

"A burger."

"Gross," wrinkling her nose.

"Not just any burger. A burger with mantou for buns."

It sounds less amazing out loud than it did in his head.

"What is man-toe?"

"You've probably had it before. It's steamed Chinese buns. But you can pan-fry it, too."

"So you want a burger with steamed Chinese buns for buns? What did you say it's called again? Man-toe?"

"Close."

"That sounds even more disgusting than a regular burger," laughing. "Who'd want to eat a man's toe? That's cannibalism."

Steve rolls his eyes.

"Steve is a cannibal, Steve is a cannibal," singing.

"Better watch out."

"Why? Are you a cannibal?"

"*Mantou*, not *man-toe*."

"*Man-toe*, not *man-toe*," giggling.

"It's delicious when it's made right, and even better with cheese, a dash of salt, a drizzle of sesame oil."

Adi continues giggling. "Uh oh."

"What's the matter?"

"I think I need to pee."

"You think or you do?"

"I definitely do. I was laughing so hard, now I need to pee."

"So no drink? The London Drugs is just right there," indicating with his chin. "We can pop in, pop out."

She shakes her head. "Do they have bathrooms in there?"

"They might have restrooms, maybe. They probably do, but they're probably pretty disgusting. Probably worse than at Starbucks. How badly do you need to go?" an idea forming. "Can you hold it a few more minutes?"

"I don't know."

"Okay," idea crystallizing. "I know where we can go that'll be clean and you can get a drink."

"McDonald's?"

"Martha's."

"Never heard of it."

"She's a member of my church and lives around here. On the other side of 41st."

"It's close?"

"Very," estimating the time by foot, adjusting for the slower pace on account of Adi being under four-feet-tall, little legs. "Ten minutes?"

"That's not close."

"Can you wait that long?"

"What if she's not at home?"

"She's always at home."

"Maybe today she went out."

"I'm sure she's in."

Steve brings Martha communion every quarter. He brings the Lord's body and blood to all his housebound members once every three months: January, April, July, October, always first Wednesdays barring something unforeseen. He visits his non-member adherents with the Eucharist, too, as time permits, which it sometimes does. Of the very few things he genuinely loves about the pastorate, this tops the list, or close to it. And of all his shut-ins, Martha is his favorite. Pastors shouldn't have favorites, he knows, they taught him this in seminary, but he does, it's the truth, and the truth shall set you free, and every pastor he knows has favorites, too. It's impossible for a pastor not to favor some people over others. It's human. There's no sin in that. At least his favorites aren't the ones who give the most money to the church.

It's the first Wednesday today, he suddenly realizes, and it's April.

"If you don't think you can hold it, we can always ask to use one of the restrooms at the medical lab over here."

"What's so special about Martha's?"

"Nothing in particular. Her house is huge, though. On a bucolic street. She's a bit of a hoarder, but her restrooms are always immaculate. Fresh soap, linens, potpourri. And I bet she has something to drink in her fridge. Her fridge is always stocked."

"Okay," moving some hair from her forehead, briefly squeezing both eyes shut. "I'll hold it."

One of these days Martha won't remember him when he shows up at her door, once her dementia gets significantly worse. She's not that close to where his grandmother was the last time she was in Vancouver, but given how fast the disease progresses she's probably not that far from it either. Durational time is relative. He should ask her again if she's thought about a transition plan, if she's gotten in touch with any of the homes on the list he gave her a few months ago. When had he given her that list? Before Christmas. Should he offer to contact them for her? Maybe he should. Had he already?

"You'll like it there."

"Does she have anything I can play with? Does she have a Wii?"

"Not the last time I was there. But she loves crokinole."

"What's crokinole?"

"Seriously?"

"Should I know what it is?"

"You're kidding, right?"

"Should I know it?"

A white sedan zips past them, eastbound, surely going too fast over the speed limit to be safe. There's no curbside digital speedometer, but it doesn't matter. A precise number is inconsequential. Steve shakes his head as the car barrels toward the stop sign up ahead at Cypress, barely slowing down before turning left through the intersection. An Audi. Of course.

"All the things you know that no other kid I know knows, and you don't know this?"

"Nope."

"Crokinole is as Canadian as curling," a breath. "You know what curling is, yes?"

"Captain Obvi."

132

"It's kind of like curling, except played on a wooden board. You flick these discs with your fingernails," doing the motion with his right thumb and middle finger. "Flick or push. Pushing doesn't hurt as much as flicking does."

"I have no idea what you're talking about."

"It's hard to describe. You'll see when we get there. It's fun." Ish.

Some people prefer using their index fingers. Steve finds it uncomfortable in the same way index finger flickers think his middle finger flicking style is unnatural.

"Are we there yet?"

"Almost. Can you hold it a bit longer?"

"I lost the urge to go."

"It'll come back."

There was a time Steve didn't know what crokinole was either. It was members of St. Joe's who introduced the game to him at a Tuesday evening potluck supper. They'd been just as surprised he wasn't familiar with the game as he was with Adi's Canadiana ignorance just now, which he ought not have been since everyone is ignorant of a particular fact until they learn it for the first time. Adi is only six, and why would an urban six-year-old necessarily have any experience with crokinole? It's impressive enough she knows what curling is.

"Have you ever curled before?"

"Played curling, you mean?"

"Yeah."

"I watched it at the Olympics. Someone gave us tickets."

"You saw it in person?"

"Yup."

"At the rink by the baseball stadium?"

"Uh-huh."

"Beside the gymnastics place?"

"Ya."

What's the name of that place? Sam and Daphne have both done gymnastics there, shouldn't he remember?—Phoenix Gymnastics.

The Flying Beaver, that's the name of the bar he used to go to with Marcel.

"Cool."

"Do you remember anything about it?" She would have only been four at the time.

"I wanted to watch hockey, but my dad couldn't get tickets."

"They were hard to get." Should he tell her he was able to get them? "I lucked out."

"You got hockey tickets?"

"I did." Favor is not to the skilled.

"Men's or women's?"

"Men's."

"Oh." Her tone is like a helium-filled balloon, mid-deflation.

"I saw all three round-robin games. Sam came with me to the one against Switzerland."

Adi doesn't seem like she cares to hear any more. "I'd rather watch the women play."

"You like the Canadian women's team?"

She nods.

"Who's your favorite player?"

"I like the goalie."

"Cool."

At the intersection Steve checks both ways. You never know when a reckless Audi is going to rip by. They begin making their way to the other side of Cypress.

You can't spell Audi without Adi, he suddenly realizes.

He puts a hand on Adi's shoulder, directing her north.

When he was growing up he couldn't keep his directions straight until one of his elementary school teachers gave his class a tip he's used numerous times since: the mountains are north: as long as you can see the mountains, you'll never get lost.

He should have figured out on his own the thing about the mountains serving as a navigational aid.

"Do your folks follow the Canucks?"

"We are all Canucks."

"Did Sam ever tell you about the time we met the Sedins?"

The light at 41st is green. Steve keeps one eye on Adi as they cross the street, another on approaching vehicles. Which is hyperbolic: both eyes are on both: it's physically impossible for one eye to be on one thing, the other on another. All the cars are coming to a stop, as they should. Steve makes eye contact with the drivers stopped closest to the traffic signal. Always make sure they see you, he tells Sam; never assume that just because it's your right of way, it's safe to go.

"It was last spring." He remembers because it was during the Canucks' Stanley Cup run. "We were outside Bluffwood, in the blue playground, the one facing King Ed, eating pizza before a PAC meeting. They used to be in the evenings. Gillian was still a baby. Sam and Daphne were playing on the dodecahedron climbing thingy. No one else was there yet because we were early. Their mom was at home napping and I wanted to give her some quiet so it was just me and the little ones. All of a sudden a black SUV pulls into the lot."

"That's only for teachers."

"I know. But it was like 5:30 or something and the lot was empty. We'd walked. So anyway this black SUV pulls in. I think it was a Volvo. A fit-looking guy comes out, red hair, not huge bulging muscles or anything, but healthy. He was wearing flip-flops, I remember. So he opens one of the back doors and out come two or three little kids, roughly Sam's age. Your age. The guy looks familiar, but I don't recognize the kids so I ask Sam if they're Bluffwood students and she says no, she doesn't think so. When they step into the playground I say hi. To be polite, you know? Acknowledge another human being, another dad. He says hi back. The kids start playing together, his and mine. I'm sitting on one of the benches, eating a slice of pizza, wondering if it would be weird if I offered one to this other dad. Because we're strangers, right? And most likely he's going to turn me down. I would never turn down free pizza, but it seems like something most people would refuse. I'm debating in my head whether or not to offer him a slice, and also there were only a couple left and they were cold and I was saving them for a midnight snack."

"What about Sam's mom? Shouldn't you have saved some for her?"

"This way," directing Adi up Angus. "We're almost there."

"Finally."

"She doesn't like pizza. I probably made her something to eat before we left, or she had leftovers. Anyway, I'm about to offer a slice to the guy in the playground when another SUV pulls in to the parking lot, almost identical to the first: black, European, but not a Volvo. It might've been a Mercedes. The driver's side door opens and out steps the same guy who's standing a few feet away from me. I mean, these two guys looked more alike than their cars. And this second guy has a few kids with him, too. And it finally clicked, who they were."

"Daniel and Henrik."

"That's right," smiling and tapping his nose. "Sam and Daphne played with their kids."

"Daniel used to be our down-the-street neighbor."

She doesn't look like she's joking. "Seriously?"

"I used to go over every week."

"Oh."

Steve's pace slows.

"Are we there yet?"

He looks up and around and yes, as a matter of fact, they are.

"When were you neighbors?" Steve has seen Adi's home. It's a townhouse.

"When we lived in my nan and poppop's basement, before Freesia was born. Then Daniel moved, and we moved, too."

"Ahh."

"Why did we stop? Are we there?" She's looking at the Tudor-style house to their left.

Steve nods. "We are."

"This one?"

"That's it."

"It's a heritage building," pointing at the city plaque affixed to the end of the five-foot-tall stone hedge dividing the property from the sidewalk, which partially obstructs their view of the house.

"Before we go in, I should let you know that Martha's quite, umm, girth-full," his arms curved as if in first position.

"You mean she's fat."

"It's why she's a shut-in. She can't really get around well."

"She's so big she can't get outside the door?"

"She has some trouble putting weight on her feet. Just don't stare or say anything about it. Be polite."

Adi nods. "Does she have scary pets, though?"

Above the heritage building plaque is another sign: WARNING STRANGE CAT, all-caps, in a narrow sans-serif typeface.

"That's always been there. Martha's got a few cats, but she's not what you'd call a cat lady. Only two the last time I was here."

They head through the open wrought iron gate, up the path parallel to the driveway, beneath a hundred-foot-tall Western red cedar. The garage, a vine maple shade of green, could do with a fresh coat of paint. The color matches the yard, sort of, filled as it is with hellebores and brophytes. All the times Steve has been here before, it's the first time he's made that connection—Connection! It must have been a deliberate choice. People put more thought into the color of their garage than they do so many more important things.

They step up the stairs, Adi first—

six

five

four

three

two

one

—then Steve.

"The rooster crown," pointing at his head.

Steve touches the excrescence. It feels like it's grown. "Hmm."

"Can I ring the door bell?"

Before he can answer she's pressed the buzzer three times.

"Enough. Stop."

"It worked. I heard it through the door."

The front door whose color is the same as the garage's.

"You know how sometimes people's doorbells don't really work so you're out there ringing and ringing, but inside there's no sound and the people are just going about their lives and no one answers because no one knows you're outside?"

"At least until you knock loudly on the window." Adi inches toward the pane of glass next to the door.

"Don't," raising his index finger like a stern church elder. "She has mobility issues, remember? It takes her a while to get around."

"What if she's sleeping and snoring so loud she didn't hear it?"

"Then knocking on the window isn't going to make a difference."

Adi presses an ear to the door.

"I don't hear anything." She squeezes her legs together, knees touching. "I need to pee."

"Let's try the bell one more time."

Steve presses the buzzer, twice.

"I can't hold it."

There's no detectable noise or movement coming from inside.

"Let's try the backyard."

It's a nice day. Maybe Martha is sitting on her patio getting some air.

They hurry down the steps—

six

five

four

three

two

one

—taking the path laid with the same type of stones as the hedge by the street, toward the backyard, going past a rabbit statue, an empty planter, another statue, of a chipmunk or squirrel, a garden hose coiled around a circular widget screwed to the side of the house, beneath an arbour separating the front yard from the back. An owl crafted out of twisted copper greets them from its seat atop a backless bench. Turning toward the back of the house, Steve pauses, taking in the simple artistry of the wooden trellis running alongside the far fence separating the property from the back alley where the garbage trucks drive, where the detached garages are. The roses will bloom soon. A charcoal-colored compost bin sits at the top of some steps leading down to the basement. And more statues: one of those spirit bears auctioned off a few years ago for charity, this one painted yellow with coniferous trees that are different shades of green tattooed on its torso; a seagull that's taller than he is, wings outstretched, perpetually waiting to take flight.

A shiver runs down Steve's spine when he touches it.

"Aren't you the cock of the walk?" Martha is on the patio, seated at an armless outdoor loveseat that resembles a Windsor chair. Her jowly face is as he'd remembered it.

"Martha," smiling a genuine smile.

"I thought you'd fallen off the face of the earth."

Steve takes Adi by the hand and leads her to the patio.

"I'm sorry I haven't been by in a while."

"I thought you were a figment of my imagination"

"Sorry."

"You have your own life, I understand. You're here now." He looks at Adi. "And you've brought someone with you." She looks at Adi. "What's your name?"

Adi's face is phlegmatic.

"This is Adi, Sam's friend. I'm babysitting. You remember Sam, my oldest?"

"Sure. Handsome little boy."

"I need to pee," tugging on Steve's sleeve.

"Would you mind if—?"

"Gogogo."

Steve slides the patio door open.

Adi steps in to the kitchen.

"The restroom is the first door on your right." The door is ajar. "Are you okay on your own?"

"Of course."

"I'll wait for you out here."

He stays put until he's sure Adi is going to the correct room, then for her to shut the door, which sounds like the French for I love you. The light comes on, shining through the quarter-inch space above the floor.

There's a low-back polypropylene chair, yellow with holes, facing Martha, that makes the most sense for him to sit on, as opposed to the identical one slightly diagonal from her. Steve takes a seat. Maybe he should have hugged her. Yes, that's definitely what he should have done, but it's too late now. Now it would be awkward if he stood up, walked over to her, leaned down and gave her a hug. Like it was an afterthought. Like it hadn't been his natural instinct to greet her with some more affection and tenderness the way a good pastor would do because that's the outpouring of his God-forged character.

"Sorry again for dropping by unannounced. We were in the neighborhood."

"Pardon me for not getting up."

He waves her off. "How have you been? It's been a long time."

"I'm old as the hills, cursed with this vile body, haven't been laid in five decades, and stopped getting on the scale once it tipped three hundred. Otherwise I'm swell, Pastor."

Steve can't stifle a laugh.

"And how have you been keeping? You look different somehow."

He takes two seconds to compose himself. "Same old."

"Life's been good to you?"

"Better than I deserve." He heard someone say that once and thought it was a pious-sounding thing to add to his own lexicon.

"You don't have to deal with the incessant fulminations of people like me every week," joking, Steve can tell.

Did she really just say fulminations? "What do you mean?"

"More of us older folks can't make it to church anymore." She sinks further in her seat. "You don't have to put up with us."

"I've never had to put up with you." Other people, perhaps, yes, sure. Not Martha. He begins to picture some of those other people's faces. Not deliberately. It just happens. How do you cast out an unwanted thought?

"What about these new statues?" turning toward the bear and the gull. Martha's gaze follows.

"Yes, they are fairly new, aren't they?"

"When did you get them?"

"It can't have been that long ago. It feels like I'm still learning to live with them. They don't have that settled air of comfort."

"That's one of those spirit bears you see around the city. There's one outside the Stong's grocery store, another at Nat Bailey. I think I saw one in Whistler somewhere. There's one on 2nd or 3rd, near Granville Island, wearing a black tank top. Not actually wearing. It's painted on."

"Is it a spirit bear or a Kermode?" Martha rubs her chin. "I can never get it straight."

"Is there a difference?"

"Has to be. I think one is always white, the other could be white. One is a subset of the other. Fruit, apple. You should know. You're a pastor."

"Could be," nodding. "What about the seagull?"

"Yes," a smile breaking out. "Do you like it?"

"It's very big."

"It's an Imredy."

"Who?"

"Pastor!" a look of surprise tinged with disappointment.

"Should I know who that is? Is he famous?"

"Elek Imredy, the Hungarian-Canadian sculptor."

The name doesn't ring a bell.

"Surely you're familiar with his work."

"His name rings a bell." Which is true in the way all names share some element of familiarity.

"He did the mermaid in Stanley Park. The one at Lumberman's Arch near the Nine O'Clock Gun."

"Yeah, okay," nodding again in spite of the fact it's not a mermaid. "So the seagull is his work?"

"He probably got the idea from seeing all the real gulls crapping on his mermaid's head." Martha bellows, her ample chest bouncing like fraternal twins on a trampoline. "It's a possibility, isn't it? It's a good story anyway. And they make a nice couple, don't they?"

"Where'd you get it?" Should he say anything about his own bird dropping experience earlier today?

"A private sale, online. Same as the bear. You know how those things are."

"I don't, actually. I've never bought any art."

"That's not true."

"It is."

"You've bought records before. Books. Watched movies. Been to the theater."

"Of course."

"That's art."

"I guess."

"Art is what makes life worth living, Pastor."

"I don't disagree, but it costs money."

"Living without art costs a great deal more."

"That's a good point."

"You can't live without art. You of all people should know that."

"You're right." Steve crosses one leg over the other.

"I took up painting recently for that very reason."

"Oh yeah?"

"I set up a little studio in my garage," pointing to the detached building near the trellis. "Takes a while for me to walk there, but I've really taken a liking to encaustic."

A small plywood structure near the garage catches Steve's eye. "What's that?" pointing.

"That's my chicken coop."

"Chickens?"

"That's another thing I started doing. Raising chickens."

"What happened to your cats?"

"Dead."

"I'm sorry to hear that."

"What can you do? That's life. Cats die, get chickens."

"Are they egg layers?"

"Mine aren't the best egg-producing hens, but they're small, which makes them ideal for urban living. Beautiful creatures." She clears her throat. "You get to be my age, Pastor, you don't have time to waste surrounding yourself with ugliness."

"You're the only person I know in the city who's got chickens as pets."

"It's responsible stewardship is what it is."

"I met a couple on Salt Spring Island who had chickens," the wwoofer couple, "but other than them you're the only person."

"You should get some."

"I doubt my condo council allows it." They let 120-pound bullmastiffs run the halls unleashed, nearly crushing his kids, but a chicken? Where would he keep it? And all the avian-borne diseases.

"You can have a parrot, can't you? Budgies? Canaries? A chicken is no different. That's what they call speciesism."

"I don't think that's what speciesism means."

"Chickens are loyal animals, and smart as a whip. Vicious, too."

"They might raise their own chickens at Marché St. George. Do you know that place?"

"I haven't been out of the house in a long time."

"Just here in the yard?"

"There's nowhere else I'd rather be than home. Why leave if I don't have to? I go out, people gawk, and it's not that easy getting around. Fall and winter are a real bitch on my joints."

"Do you keep your own bees for the encaustic, too?"

"I don't, but I should, shouldn't I? Martha B. Norton, beekeeper."

"It's got a nice ring to it."

"Beekeeper," squinting. She wipes the sweat away from the inside of her elbow pits. "Bookkeeper is the only word in the English language with three consecutive double letters. Bookkeeper and its derivatives: bookkeepers, bookkeeping."

"Is it?" Can he come up with any others? "What about committee?"

"Not consecutive."

Steve coughs into his elbow pit. What's the anatomical term for elbow pit? He should know. What did he used to say to Sam when she would sneeze into her hands?—Antecubital fossa. Does Adi know that term? How do you spell that? "Hmm."

"I know what you're doing. Don't busy your mind trying to come up with another word. There's no point. There isn't any other."

"I didn't know your middle initial was B."

"What you don't know about me, there isn't room in all the world that could contain all the books you could fill. You could try, though. Build a museum about me. A me-seum."

"We saw some missing chickens signs posted around the neighborhood."

"There's more people than you think who've got chickens in their backyard."

"Have any of yours gone missing?"

Martha does a sort of half shake of her head, which means what? no? that she's got a stiff neck? "You want something to drink, Pastor?"

"I'm fine, thanks. But now that you mention it, Adi, the girl I'm baby-sitting, she was saying before that she's thirsty."

"Who is this?"

"The little girl who's with me. Sam's friend from school."

"There wasn't anyone with you." Does her expression indicate that she genuinely can't remember or that she's pretending she can't? "Do you see dead people, Pastor?"

Steve isn't sure what to say so he sits there, lips sealed, trying to deduce something from Martha's face.

She breaks into laughter. "Of course I know who you're talking about. I'm not as stolid as you look. I'm not all gone yet. Where is she?"

"Your restroom," turning his head to see if Adi is about to come out. The door is partially open, the light off. Where is she? Giving herself a tour of the house, probably.

"Do you mind if I go check on her, make sure she didn't fall in?"

"Why should I mind? You do what you need to do," a chuckle. "I'll be right here. Go look after that busy bee you're babysitting."

"Be right back." Steve winks—*bee* right back—and stands, adjusts his pants, lifting them by the belt, pulls down on the bottom of his shirt so it's not riding up. He walks to the sliding door, wipes his shoes on the rattan mat, and steps inside the house, into the kitchen. A look over his shoulder to see if Martha is watching him.

She is.

He waves.

Martha nods, smiles.

Steve heads to the restroom, opens the door all the way. Empty. The toilet isn't making that residual flushing noise either so the restroom has been empty for some time, at least thirty seconds. Is that how long the post-flush shushing lingers? In fact, there's no evidence Adi was ever in here except he saw her go in, saw her close the door, the light go on. There's enough natural light flooding in from the hall that he can see the sink is wet, the faucet dripping, but is it dripping because Adi didn't shut it properly after washing her hands or because it's in need of repair? Or had Martha or whoever last used it not shut it properly and that's why the sink is wet? In which case it's been this way for hours, days, more. On its own the dripping faucet isn't evidence of anything. A proverb about wives suddenly comes to mind. It could get annoying, though: continual dropping of rain outside—not today, but plenty of other days; leaky faucet inside—drip drip drip. Steve pushes down on the single-handle faucet. It's wet. The dripping stops. That answers that. Now what? Should he go around the house looking for her? But the house is so big, multiple ways upstairs and down. He could go one way, she might come the other.

"Adi," a whisper.

She's not in the kitchen.

Steve calls her name a little louder, keeping an eye on Martha through the patio door. Her attention is elsewhere, looking away from the house at something; or nothing, just looking. He walks by the restroom, shuts the door on his way, heading down the hall lined by framed photographs of Vancouver landmarks, the wood floor creaking. The frames are all different, none the same. There's one of the girl in the wetsuit Martha thinks is a mermaid; one of the Olympic Village; one of the Lions Gate Bridge taken from the north side of the inlet.

At the end of the hall, Steve peeks into the formal dining room. Foot-tall piles of paper and magazines are strewn over the surface of the table that could seat eight, comfortably, were it tidy. Adi isn't hiding beneath it. She isn't sitting at one of the chairs reading.

There's a baby Steinway in the den through the dining room. If Adi were in there, she'd be playing it for sure. Three blue Rubbermaid bins are stacked one atop the other at the foot of the piano. A SPUD grocery delivery receipt is affixed to the lid of the uppermost one.

Two sets of stairs are behind him on the other side of the hall by the front entrance, one leading upstairs, one going down. There's no noise emanating from either floor.

The front door is closed and locked so Adi hasn't gone outside. She's not lost on the street somewhere. She's inside. He shouldn't be so worried. She'll come back, he'll talk to her about it later, about not scaring him by disappearing like that, about how some people might think it rude to traipse around another person's house when you're a first-time visitor, an uninvited guest at that.

"Adi," beckoning up the flight of stairs.

No response.

The light to the basement is off. It's unlikely she'd have gone down there.

He calls her name anyway.

Nothing.

Maybe if he stays extra quiet, holds his breath so the huff and puff of his inhaling and exhaling is stilled for a few brief seconds, he might hear her moving, calling, breathing. It really is a lovely house. How much longer can he stay inside before Martha wonders what's happened to them? Maybe she's forgotten he's here.

Once more Steve calls out to Adi.

He begins retracing his steps: back down the hall, a photo of Commercial Drive, an aerial shot of one of the beaches, past the restroom, door still closed, in and through the kitchen.

There's Adi, outside, sitting in the same chair as before, talking to Martha.

"You're here," stepping through the patio door.

"Where else would I be? Where were you?"

"I was looking for you."

She must have gone through the other side of the dining room, through the den and the library, through the other entrance to the kitchen and out to fresh air.

Martha pulls herself to her feet, pinches her shirt near her breasts, and fans. "We were just about to feed my chickens."

"Can you get me something to drink?"

"If it's okay with Martha."

"I've got milk, chocolate milk, orange juice, grape juice, probably, and water, but use the fridge dispenser not the sink. There may be some cranberry juice left, and prune."

"I'll have chocolate milk."

"Coming up."

"Cups are in the cabinet above the dishwasher."

Where they've always been. Steve nods and heads back to the kitchen while Adi steps in front of Martha. He can hear her hopping down the patio steps, skipping toward the chicken coop.

A red light above the water-and-ice dispenser indicates the filter needs replacing. He opens both refrigerator doors, which is what he does at home. Lola tells him to open only the one he needs, or one at a time if he's not sure which side of the fridge whatever it is he's searching for is on, but how much extra energy is he using by opening both doors the first time? Some habits aren't worth the effort to break.

Steve spots the chocolate milk tucked behind bottles of ketchup and mustard, three tubs of faux-butter, and a jug of Tropicana, all of which he has to rearrange to get at the milk. The carton feels half-empty. Half-full. Halfway to another carton. Ha! a sanitized version of a beer joke he heard a long time ago.

He sets the carton on the counter and opens the cabinet above the dishwasher. What need Martha has for all the different cups she has, four dozen at least, he has no idea. If he were single, living on his own, he'd have four to six, eight max. Who's he kidding? He'd have two. He grabs one of the small frosted glass tumblers, and with his other hand pops open the spout of the chocolate milk carton and pours until the glass is three-quarters full. Then he closes the spout and returns the milk to the fridge, pushing it in front of the ketchup and mustard and faux-butter tubs, beside the orange juice. Now he shuts both doors. He picks the glass of chocolate milk up off the counter, checks for a missed spill, finds none. Through the window above the sink he sees Adi and Martha standing by the chickens. It sounds from the kitchen like the hens are squawking, or is the term cackling? As he approaches and slides open the patio door, yes, he's certain they are. The noise reminds him of a heated congregational meeting or an extended family get-together with his cousins and uncles and aunts where each person speaks louder than the next despite the fact they're side-by-side-by-side at a too-small table. Aunt Letty is the worst. When he was three, she locked him out in the hall of her apartment once. She was supposed to be taking care of him after his daycare was done for the day; his daycare was on the ground floor of her building in Taipei. But he wasn't sharing his toys with his cousin Joan, Aunt Letty's oldest, so screw him, twenty-minute timeout in the hall. His grandmother, the one who gave him the Leafs jersey, discovered him outside the door to the apartment, on his bum, throat hoarse, eyes pink from crying.

Nai Nai was a lovely woman who hated Aunt Letty as much as he did.

No, not hate. He rarely thinks about her enough to hate her. Indifferent is what he is.

Adi is wearing only a white tank top. Her outer layers are on the lawn, next to a bush near the chicken coop.

"Aren't you cold?"

"The red was freaking them out," tossing a fistful of feed into the coop.

"That one's the alpha." Martha nods at the first bird to eat. "They're extremely sensitive to color, much more than we are. Physicists have studied them to great benefit, you know? Planck kept chickens. So did Bohr."

"I didn't know that."

"You said you're a trivia expert." Adi underhand tosses another fistful of feed.

"I was. Not anymore."

"Notice how the other birds wait their turn. The alpha eats, then the beta, and so forth, right down to the runt. Chicken broods are much more civil than human societies."

"Brood?"

"Brood, peep, flock, same thing. Don't be one of those anal types, Pastor."

Steve hadn't been trying to be precise. He didn't know brood was the collective term, that's all. "Is there something wrong with his eye?"

"Her eye. And no. Chickens don't all have symmetrical facial features."

The alpha reminds Steve of his friend Garrett, because of the eye. What ever happened to him? Are they still friends if they haven't talked in over a year? Last time they spoke was when Steve told him that Burnaby Mandarin Chinese Community Church was looking to hire a new pastor for their English-speaking congregation. BM3C. As if the M wasn't enough of a descriptor, they had to add the first C to make it as obvious as possible who the insiders are, in case anyone on the outside was unclear. Did Garrett apply for the job? Did he get it and that's why they haven't talked for so long, because he's bitter Steve suggested he work there? Steve hadn't suggested any such thing, would never do such a thing—encourage a guy, especially a white guy, but any guy, even a Chinese one, even a Mandarin Chinese one, to lead a Chinese church's English-language ministry.

There are web sites devoted to people who look like their pet dogs; maybe there's one with other animals. The more Steve looks at it, the more he sees Garrett in the alpha.

"This one looks like the one from the missing pet signs we saw." Adi is on her knees, two fingers poking through the wire mesh.

"Not surprising." Martha has both hands on her hips. "There are only so many different breeds of chicken you'll find in Vancouver."

"You can keep different breeds in the same coop, obviously?" Steve hands the chocolate milk to Adi.

She takes a sip.

"No need to segregate. This isn't church. I said chickens are more civil than humans, didn't I?

"How many different kinds do you have?"

"How many do you see?"

Adi bobs her head from one chicken to the next, then back to one she's already looked at, then another. "Three."

"Bingo. Cochin bantam, Bourbourg, Nanking."

"Is having eight chickens typical for people who raise them in their yards?"

Martha shakes her head, smiling. "Don't tell anyone, but the city only allows four."

One of them, a mostly white one, is pecking at something by the edge of the cage, near Adi's feet.

"How did you get eight if you're only allowed four?"

"How does anyone get anything they're not legally permitted to have? No one polices backyard birds, Pastor. That's why I say you can have at least a couple in your condo. No one's going to check."

She doesn't know condos, clearly, but Steve doesn't want to correct her.

Adi finishes her milk and gives the empty glass back to him.

"There's no money to pay teachers, no money to pay nurses. How's the city supposed to monitor their livestock program? They can only afford to go by the honor system, and that never works." She sniffles and scratches at a mole on her neck. "That guy who had his hens stolen, he's probably got a handful more at home."

"Could be."

It occurs to Steve that he's had many encounters with birds of one kind or another today. Frankly, it should have occurred to him sooner. Merab would say this is God trying to tell him something and if he can't figure out what it is, he'd better get praying. It could just be there are a lot of birds in the city and you're bound to come across a good many on any given day. Just because there are stars in the sky doesn't mean they mean anything.

You can make anything mean anything if you try hard enough. Preachers do it all the time: start with a topic, mine for a text. Professor Taylor warned of the temptation to eisegesis for those who don't use a weekly lectionary, those who trust the Holy Ghost alone to direct their pulpit planning.

"What if someone does come by, though? You haven't had them long. Enough time passes, you figure an inspector is going to come around at least once."

Martha frowns. "You can't worry about what-ifs. Pay a fine, have the extras confiscated, who cares?"

"I'm hungry."

"Seriously?" Steve rolls his eyes. "How many potstickers did you just have?"

"I can't help it. Watching these chickens eat has got my stomach stirring."

"There's a Papa John's nearby." Martha tilts her head in what's probably a random direction, because she's not indicating anywhere near the pizza shop.

"Gross." Steve really dislikes Papa John's. Sorry, not sorry.

"But it's close."

"Can you make me something?"

"My kitchen is at your disposal." Martha picks at the inside of her ear with a pinky.

Steve gives her a playful look.

She doesn't notice.

"What do you want to eat?"

"Anything. I'm so hungry."

"I'll take a look and see what Martha has. But you have to eat whatever I make."

"If it's tasty, I will."

"There might be some leftover Nando's in the . . . never mind. I think I finished it yesterday. But check."

"Adi's a vegetarian."

"Is that the place that makes these guys?" Adi is staring at the chickens.

"It is."

"Eww. How can you eat them when you raise them?"

"They taste pretty delicious."

"Disgusting." Adi's face is a can of two-day-old cream soda. "I don't want Nando's."

"I'll see what I can whip up." Steve heads back toward the house. Martha is telling Adi something about her hens, her voice growing fainter as he walks away. Something something porcupines something something chickens something love your enemies something something.

He should send Garrett a text, see how he's doing. Or email. He should call. At least he should put it in his calendar or else he's going to forget: schedule a time to write or phone. Not this week, though. This week is busy and almost over. Next Monday then. But it's a holiday, isn't it? Is Easter Monday a stat day? Is Sam at home or at school on Easter Monday? Is the daycare closed? The following Monday then. He should start running again then, too. He'll get in touch with Garrett the second Monday of Easter. Probably he should have deleted the job posting when it came across his inbox, or at least given Garrett a warning about the Mandarin Chinese thing, but also the pay. *Salary: TBD* is a sure sign the church is going to pay you as little as it can get away with.

There's a loaf of Heather's Buttermilk and Honey bread from Uprising Bakery on the counter, between a silver 12-quart Hobart mixer and a fennel green Le Creuset butter crock like the one he has at home in front of his toaster except his is boring blue to match all the other Le Creuset items, blue being Lola's favorite color and even though having different colored Le Creuset kitchenware is one of the points of owning Le Creuset kitchenware, diversity being almost always preferable to uniformity, he can't think of an instance where it's not, Lola sees things otherwise, prefers they alllooksame, so he defers to her: blue butter crock blue Dutch oven blue braiser blue roaster blue square skillet blue ramekins blue baking dishes blue pie dish blue spoons.

It's not just the pay, though, taking two slices of bread out of the bag, leaving them on the counter, it's what *TBD* reflects about a congregation's understanding of grace and work and rest and their unrealistic, impossible expectations of their pastor-employees.

The first drawer he tries is the one with the cutlery. Steve picks up a knife, closes the drawer. He slides the butter crock toward him and lifts the lid. He's forgotten to get a plate. He opens the two cabinet doors directly above him and there they are: plates, saucers, bowls: all bone white. A medium-sized plate should do, but he takes the largest one because why not? He sets it on the counter, places the bread on it, closes the cabinet doors. He scrapes some butter on to the knife, then smears it on the first slice of bread and starts spreading.

When she was a kid, Lola used to get butter sandwiches for lunch all the time, that's what she told him, and because of that, on days when he doesn't feel up to making lunch for Sam, she suggests he make that as a quick meal to pack her, but Steve has never done it and never will and he's not going to give it to Adi either. It's a start, a base, a foundation for something more substantial. Not a meal unto itself.

He's on the second slice of bread.

If there's lettuce in the fridge or a cucumber or tomato he could slice thinly, some cold cuts, that would be a solid snack sandwiched between some buttered bread; not something he'd ever want to eat, but objectively speaking, it would do. It's better than cookies.

A little more butter to fill in the spaces by the crust. Now over to the fridge.

On the shelf beneath the chocolate milk is a package of pre-sliced Havarti next to various tubs: sour cream, yogurt, shortening. Grilled cheese then. Next to the Havarti is an already-open pack of provolone discs. Two-cheese grilled cheese, even better. He peels back the plastic wrapping, removes a slice of Havarti. A square sheet of waxed paper keeps it from sticking to the slice beneath it. Leaving the paper on top of the next slice, and the fridge open, Steve drops the Havarti on the plate next to the bread and returns for the provolone. There's no waxed paper, but the top slice separates easily from the rest of the stack, which sometimes it doesn't, necessitating repeated attempts at picking stuck bits apart. He puts the provolone on top of the Havarti, then goes back to the fridge where he reseals the first cheese package, pressing firmly on the zip lock, once, twice, a third time to make sure it's properly closed, it is, then the second cheese package, same thing, once, twice, again, all good and sealed. He shuts the fridge doors.

About a dozen pots and pans hang from a ceiling rack suspended above the floating island. None of them are nonstick, Steve's pan of choice for grilled cheese, so he opts for a copper Mauviel, lifting it off its hook. It's small; big enough for a single sandwich, little else. Its size belies its weight. He sets it on one of the stove burners, turns the corresponding knob a touch, just until the flame is ignited, then adjusts it to medium heat. There's a kettle on the burner behind the pan he's using. He checks that it's cool to the touch, then moves it off to the side, on to the counter. Which reminds him he's got multiple pots and pans at home that need washing, that he most likely hasn't left soaking in soapy water and as a result are now caked with dried gunk that'll be a pain to get off, that he'll try removing with his fingernails before moving on to a heavy-duty scrubber.

Steve takes one of the bread slices and puts it butter-side down on the pan, which by now is on the hot side of warm. It sizzles immediately. He puts both slices of cheese on it, then sets the other slice of bread down, butter-side up. A tool crock next to the stove contains an assortment of utensils. He grabs the stainless steel slotted spatula and smushes down on the sandwich, causing it to flatten and sizzle a little louder. At home he'd do some more prep work before starting on the cook. He'd fry two strips of bacon or substitute bacon marmalade in the absence of the real thing, then an egg in the bacon fat until it's over-medium, and quickly paper towel-dry the pan. Only after that was done would he assemble the grilled cheese, with the bacon and egg in between the two cheese slices, assuming he had two to use. Havarti and provolone are as good as any, though he'd prefer cheddar and Swiss.

Steve lifts the sandwich with the spatula, holding the top slice of bread with the fingertips of his other hand. The underside is browning nicely. He flips it over, wipes his hand on the spinach green towel draped over the handle of the oven. At home he'd also sprinkle grated parm or grana padano on the butter, mid-cook, for some added texture. Then a generous glob of Sriracha on the side of the plate to finish, maybe some guacamole with pomegranates if he had the ingredients for it. But they're not at his home, they're at Martha's, and besides Adi probably doesn't like Sriracha anyway. Sam doesn't like it. Does any kid? One weaned on chilies maybe. A Vietnamese kid maybe.

South Delta (Chinese) Mennonite Brethren: now there's another terrible name for a church. Why the parentheses? If you're going to exclude around race, or construct an identity around it, which is the same thing really, you might as well do it with some chutzpah. Not be so wishy-washy. Get rid of the parentheses. Make it all caps. CHINESE. Add some exclamation marks. An even dozen. CHINESE!!!!!!!!!!!!

Steve flips the sandwich again. The side facing him is perfectly grilled. Twenty more seconds till the other side is its equal. There was a time he'd count those seconds off, one to ten, repeat. He's made enough grilled cheese sandwiches now, even if it's a foreign pan he's using, unfamiliar bread, he can more or less tell how much more time it needs. It's better to undercook, too, since you can always put it back on the stove; much harder to salvage a sandwich that's been charred. There's a parable there. He turns off the burner, slides the spatula beneath the sandwich, lifts it off the pan, and transfers it to the plate.

A slight turn of the head to look out the window, to check if Adi and Martha are still by the chicken coop. Adi is. She's crouching. Steve can just make out her head and shoulders. Martha is back on the patio, slouched in her chaise. Her eyes appear closed.

Steve takes a serrated knife from the magnetic strip screwed into the wall above the counter beneath the cabinets with the plates, saucers, and bowls. Using his left hand to keep the sandwich from moving, he cuts it in half, diagonally, into two triangles. Both slices of cheese are evenly melted. In fact, it's near impossible to distinguish between the Havarti and the provolone. There's another parable. He'd take a bite if it weren't for the fact he made it for Adi.

Steve picks up the plate. Maybe she'll save him some. Would he eat it, though? He tells Sam not to eat anyone else's food at school because of germs and because of her allergies, but he doesn't have food allergies. Adi is out of school today because she's sick, though, in theory, so the threat of contracting something from her saliva on the sandwich is real. He's got the patio door open now and steps outside. Plus, it'd probably be cold by the time she was down to her last bite. Grilled cheese is delicious; cold grilled cheese, not so much.

"Leave the sandwich here." Martha kicks at the plastic ottoman in front of her. "Bring me the crokinole board would you?"

Steve puts the plate down as instructed. "Adi," shouting. "Food's ready."

Adi, still crouching, looks over her shoulder. "I'll be right there."

"Where's the board?"

"On the dining table. It might be under some papers."

"The discs, too?"

"Everything."

"I'll be right back."

Steve slides the patio door open again, just enough that he can get through. He walks inside, leaving the door open this time: a strategic decision: thinking one step ahead.

Adi is making her way to the patio, to her sandwich.

He should tell her to wash her hands or at least use her Purell. There's no telling what she's touched, what she might catch. Do people who keep chickens in their backyards do it only for the eggs and the company, or do some people eat them? You probably need a permit to slaughter a live chicken, though. You probably couldn't just decide to kill one, then do it. Not without breaking some kind of law. Actually, there probably isn't a permit for something like that. Not that a regular person could get. A farmer out in Langley, that's one thing; not a woman who lives in a house in the middle of Vancouver.

Steve doesn't particularly like chicken. It's hard to cook well, for starters, and even a perfectly cooked chicken doesn't taste that good. Wings being the exception, and Buffalo wings especially.

Once, not that long ago—when was it? the last time they visited Toronto or the time before that?—he was at the Pickle Barrel by his cousin Timothy's house in the suburbs to order Buffalo wings, two pounds of them, because Pickle Barrel made the best ones he'd ever had and two pounds was a better deal than one, it was something like $16 for two pounds and $10 for one, something like that, and when the two teenagers working the take-out counter, one white, one black, high school students probably, finally asked what he wanted, this after he'd been waiting nearly five minutes for them to quit talking to each other about the girls they were wheeling or whatever, he told them what he wanted, and one of the teens, the white one, looked at him like he'd spoken Cantonese and said, We don't have Buffalo wings, we only have chicken wings, and Steve couldn't believe he was serious except he totally looked like he was, like he really thought Steve thought buffaloes have wings or that Steve was pranking him, and after a few seconds of silence, Steve clarified what he meant, saying something about Buffalo-flavored chicken wings; no not Buffalo-flavored, that's not what he said, that's stupid, what flavor does Buffalo have? Buffalo-style is probably what he said, something like Buffalo-style chicken wings, and only then did the white student tell him they only served four kinds of wings, none of them Buffalo-style: mild, hot, barbecue, and honey garlic, so Steve ordered the hot wings, walked back to his cousin's place, and they were terrible, and he thought what a shame that two pounds of wings worth of chickens had to die for such an awful Styrofoam container of food. How many chickens have to die for two pounds worth of wings? Figure eight wings in a pound, sixteen in two, two wings per bird, that's eight chickens. Eight chickens, give or take, died for those hot wings.

"Here we go," setting the octagonal crokinole board on the patio ottoman.

"What's that?" Adi is sitting on one of the plastic chairs, plate on her lap. Half the grilled cheese sandwich is gone, working its way to her stomach, presumably, unless she dropped it somewhere.

"Crokinole."

"That's the thing you said is like curling, right?"

"It is."

"Can we play?"

"You two can," pointing at Adi, then at Martha.

"What about you?"

Steve isn't in the mood to play crokinole, and to play crokinole you really should be in the mood. He's not sure why he isn't, though he did just punch Marcel in the nose not that long ago.

"He can get communion ready while we do battle." Martha wags her finger at Adi.

Steve nods.

"Use the same bread you used for her sandwich." Martha isn't looking at him.

"And wine?"

"There should be an open red in the fridge, against the door."

"What are you getting?" Adi looks up from the board.

"Communion it's called," standing. "Bread. Wine. It's a church thing. I'll explain later. Martha will teach you how to play crokinole."

"Okay."

"And close the door on your way in, would you?

He nods.

Were the Pickle Barrel wings really $16 and $10? That seems too disproportionate. You expect a better price-per-wing ratio when you order more, but that's a little too good a deal.

He shuts the patio door.

Maybe it was $9 for one pound, or $8.99 is what it probably was, or $8.95. And he was wrong, before, in his calculations, too: two wings per bird, yes, but also two drumettes. So: sixteen wings, loosely defined, four appendages per bird, equals four birds. Four dead chickens for two pounds of those newish hot wings. Better than eight, but still four too many.

Steve is holding two tumblers he's taken from the translucent cabinet above the microwave. Translucent cabinets are classy. He sets the tumblers on the counter beside the fridge, which he swings open. Classy is an overused word. The wine is right where Martha said it'd be. It's about two-thirds empty judging by its weight. One-third full. What's another word for classy? Sophisticated. Posh. He pulls the stainless steel stopper out, rests it sideways on the counter next to the tumblers as he nudges the fridge closed with his elbow. Tony, that's another synonym. Now there's a Chinese boy's name if there ever was one. Mandarin Chinese and Cantonese Chinese. Steve pours. Two ounces, give or take, in the first glass, another two in the second, then a splash more. Thank God his parents didn't name him Tony. Tony Tu. Ha.

A single slice of the buttermilk and honey loaf will be more than enough. It might even be too much. It might be better if he pre-tears it, avoiding any potential awkwardness about how much to break off and what to do with the unfinished portions. Then again, to break a piece off an untarnished, wholly intact slice as he's serving it, the body of Christ, has more visceral power. A slice isn't a whole loaf, but it's better than a slice of a slice. That's what he'll do then. They can feed the leftovers to the chickens. Is that too irreverent? Chickens eat bread, don't they? Actually, Tony Tu doesn't sound that bad. What if Adi asks for some? The wine, that's easy enough to dismiss, but the bread? When St. Joe's kids ask to eat the uneaten sacramental bread, he always lets them because it'd be wasteful just to chuck it, but he's never felt entirely good about that either because it seems inappropriate somehow, but on the other hand he never feels entirely right about not feeling entirely good about that because it seems to border on the superstitious. He doesn't believe in transubstantiation so why should it nag at his conscience? Still, best if he tells Adi no. If she wants a piece of bread, there are more unblessed slices in the kitchen. Martha probably has Nutella. How does she pronounce it, he wonders. *Nut* or *new*?

Back outside, Steve sits next to Adi, balancing the tumblers in one hand, the bread in the other. Adi and Martha each have one disc left to shoot.

Adi steadies her middle finger against her disc, a red one, takes aim, flicks. It passes two other discs, one red, one yellow, and lands in the center hole.

"Nice shot."

"Your turn."

Adi takes the disc from the hole, puts it with the two others next to her on the ottoman.

Martha shoots. The disc ricochets off a rubber-covered bumper and comes to rest just shy of the target.

"Not bad."

"Not good."

"Did I win?"

Martha begins to gather the discs on the board. "We'll keep score next time. This was a practice round."

Adi glowers.

"Ready?" Steve holds up the elements.

"Do it."

He puts the tumblers and the bread on the now-bare crokinole board.

"Shall we pray together?"

Martha bows her head, closes her eyes.

"We're going to pray."

Adi shrugs and picks up a crokinole disc.

"Our Father which art in heaven, Hallowed be thy name. Thy kingdom come. Thy will be done on earth, as it is in heaven. Give us this day our daily bread. And forgive us our debts, as we forgive our debtors. And lead us not into temptation, but deliver us from evil: For thine is the kingdom, and the power, and the glory, for ever. Amen."

Steve has the slice of bread in his hand.

Adi flicks the disc she'd been holding. It hits a bumper, halts.

"Our Lord Jesus on the night when he was betrayed, took a loaf of bread, and when he had given thanks, he broke it," tearing the bread in half, "and said, This is my body that is for you. Do this in remembrance of me."

He rips off a smaller piece from one of the two halves and puts it in Martha's open palm, then tears another for himself, leaving it in front of him on the crokinole board.

"In the same way he took the cup also, after supper, saying, This cup is the new covenant in my blood. Do this, as often as you drink it, in remembrance of me."

He picks up the tumbler nearest Martha and hands it to her, then he puts his piece of bread into his mouth while she does likewise. He chews. There's a hint of sweetness, delicious for plain bread, swallows some, raises his tumbler, drinks, swallows again, the rest of the bread goes down, takes another sip, finishes the rest of the wine, one last swallow.

"Amen," wiping the corners of his lips with the thumb and index finger of his left hand.

"How do you remember all the words?" Martha sets her tumbler down. "Is it like riding a bike?"

"In some ways."

Steve used to rehearse the words of institution in his office with the doors closed each Sunday morning before worship service began and most of the time he'd get them at least 80-percent right and what he forgot was easy enough to improvise.

"Your memory is better than mine." Martha squeezes her scalp.

"That's not really someone's body." Adi is peering at the leftovers. "It's just bread."

"You're right."

"So that's not blood either."

"It's wine."

"Why did you say those weird things?"

Steve gives it a moment's thought. "Ritual. Signs and symbols."

"Weird."

"There are people who really drink blood, though, did you know that?" Martha straightens her back. "Not human blood, but animal. Quite a number of people."

Adi contorts her face, the universal look of disgust.

"It's true."

Steve nods.

"Who drinks animal blood?"

"Your ancestors did," pointing a finger in Adi's direction. "And if you have relatives, extended family in Asia, them, too, in all likelihood."

"What are you even talking about?"

"In fact," her pitch increasing, "it's possible you have relatives on both sides of your family who consume animal blood. You're happa, right? Which one of your parents is, what, Chinese?"

"My mom."

"And your dad is from where?"

"Vancouver."

"Where are his parents, grandparents, great-grands from? That's what I mean."

"My nan and poppop are from Wales."

"He's definitely had blood pudding, then."

"Pudding made with blood?"

"It's a sausage made from pork blood," scratching his chin. "People eat it warm, don't they?"

"Not just warm. Cold, too. It's common in the Maritimes."

"Martha was born there. Cape Breton, right?"

"Raised, too," slowly nodding. "Lived there nearly eighteen years."

"You've eaten blood before?" Adi's eyes are wide with anticipation.

"Eaten, drank, you name it."

"From what animals?" She looks like a mouse.

Martha sighs. "If you've got time, I could try to name them all."

"Why would someone want to drink blood?"

"Blood is life. You'll understand when you're older. When people get older they wish they were younger. It's a universal condition."

"It's not safe, though. Or hygienic. People get sick from drinking blood."

"The risks are overblown, Pastor. The Japanese drink chicken blood, did you know that? And not just them. I was reading about these Pacific islanders, a small tribe where everyone lives to be at least a hundred. If you die in your nineties, you're young. They drink chicken blood, too. The Chinese have known about it for ages."

"You're kidding."

She shakes her head. "I'm surprised. You should know this."

Why should he know this? Because he's Chinese? Because he's a pastor and therefore should know these kinds of things?

"Ask whatshername. She'll know what I'm talking about. It's the cutting edge in medicine."

That's why he should know.

"They're doing all sorts of exciting things in metazoic hematology nowadays and in avian genetics in particular. With galliformes especially."

"Galliformes are chickens," turning to Adi, "turkeys, those kinds of birds."

Adi nods.

"They're saying that by injecting purified chicken blood into humans they can prolong human life by decades. Even reverse some of the effects of aging. Dementia even. Would you believe that? Something to do with DNA compatibility. Who knows what they'll come up with next. Peafowl? Pheasant? Wild ones, never been domesticated before, in a jungle somewhere? Wooeee. On the internet chat forums some people are saying it's the key to immortality, the fountain of youth. I wouldn't go so far as that, of course, but it's exciting."

"Sounds specious. Sounds like pseudo-science."

"Nothing pseudo about it. The Chinese have been injecting themselves with chicken blood for centuries. For millennia."

"I've never heard of it."

"Broaden your thinking, Pastor. Behold the expansiveness of the horizon." She spreads her arms open. "There's wisdom in traditional Eastern medicine. Jesus was visited by Eastern healers as an infant, after all. There's common grace."

"We're not built to live indefinitely."

"Of course we are. Why else would we avoid death the way we do? Remember the Garden, Pastor. Remember the serpent."

"Hmm."

"Won't heaven be infinite?"

Steve is thinking of a response.

"And aren't we to pray God's kingdom come and will be done on earth as it is up there?" looking skyward.

"Okay."

"Prolonging human life: what is that if not bringing the kingdom of God to earth?"

"There's a hole in your logic."

"You know, Pastor, even in the sporting world—you like sports don't you?—they're doing this very thing. Blood spinning, have you heard of it?" She twirls her index finger like she's unspooling thread. "Has to do with separating out the platelets and plasma."

"Wait," pausing to formulate his thoughts. "That's not why you keep chickens, is it?"

Martha laughs. "Chicken blood is naturally rich in a particular kind of platelet that helps in healing. You know that thing where a chicken can run for hours with its head cut off? The blood's the reason. Scientists think if they can engineer it somehow so that human and chicken blood could be—I don't remember what the technical term for it is—mixed together, co-mingled, they could tap into a limitless therapeutic resource. After all, if merely drinking chicken blood has diverse health benefits, how much more would mainlining it do?"

"You're not joking about this."

"Do I look like I'm joking?"

"Can we play crokinole again now?"

"Sure." Martha shifts in her seat. "Gather your discs."

"Did you finish your grilled cheese sandwich?"

"Yeah."

"Where's the plate?"

Adi looks quickly in a few different directions before spotting it beneath Steve's chair. "There," pointing.

He leans forward, head by his knees. "I'm going to bring this and the cups inside."

"Can I have the leftover bread?"

It's still on the crokinole board, surrounded by crumbs.

Steve picks it up and hands it to her, then sweeps the crumbs into his palm. He scatters them on the patio. "Hold on to it for now. But don't eat it. Let's feed it to the chickens when you're done your game."

Adi purses her lips. "I just fed them, though. They're not going to be hungry already."

"You were hungry not long after having all those potstickers."

"I guess."

"Keep the bread. I'll be back in a moment."

Plate and tumblers in hand, Steve heads back inside, once more through the patio doors. He turns on the faucet, producing a stream of water, cold, slowly warming. It won't take long to rinse and wash the two tumblers and the plate that carried the host. He runs the first cup under the water, swirls it around, buffs the rim, turns the cup upside down, shakes, transfers it to the drying rack next to the sink. He runs the second cup under the water, swirls it around, buffs the rim, turns the cup upside down, shakes, transfers it to the drying rack next to the sink, so that it's leaning against the first cup. Then he splashes running water on the plate, quickly polishes it with his bare hand, just long enough to be sure he's gotten rid of all the crumbs. He sets it on the rack.

Outside, Adi and Martha are immersed in their game.

Steve takes his phone out of his pocket as he walks toward the patio. It's 1:53. He unlocks it, taps the camera app. They need about twenty, twenty-five minutes to get to the school. A half-hour to be safe. More wouldn't be bad. Adi could play in the playground while they wait. He could chat with whatever parents are early for pick-up. That still leaves them plenty of time. They could stay at Martha's a little longer, even go somewhere else, though if they went somewhere else it'd have to be on the way to Bluffwood or just a brief detour. If they did run late, he could text May, ask her to watch Sam for a few minutes. Does Hailey have any after-school thing going on today? She's got something everyday: skating, swimming, dance, music, Spirit of

161

Math, horseback riding; but a couple of those things don't start right after school. Which days is it again that Sam usually stays after class and plays with her? Wednesdays is one of them, isn't it? Hmm.

He taps the screen to focus, again to take the picture. Neither Adi nor Martha notice. He takes another, just in case, scrolls back to the first one, comparing it to the second. The first is better, sharper. He taps the share icon, then the white-on-green text message balloon, M-A-R-Y. Send. Sending. Swoosh. He puts the phone to sleep and back in his pocket and suddenly has a craving for Buffalo wings.

Before he discovered the Pickle Barrel wings, Steve and his cousin Timothy and Timothy's best friend Adam used to have grilled cheese sandwiches there every time Steve was back in Toronto. Steve would get the triple decker grilled cheese, with bacon for an extra buck. So would Timothy. Adam, just the triple decker grilled cheese, no bacon. Most of Steve's Jewish friends growing up kept kosher like Adam did. The only one he can think who didn't is Sylvan, who liked his pizza with pepperoni. For Sylvan's bar mitzvah Steve got him a bar of gold. Not a whole bar. A mini bar. Ha. A bar-ette. Haha. Or is it barrette with two Rs? Look it up later. For Omri, another one of Steve's Jewish friends, a framed print of da Vinci's Vitruvian Man. His mom liked the frame, Omri told him the next day at school. Some of the girls in his class pitched in to get him a sweatshirt with a picture of his head ironed on the front.

Martha appears to be winning the crokinole game. She's not the kind of person who'd let a kid beat her, apparently. Nor is he? Kids should learn failure at a young age, then go on re-learning it.

"I still remember your funeral sermon for John. Absolutely lovely."

Steve smiles. Was that the last time Martha was inside the church building? "I'm not officiating, but I'll be speaking at my sister's wedding in a couple of weeks."

"You're preaching? Or something else?"

"Something else, I guess. They're not going to have a real sermon per se." He pinches his shirt at the chest and tugs at it a moment. "It's not coming along so well."

"What's wrong?"

Steve shrugs. "Writer's block."

"Your creativity is constipated, is it?"

The metaphor reminds him of those two Taro Gomi books Daphne loves. "My sister wants me to tell a story or recite a poem."

"What are you going to do?"

"What I was thinking is, I heard this fable, I guess it was, when we were in Maui on vacation. We were sitting at a luau with a couple who were on their wedding anniversary. The wife told it to us. I remember thinking at the time, What a lovely story, maybe I can share it at the next wedding I officiate, but by the time I had a wedding to do, it was a couple years later and I didn't remember it until the day after the wedding when I was mailing in the marriage registration form that officiants have to fill out. So I kept it filed away. Not literally. I don't have a file for sermon illustrations. I thought, I'll save this story and if ever an opportune time comes to tell it, the Holy Spirit will bring it to mind. And now is that time."

"So what's the problem?"

"I remember all sorts of details. When and where I was when I heard it. I can tell you about the drinks I had at the luau, the food, the dancers, the sunset. But I can't remember much about the fable except it has to do with a bee, and it's an origin story for the wedding lei, which is usually made from this flower whose name escapes me. It's not an iris."

"Plumeria." Martha wrinkles her nose, then flicks a disc. "I win."

Steve sounds it out in his head, twice. "That's it."

"I know that story."

"Yeah?"

"My memory may not be what it once was, but yes. Some things stick for whatever reason. Not to mention, I'm a gardener. Which probably helps it stick a little better."

"I'm going to look at the chickens." Adi stands up.

"Alright. But we have to go pretty soon." Steve slides the phone out of his pocket. It's 1:58.

Adi is down the patio, making her way to the chicken coop.

"It's a Hawaiian wedding custom for the couple getting married to exchange leis." Martha mimes the gesture. "You know why they use leis?"

Steve shakes his head.

"You've got an imagination. Why do you think?"

"It could be anything." He shrugs and gives it some thought. Flowers are pleasing to the eyes and the nose, but they don't live long, especially after they're plucked. "The beauty and impermanence of life?"

"That's pretty much it." She extends a finger toward Steve. "Life is fragile, temporary, like the lei. When one partner gives the other a lei, she's promising not only her love now, in the moment, but for the span of her life, however long that might be. It's a lovely symbol, don't you think so? A little saccharine, sure, but it's impossible not to be when we're talking about love."

"Good point."

"The traditional wedding lei consists entirely of fresh plumerias. You can use other flowers. People do. But the plumeria is the most beautiful, the most fragrant. Today, plumerias don't produce nectar. But many years ago, so the legend goes, they did. Just a droplet. That single bead of nectar is what gave them not only their bright colors and sweet aroma, it was also the source of its life. Its blood, so to speak. Bees always knew better than to try to gather this nectar. They were too big to travel through the plumeria's bloom to reach its stamen. That's where the nectar and pollen are produced."

"Sam learned about flower physiology at her old Montessori pre-school," nodding. She used to show off to him what she knew. She's probably forgotten all of it, other than petal and stem.

"She can always learn it again." Martha looks over her shoulder toward the chicken coop where Adi is standing, hands on the side of the cage. She has her shirt and jacket on again. "There was one bee," turning back to Steve, "legend goes, that spent good portions of its nectar- and pollen-collecting days hovering by one particular plumeria, doing nothing but admiring it. One day, as it exited its nearby hive, this bee noticed the flower bending, lurching in an unusually aggressive manner. As it approached, it saw the cause: a giant moth trying to reach in and extract the nectar with its, what do you call it? Not nose."

"Proboscis."

"Maybe. But if you use that word at your sister's wedding no one will know what you mean. You want your audience to understand you."

"I think I'd rather be precise."

"Just say long nose," touching hers and pretending to elongate it. "The bee flew to the flower's defense, but the moth was too fierce, too powerful, determined. In short order the bee's wings were clipped." Martha mimes a slicing gesture at her shoulder blade. "In a last-gasp act, as it fell from the sky, the bee lunged and stung the moth, sentencing both insects to their death. Critically wounded, the moth flew off, never to be seen again. As for the bee, it collapsed on one of the plumeria's petals, death mere seconds away. Moved by its self-sacrifice, the plumeria released its single droplet of nectar to the bee, which drank. And in both their final earthly moments, the bee and the flower were happy like they'd never been. After that, plumerias stopped providing nectar: a memorial to that sacrificial love." Martha smiles. "And that's why the plumeria is the customary flower for Hawaiian wedding leis."

"So the point of the fable is that marriage is founded upon the kind of costly, other-centered love exemplified in the legend."

"Love that offers nectar to a bee which has no wings."

"I like it."

"Will you remember it well enough to tell it at your brother's wedding?"

"My sister's," nodding. "And yes, I think I will."

"Good."

"You said your memory isn't so sharp anymore. Are things getting worse? You were able to remember that fable."

Martha waves a hand dismissively. "I'm old, frail. Those things are predestined."

"Can I ask how old you are?"

"Pastor," her mouth agape. "You can't ask that."

"Sorry."

"I'm teasing. I think I'm eighty-five. Thereabouts. Next year, I might not know the answer to that anymore. Women younger than me, they don't like to tell people their age, right? But you get older and the things you worried about as a young woman, a young person," she clears some food that had been stuck between two teeth—the Eucharistic bread, by the looks of it, "they just don't matter so much anymore. There's not enough time to waste on those things."

"That's a healthy perspective."

"The trick is getting it without waiting to grow old."

"I suppose."

"When I was younger, I used to see people as old as I am now, and I'd think, God, I hope I don't end up like that." Martha laughs and goes on talking, but Steve's mind is elsewhere.

He's looking at her and nodding, but what he's doing is he's trying to visualize his kids—trying to, failing, he can't, not even their heads, he can't summon them without closing his eyes, and to close his eyes now, while Martha is talking about, what? her nephew? she said the name Fred. Is that a friend? would strike her as pompously rude of him, surely. He nods some more. Dear Lord, he thinks, or is this praying—if I forget everything else, please let me remember this: how much I love my girls. So treacly. Steve can feel the tears beginning to well at the bottom of his ducts.

There isn't one Sunday at St. Joe's that goes by without some person shutting their eyes. Is that rudeness? sleepiness? boredom? Steve always assumes they're deep in thought. Why shouldn't he? He doesn't know. He could close his eyes now, shut Martha's voice out, picture his kids, continue nodding. Martha might assume the best in him. She'd be wrong, but she wouldn't know.

"Do you want to see a photo of the kids?" He takes his phone out of his pocket.

"What do you think about what I told him?" holding out her hand, keeping it in front of Steve.

It's 2:03.

"What do I think?" It's almost time to go, even though they could stay another half-hour and still make it to school before the closing bell. Twice the amount of time needed to arrive at a destination without stress is when the stress hits him, almost always. "It's a tough one, that's for sure."

Martha takes the phone from Steve's hand. "They're older than I remember."

"It's from Harrison Hot Springs, back in February."

Martha gives him back the phone.

He studies the picture, a good one, unposed, natural. They're laughing legitimate laughter, not smiling for the sake of another one of Daddy's photos. He can almost hear their giggles.

"He thinks because he's named after the Eliot poem he's qualified to be a flâneur, that he's got some kind of Maritainian poetic intuition."

"Which poem is that again?" And who are you talking about?

"Prufrock," her voice betraying annoyance, but mild. "Pastor, have you been paying attention?"

"I'm just now connecting the dots."

"Look it. There's only one way I'm leaving this house, you know what I mean? Is it going to be any safer for me someplace else? Come on. It's not like I'm driving anymore. I wasn't born yesterday. He thinks with me out of here, he's going to move in. One day it's to help me downsize, the next he's king of my castle. It's only a matter of time before the moving trucks come for my things. My things, Pastor." Her nostrils flare. "No. I'm not leaving."

"Hmm."

"And it's not like it's all gone yet," pointing a finger at her temple. "Medical advancements are being made every day. Literally, not a day goes by that they're not coming up with something that pushes back the clock."

"Like the chicken blood thing?"

"The internet is making it now so that all the relevant information is at everyone's disposal. It used to be that breakthroughs revolved around the time some researcher somewhere could put in. But he's got to go on vacation, sleep. Now? You have Wi-Fi, a sense of determination, a will, some modicum of intelligence, you don't need to wait for that guy to wake up or come back from holiday. DIY. The world belongs to amateurs. All a girl needs is the physical apparatus to run tests."

"You mean chickens?"

Martha straightens her back. "I meant laboratory space. Microscopes, micropipets, centrifuges, vortexers, mixing devices. That sort of thing."

"Oh."

"But test subjects, sure. Those, too."

"You've given this a lot of thought it sounds like."

"What else do I have to do all day except think? It's good for the old brain, too. And if I'm going to think all day, might as well think about this. What better thing could I be thinking about?"

Something from the last chapter of Paul's letter to the Philippians comes to mind. "Nothing, I guess."

Adi is back, holding a feather in her hand. "Can I keep this?"

Martha takes it from her and presses the shaft gently into her palm. She swirls it around as if writing. "You didn't pluck this from one of my birds, did you?"

"It was just laying there."

"Lying."

"I'm not."

"I mean, you meant to say the feather was just lying there. Not laying. Laying is something hens do with eggs."

"With?"

"To?"

"Anyway," Adi reaches out her arm, "can I have it?"

"Here." Martha passes it to her. "It's yours."

"What do you say?"

"I was just about to," rolling her eyes a little before looking at Martha. "Can I have another one? Can I have one from each of the different birds?"

"Thank you," exasperated.

"Thank you, Martha. More please?"

"Help yourself to whatever you can find on the ground."

"I think one is enough," before Adi has moved toward the chicken coop. "What are you going to do with more feathers?"

"Lots of things."

"Like what?"

"Lots of things."

"Just one more. Maybe from one of those orange hens, so you'll have a white one and an orange one."

"It's called buff."

"But there are different whites. I need one from each."

"The feathers all look the same, though. Don't they?"

"To the layperson." Martha scratches her left eyebrow. "To an ornithologist the differences couldn't be more obvious."

"Even I can tell."

"Fine," scratching just above his ear. "Go grab whatever Martha will let you take."

"Take however many you want."

"Thanks, Martha." Adi darts toward the coop.

Steve watches as she scuttles away, slightly worried she's going to trip on the walkway or her own feet and break an arm or wrist or chip a tooth, and then how will they get to school on time? She reaches the chicken coop in one piece.

"Once she comes back we should get going."

"Already? Have you been here even an hour?"

"I have to make it back to school for pick-up. And even though she ran there pretty fast," nodding in Adi's direction, "it's been a long day and she doesn't normally move that quick. Her stride is—" holding his hands about a foot apart.

"You and I didn't get to play crokinole."

"Next time." Steve picks up one of the discs. "I'll practice in advance so you won't steamroll me like last time."

"Did I?"

Steve nods. "You decimated me."

"Sounds like something I'd do."

"I'll give you a better fight when I'm back."

"When will that be?"

"A few months? Is that okay?"

Martha nods.

"I can come before that. Anytime you need anything, give me call."

"I might."

"Do."

"Do people ever, though?"

"Sometimes."

"They do?"

"More often than you'd think."

"Don't people feel bad about imposing on your time?"

"It's no imposition. I enjoy meeting up with people."

"You have to say that, though. It's your job. Tell me the truth, Pastor. You enjoy coming here?"

"Most of the time," smiling. "Especially when there's fresh food in the oven."

"Had I known you were coming, I'd have prepared something."

"Next time."

"How about a pie?"

"Anything you want. Don't put yourself out."

"Sweet? I can do apple, blueberry. Or savory? Chicken pot pie?" she eyes the coop.

"Surprise me. But not chicken."

"If I remember us having this conversation."

"I'll probably forget, too."

Steve stands as Adi approaches, three feathers in her hand, one of them orange. Buff, is that what Martha called it? He reaches instinctively for the top of his head, running his hand from back to front, tracing the ridges of the excrescence with his fingertips. It feels even larger than before. He's about to ask Martha about it, what it looks like to her, has she ever seen anything like it, when Adi announces that she's ready to go and says bye to Martha.

"Alright then," nodding as Martha waves and thanks them for visiting. Steve bends down and hugs her with his right arm, his left dangling feebly by his side. If he brings up the bumps on his head now, it's only going to delay their departure. He's already on his feet, Adi's got her souvenirs, they've just said their goodbyes. It's definitely time to leave.

They step off the patio, onto the cement path. Steve looks back at Martha who isn't looking at them, and they make their way past the seagull statue with the outstretched wings, then the yellow spirit bear that might also be a Kermode; Steve should look that up later, along with all the other things he's supposed to look up. What were they all? He could look it up now, in fact, on his phone, but that would be impolite, setting a bad example. His feet tap against the ground as the two of them make their way toward the front of the house. When he was a boy, his mother would tell him to stand up straighter, not hunch his back. To lift his legs. It didn't stick, obviously. Captain Obvi. Connection! They pass the copper owl, cross from one side of the arbor to the other, and there's the street a little farther ahead.

"What time is it?"

Without breaking stride Steve takes his phone from his pocket. "It's ten after two."

"You mean 2:10?"

"That's right," slipping his phone back in his pocket. "More than enough time to get to school."

They step onto the driveway. Steve adjusts the angle of his phone so it's closer to being parallel with his leg. He and Adi head through the open wrought iron gate and make a left on to Angus.

"Martha is weird." Adi is looking straight ahead, expressionless.

"Everyone is a little weird."

"She's extra."

"Only because you're a kid so you don't know that many people yet. As you get older you'll meet more people and discover that everybody is strange. That's what makes people so interesting. You could spend a lifetime trying to get to know a person, and only scratch the surface."

That sounds lame.

"Yeah, but Martha is still extra weird."

"Not really."

"And I know lots of people. I know everyone at Bluffwood."

"All the kids?"

"And the teachers."

They lock eyes.

"So if you saw someone from school at Safeway, you'd know their name?"

"First and last. And what grade they're in. And who their teacher is."

Steve nods. "If you know their grade, the teacher isn't that hard. There's what, two or three teachers per grade, max?"

"Like I said, I already know lots of people. Some of them are weird, too. Like Evan. You know Evan? From my class?"

"He's the one who drinks puddle water with yogurt containers he finds lying around outside, right?"

"Lying or laying."

"Lying."

"That's him."

"That qualifies as weird."

"Martha is way weirder."

"What?"

Adi is about to say something judging by the way she's opened her mouth, but she's silent. Composing her thoughts, probably. Rare for a child her age to think before speaking. Rare for anyone to do that, come to think of it.

"You know how I went to the bathroom and didn't go back outside for a while?"

"Where did you go?"

Adi looks up at him.

"Did you get lost in the house somewhere? It's a big house."

"I went to the basement."

"By accident? Because you got lost?" Steve wonders how getting lost from the bathroom to the backyard would be possible. "But you didn't have to use any stairs on your way in, and we were literally right outside so you shouldn't have gotten lost."

"I wasn't lost. The basement was on purpose."

"I looked, though. The lights were off."

"Not all of them."

"Why did you go down there?"

"Have you ever felt like you were meant to go somewhere? Like someone is calling your name, but not in a voice you can hear?"

"No."

"Then you wouldn't understand."

"You heard something in your heart calling you down there?"

"Something like that."

"Alright. And?"

"Have you ever been down there?"

171

Steve tries to remember. He's been to Martha's a couple dozen times at least. Yet he can't recall ever being anywhere except the ground floor and the yard. Not that there's anything peculiar about that. "I don't think so."

"You would remember. She's so weird. I like her, though. She's just weird."

"What's there?"

Adi looks behind her, as if checking to see if they're being followed.

Steve looks, too. "No Alfred Bester."

No one else is on the street at all. Which isn't surprising. It's a quiet residential road, middle of the day, more or less. People are at work. Just like he is.

"She has chickens in her basement."

"Like the ones outside?"

"Except dead."

Steve furrows his brows. "You mean in a fridge or freezer? Chicken legs, thighs, breasts, nuggets? Wings?"

Adi shakes her head. "Some of them still had their feathers. Some didn't."

"What do you mean? There were just dead chickens laying on the basement floor?"

"Lying."

"Wait. You're lying? Or you're correcting me?" Steve replays, best as he can remember, what he just said. "Did I say laying?"

"You did."

He doesn't think he did, but doesn't want to belabor it. "There were just dead chicken carcasses in her basement?"

"Maybe ten of them."

Steve grimaces. He doesn't believe her, not fully. But he can't think of a reason why she would lie. Then again, does a person need a reason to deceive? Maybe the reason is she's a person and lying is what people do.

"Weren't you scared?"

Her eyes shift to the side. "A little at first. But they were all dead. What could they do to me?"

"You should've asked Martha about them."

"Then she'd know I was in her basement."

"You could have told her you got lost. If you saw that many dead birds, wouldn't you want to know why they were there?"

"You shouldn't encourage me to lie. There was all this equipment there, too. Like the kind Mrs. Canard let us use when we looked at bacteria," gesturing as if she's peering under a microscope. "And other machines. Big ones, some of them. One was as big as a refrigerator."

"Maybe it was a refrigerator."

"But it had a bunch of doors and lots of buttons on the front and on the side."

"You should have said something before we left."

"I'm saying something now."

They're rounding the bend, headed northeast toward 37th.

"What do you think all that stuff is for?"

"I have no idea."

"Think of something. You're the smartest kid in class, aren't you?"

Adi looks like she's thinking. "To keep her old pets that have died, maybe."

"Maybe she eats them. I'll ask her the next time I'm over."

"Gross."

"Have you had iguana before?"

"Eww."

"They say it tastes like chicken."

Adi looks at him like she thinks he's making it up, her head tilted slightly.

He's not making it up, though. Though it might not be true. It's what one of the characters says in *The Night of the Iguana*, starring that guy who was married to Liz Taylor—whatshisname, he plays a disgraced, drunkard Episcopal minister in it. So there's at least one movie with the inebriated minister trope. Is that line about iguana tasting like chicken in the Tennessee Williams play which is the film's source material? Steve doesn't know, having never read it nor seen it performed. He'd found a used copy of the movie at Videomatica on 4th Ave, not knowing anything about it except Sue Lyon was in it, whose name he recognized from her role as Lolita in Stanley Kubrick's version of the Nabokov novel. He bought the DVD for no reason other than that. Now there's a fine name for a boy if he ever has one. Stanley. Like the Park and the Cup. Richard Burton, that's whatshisname's name. Richard isn't as good a boy's name as Stanley. Because the nicknames. Vladimir, on the other hand. There's a good name, too. Vlad. A good, supernatural-sounding name. Just not for a Chinese boy. Nabokov was one of Steve's favorite novelists when he was a high school student, and

Lolita one of his favorite novels. His absolute favorite, though, was *Pale Fire* because of how novel it was when he first read it, and that's what novels should be after all, isn't it? Novel. If Steve ever writes a novel, he'll try to do something original. Provocative would be a bonus. Maybe like *Lolita*, with an underage girl, but even younger. Or *The Night of the Iguana*, with an older, but maybe still youthful girl. Maybe the former in a first novel, the latter in a second or third. Maybe a supernatural element or two somewhere. If there are too-young girls, there needs to be a too-old male. Before he lets his mind wander too much, Steve realizes it's a stupid dream. When is he ever going to have time to write one work of fiction, let alone two? Maybe he'll write about preaching. A novel take on the topic. Any fictional exploration of preaching would be novel, wouldn't it?

"Besides, I've seen lots of dead chickens before."

Back to reality. "You have?"

"At the grocery store, duh."

"Hmm." A few houses ahead a silver Tiguan like the one Mary drives backs out on to the road. Steve is suddenly more mindful of the hidden driveways they're mindlessly crossing. "Have you ever seen this old television show called *Crocodile Hunter*?"

"What's that?"

"An old Animal Planet show. This Australian guy, Steve Irwin, would tell jokes while wrestling crocodiles. Crazy stuff like that."

"That's stupid."

Steve shrugs. "One time he was holding his baby in one hand and feeding a dead chicken to a crocodile with the other."

"That's extra stupid."

"He got in trouble, I think."

"Good."

"When I was in my last year of university, during final exam time, I used to study in the fine arts building. Meyerson. There's this big lecture hall in the basement, room B-1." The things you remember. "It had a television hooked up to this giant screen and in the middle of the night, like two or two-thirty, I'd take a break from studying, turn off all the lights, turn on *Crocodile Hunter*, watch an episode, then take a nap on the stage, and wake up to study some more."

"That sounds stupid, too."

"A bit," nodding. "I used to bring my sleeping bag with me all over campus. For convenience. So I could sleep anywhere, anytime. One night after a *Crocodile Hunter* episode, I fell asleep in it, on the stage. There were these motion detector lights that automatically turned off when there wasn't any movement. Which helped me sleep. But this particular night, they turned back on. Which woke me up. Two cops had come in. Apparently there'd been a report of a homeless person sleeping in the Meyerson basement. They meant me."

Adi laughs.

"I told them I was a student and offered to show them my student card, but they saw all my textbooks open and didn't bother."

"You carried a sleeping bag with you?"

"Just at exam time."

"You're weird, too."

"It's a good thing the cops didn't take me up on my student card offer, though, because as soon as I told them I could show it to them to prove I was a student, I remembered I'd forgotten my wallet back home and I'd used Sabrina Li's to get in."

"Who's Sabrina Li?"

"An old friend." Are they still? Facebook friends, anyway. That's not nothing, necessarily.

"Do you think the chickens in Martha's yard that are still alive will end up in her basement?"

"Literally or metaphorically?"

"I have a feeling they will."

They cross an empty back alley as they approach 35th. If they could afford it, the houses here would be perfect for Steve's family. Large enough for the five of them with room for more. Room for a Stanley.

"Did I tell you my Chinese name sounds like the words for *chicken poo*?"

"Really?"

"Slightly different pronunciation. Ji Fun. That's my name. *Jī fèn*. That's chicken poo."

"Sounds the same to me."

"You know what else?"

"What?"

"Your mom's car sounds like the Chinese words for *shaved head*."

"Volkswagen?"

"Tiguan."

"My mom drives a Volkswagen."

175

"Tiguan technically sounds more like *to shave off*, not specifically a shaved head. *Shaved head* is *tì tóu*."

"Like man-toe," laughing.

"Kind of," laughing.

"Before when you said your hair was down to your shoulders before you shaved it, were you lying?"

Steve shakes his head. "I kept it that long for about a year."

"Why? Long hair on boys is ugly."

"It was trendy then. I could ponytail it, tie it in a bun."

"So lots of boys had long hair?"

"In some," trying to think of the word, something like cliques or groups, "circles. Some of them did."

"None of the boys in my class has long hair. Or any of their dads."

"It's not fashionable right now. In a few years, though, it might make a comeback."

"Martha is really fat."

"That's not a nice thing to say."

"I didn't mean it as an insult."

"When I was at Penn I had a friend, a guy named Fadi."

"Why would someone name their kid that?"

"Not fatty, F-A-T-T-Y. F-A-D-I. Once I thought I saw him in the library, studying. His back was turned to me, but he was wearing this Wharton hoodie he always wore with the hood pulled over his head. I called to him, Fadi! Fadi! He didn't turn around so I went right up to him and tapped him on his shoulder. Hey Fadi! And it was a girl."

Adi laughs hysterically. "She thought you were calling her fat."

"I was so embarrassed."

"Did you say sorry?"

"Right away. And I explained that I thought she was my friend. Because she was wearing the same hoodie."

"What did she say?"

"She didn't look like she believed me."

Adi laughs some more. "What kind of hoodie did you say it was again?"

"A Wharton hoodie. That's the name of the business school I went to."

"So not a lot of people wore it?"

"Actually," come to think of it, "lots of people did."

"Did you know who she was?"

"Nope."

"You probably made her feel really bad."

"I know."

"She probably cried after."

"I hope not."

"She probably felt bad about her body."

Steve sighs.

"Was she actually fat, though?"

"A little?"

Adi's face is the face of someone who's just been served the corner piece of lasagna. "You're so mean."

She means to be joking, but she's right. She's understating, in fact. He's much worse than mean. He just slugged his old parishioner in the nose and doesn't even feel bad about it. Or does he? Does his self-reflection about his temper, his lack of self-control, mean he's not as mean as all that? That he does feel bad? Does he, though? Had he even lost his temper? It was just a physical reaction, wasn't it? Instinct. Hadn't he felt bad immediately after? He'd apologized, anyway, and surely that counts for something. He hadn't been too proud to say sorry.

"Why are there more stories about pigs than chickens?"

Steve looks at her, confused. "What?"

"There are lots of pig stories and pig characters, right? *Peppa. Babe. Olivia.* The one in *Charlotte's Web.* The three little pigs. The little piggies who go to the market. The pig from the *Toy Story* movies. Piglet. Miss Piggy."

"Porky Pig. All the pigs from *Animal Farm.*" That scene in *Lord of the Flies.*

"Yeah. But there aren't that many with chickens."

"There's another pig story. *Mackenzie and Pig.*"

Adi shakes her head. "I don't know it."

"You want to hear it?"

"Okay."

"There was a girl named Mackenzie. For her eighth birthday, I think it was—it's not important—her parents got her a yellow pig as a gift."

"Seriously?" looking unimpressed. "A pig?"

"It's a story."

"Fine."

"What are you going to name him? Mackenzie's father asked.—I don't know, she said. I have to think about it.—How about Bacon? her big brother

Topher suggested.—That's not funny, Mackenzie said.—How would you like it if I called you Tofu?"

"Tofu is yummy," grinning.

"I'm sure you'll find the perfect name, Mackenzie's mother said. Mackenzie hoped she would. Finding the perfect name for her things was a great responsibility. She took it very seriously. For her last birthday, her parents gave her a blue teddy bear. She named him Pablo, after her favorite painter. For Christmas, her parents gave her a baby doll. She named him Billy Reuben, because she had jaundice when she was a baby. When she finished second grade, her parents gave her a bicycle with roses painted on it. She named it Juliet, because what's in a name is everything. Every one of Mackenzie's things had a carefully chosen name, and it was only after she named them that she felt they truly belonged to her. But finding the right name wasn't always easy, and Mackenzie spent the rest of that morning thinking of different names for her pig. Lemon? Too sour. Mustard? Too spicy. Sunshine? Too sweet. Roast? Too salty. Wilbur? Too obvious. Freddy? Too old-fashioned. Napoleon? Too Orwellian. Spivak? Too obscure."

Steve looks at Adi, making sure she's close and safe as they cross 33rd where the light has just turned green. She's rapt. He's trying to remember how the rest of the story goes.

"By lunchtime Mackenzie still hadn't come up with the perfect name for her pig, but she had to take a break because she was hungry from all her thinking. She walked into the kitchen and asked her parents what was for lunch."

"It was her birthday so they were probably making her favorite food."

Steve points at her, impressed by her thinking. "It's a surprise, her mother said from behind the counter. Mackenzie sat down at the table, holding the pig in her lap.—Topher! her father shouted up the stairs. Time to eat. He set two bowls on the table. When Mackenzie saw what was for lunch she was so happy. Just like you predicted. Mackenzie's pig saw what was for lunch, too, and jumped out of Mackenzie's arms, on to the table. He stuck his yellow snout in Topher's bowl.—Does your pig have a name yet? her father asked. Before she could answer, Topher walked into the kitchen.—Hey, Mack, he said, your pig is in my bowl.—Excuse me, Tofu, Mackenzie said, but he has a name. It's Queso."

"That's a funny name for a pig."

"*Queso* is Spanish for *cheese*."

"I know."

"Queso looked up from his meal, his face covered with the mac and cheese that had been in the bowl. He squealed at the sound of his name, smiled at Mackenzie, and returned to his lunch."

"Then what?"

"The end."

"What happened to Tofu?"

"Nothing. I don't know. The story is over."

"That's dumb."

"Every story has to end somewhere. The trick is figuring out where."

"Who said they have to end?"

"Because you can't go on listening forever. It has to stop. You have to live."

"But I want to know if Tofu got any mac and cheese. And what happened to the pig? Did Mackenzie bring him to school for show and share? That would be so cool."

"If you imagine her bringing him to school, then she did."

Adi looks unconvinced. "What color is Mackenzie's hair?"

"I didn't say."

"That's why I'm asking."

"What color do you think it is?"

"It should be pink. Because pigs are usually pink and the girls in these stories always have blond hair. But in the story, the pig is the one that's yellow, so the girl should have pink hair."

"I like that logic."

"But what color is it really? In the book."

"There is no book."

"You said it was a story."

"A story I've told Sam at bedtime before."

"You made it up?"

"It's undergone some different drafts, and I don't always tell it the same way, but yeah. I made it up."

Can it be? Adi looks impressed.

"My dad is usually at work when it's my bedtime. Or traveling."

"So your mom tells you stories?" Sam should get Adi Anthony Browne's *Gorilla* for her next birthday.

"Sometimes."

Steve isn't sure if he should press the question any further.

"Sometimes she'll tell me a story. But she doesn't make them up. She reads them from books."

"I do that sometimes, too."

"The one you made up is better."

"Thanks."

"Even if I didn't understand all of it."

"That's okay."

"You should turn it into a book."

"It's not that good."

"And I could draw the pictures. I'm a good artist."

"Okay then. Deal."

"Also her nickname should be Zee, not Mack."

"I'll think about it."

Adi looks happy. "Do you know any other stories?"

One comes to mind straight away. "I've been working on something, but can't figure out how to end it."

"Don't end it, then."

"You want to hear it?"

"Yes, please."

"We pick things up *in media res*. Zinnia and Peru were making their slow daily trudge through the forest, searching for mushrooms in all the same old spots, when they heard the voice. Only Peru heard it at first because sasquatches have sharper hearing than nine-year-old girls, but as they approached a clearing in the trees, Zinnia heard the voice, too.—Help!—It's coming from over there. Zinnia pointed toward the river beyond the clearing, by the base of Mount Berg.—We should check it out. Peru was scared. The sasquatch hunters no longer searched the Cascadian woods like they used to, but Peru had become cautious since having his photo snapped by a hiker years earlier. He used to be curious about the world.—Wait here then, Zinnia said, pointing to a large fir at the forest's edge. I'll let you know if it's safe. Her pace quickened as she neared the river.—Hello, she called out. Is someone hurt?—Over here. Zinnia followed the voice to a circular rock formation by the river bed. A salmon was floating among some reeds. She picked up a stick and gave the salmon a gentle poke.—Hey, the salmon said. I'm not dead yet. Zinnia apologized.—Never mind, the salmon said. My name is June. Can you help me?—What's the matter? Are you stuck?—Not stuck. I've just spawned, and while I'm not dead yet, I am going to die soon. This is where I was born and where I will die. It's the salmon way.—I don't

180

understand, said Zinnia. How can I help you?—All my life, I've only ever known the water. I've always ached to see the stars.—Can't you just look up? Zinnia asked.—It's too high, June answered. I need to get closer.—What do you mean?—I need to get up there. June rolled her eyes and splashed her fins in the direction of Mount Berg. Can you take me? Zinnia stared at the mountain soaring above the river.—I've never been up there, she said. But I have a friend who might be able to help. Zinnia turned toward the forest and waved her arms, mimicking the branches of a tree being blown by a great gust of wind. Peru came bouncing from the woods. Zinnia introduced him to June and told him her dying wish."

"Wait." Adi looks concerned. "Where are Zinnia's parents?"

"I don't know."

"Maybe they're working."

"Yes. Maybe."

"Okay. Go."

"What do you think? Zinnia asked. Can we do it? Can we help her? Peru looked at the mountain, then at June. He knelt down, dipped his big furry brown paws into the water, and scooped her out, clutching her against his chest. He was instantly emboldened.—It's been too long since we last went exploring. With that, the three of them began their ascent up Mount Berg, June resting in Peru's arms, Zinnia riding on his shoulders.

The climb took all day and all afternoon, but for Zinnia, Peru, and June, it seemed time stood still. June regaled them with tales of the deep blue sea, harrowing escapes from great white sharks, and swimming with schools of mermaids. They took breaks along their trek to snack on the mushrooms that lined the way. There were scrumptious species that Zinnia and Peru had never tasted or seen before.—To think: these mushrooms have been here all along, Peru said with his mouth full of pink and purple honeycomb-shaped morels. And we've been eating the same old portobellos and chanterelles from the forest floor. Zinnia nodded in agreement, too busy eating to answer."

"What if they were poisonous?"

"They knew they weren't."

"How did they know?"

"I don't know."

"You should figure that out for the next time you tell it."

"Sure. Do you want to hear the rest?"

Adi nods.

"Between June's stories and the wild mushrooms, they didn't notice it was dark until they reached the summit, minds and bellies full.—We've arrived, Peru said. Zinnia hopped off his back as he bent down to place June on the snow-covered peak. All three lifted their eyes toward the nighttime sky.—It's too cloudy, Zinnia complained, her voice rising. June sighed.—Wait, Peru said. Look."

Steve and Adi turn right at 29th, toward Marguerite.

"He pointed to a faint twinkling light between two dissipating clusters of clouds.—Is that a star? June asked, eyes fixed on the spot where Peru was still pointing.—It is, Zinnia said when she saw it. At least, I think it is.—I am. The voice seemed to come from every direction. June gazed at the flickering diamond in the sky.—Star?—Yes. Zinnia and Peru stood with their mouths open, speechless.—You can talk? June asked, still staring up, up toward the light.—Yes, said the star. But I don't have much time.—Much time for what?—I'm not really here, the star answered. I died millions and millions of years ago.—What do you mean? asked June. If you're dead, how can we see you and talk to you?—Because I'm billions of years away, the star explained. It takes time for light to travel. Mine has already gone out, and soon it will be gone altogether. Best if you speak quickly. June thought for a moment about what to say, then asked, What is it like to be dead?—It's not something that can be put into words, the star began. I'd need to paint you a picture, or play you a symphony.—What do you mean? There was silence. The star was gone. Zinnia, Peru, and June remained at the crest of the mountain, gazing skyward, watching the spot where the star had been, hoping it would reappear. It didn't. Instead, the dissipating clusters of clouds continued dispersing, and soon the celestial curtains were pulled all the way, unveiling a cosmic stage filled with vibrant, shimmering, luminous stars, dissolving the darkness, filling the sky with music, soft and langorous. As the sun began to rise, June broke the silence.—Goodbye, goodbye. Thank you so much. She was gone. Zinnia and Peru decided not to return to the forest yet. There was so much more of the mountain to explore, and so they did, wandering and wondering together."

Steve and Adi turn up Marguerite, the final familiar stretch, some four minutes, probably, before they reach the school. Steve checks his phone. It's 2:32. They'll be almost a half-hour early.

Steve looks at Adi.

Her eyes are glistening.

"That's all I've got so far."

Adi blinks her eyes a few times in rapid succession, then squeezes them shut for two seconds.

"I know what you should do."

Steve waits for her to continue.

Adi is staring straight ahead. "You should have another little girl and another sasquatch appear out of nowhere, on the mountaintop with Zinnia and Peru."

"Hmm."

"That would explain where the two of them came from. Girls are just stars that have died and been reborn. And sasquatches are salmons. Or the other way around."

Steve is drawn to the elegance of Adi's suggestion. It doesn't square with his worldview, doesn't align with the most fundamental things he believes about life. But who says fiction has to cohere with what a person actually believes? He's trying to tell a bedtime story, not write propaganda.

"You shuffle your feet when you walk."

"No I don't."

"Listen to that noise."

Steve continues walking as the two of them tilt their heads slightly, each with an ear angled downward.

"It's your shoes against the ground."

Steve continues walking, one step, the next, so on. Sure enough he's dragging.

"You should lift your legs a little higher."

"I didn't know I shuffled."

"My mom is always telling me and my sister to lift our legs and straighten our backs."

"That's good advice."

"You walk with your shoulders kind of slouched, too."

"It's because we've been walking all day and I'm tired."

"Eww." Adi slows and points at a dead worm at the edge of the sidewalk, by the front lawn of the house they're passing.

"Are you afraid of worms?"

"It's all dried up and yuck."

"So you're not afraid?"

"Freesia is really afraid. She cries and won't walk when the worms come out after it rains."

"My sister was scared of worms, too."

183

Steve doesn't tell her that when he was younger he would sometimes mercilessly stomp worms flat until their insides were their outsides. Boys are made of things like worm innards, and snips and snails. Little girls, though, are made of all things nice. They don't like worms. That's one explanation. Emily used to be terrified of worms when she was Adi's age. Even though she outweighed them fifty pounds to fifty grams, they were the stuff of her nightmares. Fifty grams? That seems too heavy for an earthworm. She was only six, though, so Steve never thought it was a thing to laugh about. And she's long since outgrown that fear. It's given way to real ones. He remembers more than one spring afternoon, after school, terror all around them. The two of them stepped off the school bus, a few blocks from home, the air redolent of fresh, squirming earthworms. Emily's eyes welled with tears. It was less than a ten-minute walk to their place, and once they were through the front doors of their parents' modest two-story townhouse, she'd be safe and secure from all alarms. Still, it was an almost ten-minute walk, and his sister had little legs. A six-year-old can only walk so fast, a thing he's been reminded of today, and the worms were everywhere. Where were the birds when they needed them? Steve used to tell his sister not to worry, everything would be all right. He really believed it back then. He was her big brother. That used to be his job. It was his calling when they were young. He wasn't about to let those menacing, ungodly creatures harm her. He'd bend down, tell her to hop aboard, and proceed to piggy-back her to safety. Her knight in well-worn gray sweatpants. During the trek home he'd navigate the worm-swamped pavement with skill and ease, deftly maneuvering between the hoards of invading annelids. Every now and then when one dared attack, he'd squelch its offenses. Squash it with all the fury of his left Reebok sneaker, or maybe it was a Tretorn, which he also used to wear, or a K-Swiss, not the Vans or PF Flyers or Onitsuka Tigers he wears these days, and yell a triumphant victor's yell. He was Goliath. The worms had no David to stand as their federal head, their covenant representative.

"Is Sam going to be a flower girl?"

"Sorry?"

"At your sister's wedding."

Steve nods. He used to tell his sister stories, too, like he tells Sam and Daphne and, when she's willing to sit still, Gillian. Now Emily is getting married. The two of them were almost always the first to get to school. Their parents would drop them off on their way to work, which meant they were there early, by eight. The caretaker—what was his name? something like

Mr. Ross or Mr. Russ, or was that in fact his first name?—he used to unlock the building just for them and they would wait together in a narrow hallway outside Emily's classroom. Sometimes when the doors remained locked because Mr. Ross hadn't opened them yet, they'd wait outside on a bench, in a little alcove. While they waited for her teacher to arrive, Steve would spin his fatuous tales. The main characters in those stories had names like Lumpy Grape Emily, Apple Tyson, Banana Tyler, and Peary Chunky, who was based on their next-door neighbor piano teacher Mrs. Duncan. The stories were probably as good as one would expect from a fourth grader, but the memories of those mornings, memories that Steve didn't know he still had until just now, of laughing and making his sister laugh, are better, truer, than his juvenile self could have imagined.

They've crossed the crosswalk at Nanton.

Adi asks if she can run to the playground.

"Go."

She takes off in a full-on sprint and as she nears the opening in the fence leading on to school property Steve suddenly remembers one of his sister's birthdays not that many years ago, when he bought her two artsy DVDs thinking she'd enjoy them. You don't know me at all, she'd said. When they were younger, but not that young, he'd punched her once in the stomach. Another time he accidentally cut her on the thigh with a pair of carelessly thrown scissors. Both times he'd felt remorse straight away. Like today with Marcel. It was worse with the DVDs. Had she been right? Did he not know his little sister at all? Are he and Sam destined for the same end? Is the fate of every father-child relationship the same as a brother and sister's?

Adi is on the swings.

May is sitting alone on a bench, looking at her phone. She hasn't spotted Adi yet, or Steve, who has his hands in his pockets, back slightly slouched, shuffling his feet across the grass, conscious of both his posture and his gait, which are exactly as Adi described, but is he walking this way because of what she said?—her words having a causal effect—or because it's just the way he walks?—her point. He straightens his back, deliberately raises his legs a fraction more with each subsequent step. It doesn't feel as natural, though. It's uncomfortable, in fact. He reverts to his old form.

May looks up from her phone and sees Steve a few steps away. She smiles. "Hi there."

"Hey."

"You're early."

"We've had a long day." He nods in Adi's direction as he sits down.

"What's Adi doing outside already?" spotting her thanks to Steve's physical prompt.

"She hung out with me today."

May parts her upturned lips a little, expressing her surprise. "How did that happen?"

"She wasn't feeling that well this morning when I dropped Sam off, and Mrs. Canard didn't want her staying and getting the other kids sick."

"And Mary couldn't take her?"

"Yeah. And Adi's dad is on a business trip."

"So you volunteered," a statement not a question. "Aww. That's so sweet."

Steve shrugs. "I had a fairly free day. She just tagged along."

"What did you two do? You must be so tired."

"Not much," beginning to replay the last five hours. "We got something at Starbucks, picked up some stuff at the pharmacy, had lunch at the potsticker truck, met with an old friend, visited the home of a woman from church. Then back here. That's all."

"Sounds like a lot." May crosses one leg over the other. "Is Adi feeling better?"

"She's alright," remembering now that May used to be a nurse before having kids. "She doesn't seem the least bit under the weather right now."

"A lot of people have been sick lately."

Steve nods. "Apparently."

"I hope you didn't get Adi the special potstickers," smiling.

"Her mom would kill me."

"Definitely"

Steve smiles.

"It sounds like you had a great day."

"It was fun."

Should he tell her about following Alfred Bester? Probably not. Probably if he told her, she'd think it weird or worse, creepy. Even though it was entirely innocent, outsiders don't understand about these things. But it was just as harmless and sweet, even, as the time he and Emily followed their grandfather that one morning, on his last trip to Canada. It's one thing to enjoy long walks on a familiar beach in the south of Taiwan, or even the crowded dirty streets of center city Taipei. It's quite another to walk on your own in a tree-lined suburban neighborhood in Vancouver. Steve and Emily had feared for their grandfather's safety. He might have lost his way. Steve had just read *Harriet the Spy*, though, so he was inspired. They gave him a head start, then set out to track him down. It wasn't hard. He was on foot. They were on bikes. He was old. They were young. He wasn't even at the corner of 16th and Quebec when they saw him. But they kept their distance. He didn't know they were following. What kind of spies would they have been if they were made by an old man who walked with one hand in the other, both behind his back? So they'd circled around, bided their time, detoured down one street, then another, rested at Grimmett Park for a spell. Marcel owns a house there? By the time they found their grandfather again he was heading north up Manitoba. It was still too soon to reveal themselves. Again they turned around, which they realized in hindsight was a mistake because when they decided to find him again, they couldn't. They didn't for some time, not until he'd reached the traffic lights at 4th and Cambie. They got to him before the lights changed, and good thing, too. Had he crossed the street he would have been lost for sure.

"Hailey told me about Sam's All About Me project."

"Which one was this?"

"The shoebox."

Steve is almost certain he hasn't heard about this before. "Uhh."

"You know, the kids had to bring in five objects and use them to talk about themselves." A question or a statement, he's not sure.

"She never told me."

"Really?" May looks surprised.

"Really. What did she do?"

She still looks like she doesn't believe him, but they're pretty good friends, Steve and May, she should know he wouldn't lie, not about something like this. "Hailey said she brought a shoebox with five different shoes."

"That's clever."

"I know. I was like, wow, Steve is really creative."

"It wasn't me."

"Maybe Lola?"

"Maybe." He turns his attention to the playground where Adi has moved to the monkey bars. "Do you know what shoes Sam brought?"

"I think Hailey said there was a swim flipper, a ballet shoe, something someone knitted her when she was a baby. A wool baby bootie maybe." She looks like she's trying to remember the rest of the items. "A couple of other things."

"Wow," impressed.

"Oh, and the old sneaker Hailey gave her with the shoelaces."

"It was her first non-velcro running shoe."

"Such a unique idea. And she told a story with all of the shoes, too. So there was a whole narrative. She didn't tell you?"

"Honest." Steve crosses his heart with his right index finger.

"Hailey brought a doll, a blanket, an old t-shirt, nothing nearly as special as Sam."

"I'm sure it was great."

"She didn't put her things in anything special either. Just a paper bag from Choices. Sam was the only one who brought a shoebox. She's so smart." May's eyes have a twinkle to them.

"She doesn't get that from me, that's for sure."

"Don't be modest, Steve."

It's not just an act, though. Is it?

"Hi you two." Shelby, Bella's mom, sits next to May at the other end of the bench.

"Hi Shel." May scoots over a bit, giving Shelby some more room.

Steve gives her a polite wave.

Shelby reciprocates with a nod and smile. Steve has never met her husband who, he's heard, works most of the year in China. She's a pharmacist. They live just down the street from the school in a massive house, more space than they need for Bella, who's an only child.

Steve sighs.

Neither woman notices.

Sometimes, as is the case right now, he thinks about what he could be doing with his life if he weren't a pastor, not that working in China or as a pharmacist appeal to him, but he wonders what he'd be doing instead if he weren't bound by divine call to Vancouver, which is the most expensive city in Canada to live in, a city where you can't get a detached house for under a million dollars and even a million dollars won't buy much, maybe a two-bedroom, one bath, rundown crack den in the worst part of town, view of chalk outlines and yellow police tape if you're lucky, so they live instead in a 700-square-foot one-bedroom condo with a walk-in closet, barely large enough to fit the bunk bed they put in there, which serves as Sam and Daphne's room, though getting this place was their mutual decision, they could have bought something else, something slightly more spacious, some place friends wouldn't have called them out of their minds for purchasing, as if fitting a family of four, which their family was before Gillian was born, in a space so small was unheard of, insane, they must not be thinking clearly, when in fact most people in the world do with less, significantly less, a fact Steve knows well because of the summer he spent volunteering at a girls' orphanage in southern India and ninety-three girls were there at the time, with hundreds more on a waiting list and all that was needed to get these girls off this waiting list was more money to build more dorms, with each dorm able to hold one hundred girls, but it cost two hundred and fifty thousand US dollars to build one, and fundraising in the developed Western world, which is the minority world, was hard, all of this Steve thought about when it came time to buy a place for the first time, so though Lola had wanted a larger condo or a townhouse even, they ended up at their current place, allowing for continued support of the orphanage and other charities, but despite the fact they live fairly modestly, he's not actually as pious as he seems, a fact he'd like to confess with brutal vulnerability to May right now, but she's not safe, she might gossip, word might spread that sometimes he wrestles with whether or not they should move, get a real house with a bedroom for each kid, and a guest room, two-car garage, a backyard, and these thoughts quickly turn to thoughts about his job, his ministry among people who for the most part don't care much about anyone other than themselves, who talk a good game, but when push comes to shove, they'd rather be the one pushing, shoving, and when he thinks too much about this, everything he's done feels pointless, his life feels pointless, devoted as it's been to trying to help people not shove others so hard, and in those moments, which come too often and linger too long, if he's honest about it, he wants to quit, wants to slug obstinate, truculent people like Marcel on purpose instead of by instinct, though that's not really true, that's a violent fantasy born of sin, he's much too much of a pacifist at heart to ever really do that, but he does imagine quitting, returning to work in finance or something else his old Wharton buddies are doing, make guap, build orphanage dorms, do real worthwhile tangible acts of kindness mercy justice for others, vacation anywhere in the world, any time of the year, instead of spending too many nights out each week at this or that unnecessary meeting, too many days spent fielding and juggling and botching complaints, not enough evenings at home with the kids, no more sleepless panic-filled nights worrying about God's eternal evaluation of his deeply

flawed pastoral care, worrying about how Blair is doing in the abusive relationship she refuses to leave, how Gabe is faring in his addiction struggles,
no more elders asking him with incredulity after the announcement of a
new pregnancy how another mouth to feed and more diapers to change is
going to effect his ministry, instead of offering congratulations, he won't
have to bite his tongue as often, not that he bites it that often right now, he's
too stubborn and proud, too poor at listening to other people's ideas especially when it's obvious they aren't as smart as he is, he needs to learn he's
not actually the smartest person in every room he's in despite what Dr.
Siegel told him once, and goodness if he weren't a pastor anymore he
wouldn't be so physically and emotionally exhausted all the time, though
maybe that wouldn't change at all since he'd still have three kids under
seven not to mention Lola, who's currently requiring something close to
parental care, yes, certainly wouldn't change at all, and if he really thinks
about it, the benefits not just the costs, the blessings as well as the curses,
not that they're actually curses, his schedule is more flexible than just about
anyone else he knows, like, he can do drop-offs and pick-ups and supervise
class field trips, babysit on a moment's notice, not many other people can
do that, certainly no other dads, it's always moms who do the heavy lifting
at Bluffwood, moms like May and Shelby, and the BPA women, he's still the
only male on the BPA despite some admittedly half-hearted attempts at
recruiting the other dads he occasionally runs into at the school or Safeway,
Starbucks, Quilchena Park, in the neighborhood, everyone he's ever approached has brushed him off because they're better at saying no than he is
and he should learn from them, learn to say no, not have his sense of worth,
his identity, his cosmic significance bound up in other people liking him,
he should know better, feel better, he shouldn't care, he should recognize
the miserable comforters he relies on, at school and at church, he should
say no more often, say it emphatically, but the truth is he likes the things he
does at the school, for the school, they fuel him, better to give than to re-
ceive after all, and if he could, if for instance he wasn't pastoring, he would
be a full-time part-time volunteer, which he kind of is already, because he
does, in fact, love it despite the pretense he makes too often of being over-
worked, it's a legitimate consolation for him, these hours he spends each
month on Bluffwood business, though they would still have need of an in-
come especially with Lola on medical leave, so he couldn't really volunteer
that much time, he'd still need to work a wage-paying job, assuming he
could find one, there should still be a market for a Wharton grad, even one

ten years removed from the traditional work force, and if he found a job, he could maybe go to India again and spend some time at the orphanage, track down Elizabeth the little girl he fell in love with there, or visit some part of the world Lola has never been before, which might be able to expel the sad things, at least for a bit, some temporary scaffolding, maybe Australia, the only non-Antarctic continent she hasn't visited, and if they were to go to Australia he could rewatch some *Crocodile Hunter* episodes in preparation, to set the mood, call attention to off-the-beaten path destinations, it's a huge country Australia is, coast to coast probably as wide as Canada, nearly, he used to know when he did *Reach For the Top*, so they could really explore the land, take their time, no rush, he could lay out his plan before signing an offer somewhere, and perhaps in lieu of a signing bonus, whatever firm that hires him will give him more vacation days than normal, at least for the first year, or he could just start working a few months later and take those months between his resignation at St. Joe's and the start of his new job to travel, the kids would love it, he could give his notice right after Easter, find a new job, leave the church at the end of June, spend July and August Down Under, be back for September at which point everything could begin again, anew, and maybe Lola will be good enough by then to return to work, it's possible, but he doesn't really want to quit, despite how often he thinks about it, he couldn't do that to his congregation, leave them in a lurch like that, without anyone to bury those in the winter of their lives, but he could maybe go back to school while he continues to pastor, open a few new career doors, possibly study English like he'd wanted to when he was a high school student but hadn't because he'd been too scared of failing, a feeling he hopes Sam, Daphne, and Gillian never feel, or if they do, which they almost certainly will because fear is probably the most primal human emotion, he hopes they'll have the courage to act in spite of those fears, to pursue their dreams, to know they have his full support and encouragement whatever they want to do with their lives, be it writer or pastor or food truck owner/operator or documentary filmmaker, that's the kind of father he wants to be, who gives ten yeses for every no and shows up at every school event and extracurricular activity, everything from Bluffwood talent shows to DanceCo ballet performances, violin recitals to swim meets, he wants to be at everything cheering his girls on, elementary to high school, through university and beyond, walk them down the aisle and officiate their weddings, if they should get married, a prospect he'd rather not think about, but too late, he's already started, and it's only going to get worse as the very boys in Sam's class, should she stay with the same peers for the next eleven years, are the same boys who are going to try and sleep with her, with Adi, too, whose face is moliminal, preparing to go another round on the monkey bars, then another in all likelihood, and another, until she stops, she can't go on forever, *tempus edax rerum*, just as childhood can't continue in perpetuity, and the truth is, Steve doesn't want to keep his kids from growing up, growing up is good and necessary, it's the pain and suffering that comes with being human that he fears, the knowledge that his girls will get hurt, get sad, get sick, and one day won't get well, a fact he ought to have known when he decided to become a parent, that the nightmares will all come true, but instead of staring the fear in its devilish face, he distracted himself from the serious business of life by not thinking about its end, his end, Sam's end, and on those occasions he's tried talking to friends about it they've labeled him morbid and morose, without ever getting to the heart of the problem so the fear has never gone away, and the only thing that seems to help is prayer, which even then only helps a bit, though he'd never admit that to his church, but it's the truth, just a bit, but a bit nonetheless, to give that fear to God, it's not nothing, it's something, maybe it's everything, no that's hyperbolic, nothing is everything, but maybe it's all a parent has in the end, to combat the ever-encroaching shadow of death, which is always nearer today than yesterday, to choose either God or distraction, and opt for God even if that means choosing tears over superficial happiness because it's better to go to the house of mourning than the house of feasting, though no one actually believes that sorrow is better than laughter, even Steve isn't sure he believes it because laughter is the best medicine they say, remembering how Sam called the IKEA ice cream treat a dingleberry sundae, remembering the story Bella told him the last time she was over for a playdate with Sam, about Anil being made by Mrs. Canard to stand outside in the hallway until he finished farting, he farts all the time, Bella had said, and they smell bad, so he has to leave the classroom and once he didn't and everyone laughed except Mrs. Canard, who didn't laugh, she got angry, her face turned beet red, which weren't Bella's words, Bella had just said red probably, and Mrs. Canard told him never to pass gas in class again and the kids had all laughed harder because she said pass gas in class, three rhyming words, and Steve had laughed out loud when Bella told him this story, just as he had when he first heard Sam call it a dingleberry sundae—*Sursum corda*—he wonders if Shelby did, too, or if maybe Bella hadn't told her, which is possible because Sam doesn't tell him much, like when she started kindergarten Vanessa's mom had said isn't it so much fun when they come home and tell you all the gossip, share everything they've done and learned, which Sam never did, and maybe Bella is like that at her own home, too, taciturn, even if she isn't at his, after all she's told him some of her family secrets before, which aren't really secrets, like how her dad, Steve doesn't remember his name, packs the same meal every day for lunch, something like apples, carrot sticks, Greek yogurt, and salad, and how her mom is addicted to shopping across the border at Bellingham, a fact that didn't surprise Steve at all, she's exactly that kind of person, the kind who tells him he should enjoy his kids as if he doesn't want to, the way she did once when he told her in a moment of uncommon openness that he was sad thinking about Sam eventually dying, but then she doesn't say how, exactly, he's supposed to do that, i.e., enjoy his kids while he can, when he knows what awaits them and knows, too, that he's impotent to stop the suffering, unless he could create a time machine, go back to the past, not have kids, what Veronica said, but this is real life not an Alfred Bester story, assuming those are the kinds of stories he wrote, or writes, not one of Martha's pseudo-science experiments, and in real life the best he can hope for is to one day enjoy the present, savor the moments more, which is a small grace, because real time is flying, doesn't rest, still you should enjoy her while she's young, is what Shelby said and people like her say, full of shoulds and oughts and musts, as if the faintest glimmer of an opportunity to give advice means she has no choice but to interject, but she's at least got the right idea, everyone wants to be happy, it was Steve's elementary school ambition from what he can remember, the answer he'd given when his fifth-grade teacher Ms. De-Castro had asked his class to write down what they wanted to be when they grew up, and while other boys wrote things like hockey player, fireman, dentist, astronaut, Steve had written happy, actually his first answer had been loud, which he erased as soon as he thought of something better, more fantastic, less realistic, he rubs at the callus beneath his wedding band, surprised he hasn't had to do it more often today, but that's what happens when you're distracted, you forget the minor nuisances, even the big fat existential worries, if the distraction is distracting enough, and he's trying to think what kind of distraction might be suitable to do a job like that as he touches the top of his head, his fingertips feeling wet all of a sudden, like the excrescence is suppurating, but bringing his arm down and looking at his hand now, his fingers are dry, he must be imagining things, he touches it again and again it feels wet, but still his fingers are dry, maybe the whole day is make-believe, but that's silly, the pills he picked up at the pharmacy are in his pocket, he hears them rattling, which reminds him Adi still has the stone and he should make one more attempt at getting it from her to give to Sam, who would appreciate it were he to remember to use it as an object lesson about trying hard, never giving up, digging deep, she'd certainly appreciate it more than Adi, who's probably going to end up throwing it away or forgetting it in her pocket along with the chicken feathers, only to have them inadvertently washed with the laundry, it's probably her mom who does the laundry, Mary whose name is actually Marigold, she probably hasn't gone by Marigold since she was something like Adi's age, when it would have been cute to be named Marigold, nicknames are strange things, which ones stick, which don't, like Teddy in Sam's class who the kids call Three Slice because once he ate three slices of pizza on Pizza Day, which is next Tuesday, also the day of the next elders' meeting at St. Joe's, Pizza Day is always the Tuesday after Hot Dog Day, once Teddy had eaten three slices, not even twice, and now all the kids call him Three Slice, which is a pretty awesome nickname, but he could have been something else like Cheese or Fromage or Queso because the three slices he had were cheese slices and when he was in the seventh grade Steve called his friend Jason Chao Cheesepuff and it stuck for the next ten years at least, since the last he'd heard about him was after Cheesepuff had graduated from UVic and their mutual high school friend Ben had told him what Cheesepuff was up to and that's what he called him, not Jason or Chao, which would have been a natural nickname because it's a homonym for chow, but Cheesepuff is what Ben called him still after all those years, and what Cheesepuff was up to was grad school, which was anticlimactic given the excitement in Ben's voice when he asked Steve if he'd heard what Cheesepuff was up to, and Steve had assumed it would be something like prison guard or forest ranger, a unique thing like that, out of character for a book-smart bespectacled Chinese male, not grad school, which is what like half of all undergrad students wind up doing, the book-smart bespectacled Chinese male ones anyway, but nicknames can really define a person, more than actual given names even, because nobody calls a person by their actual given name if there's a catchier nickname alternative, nobody calls Steve Stephen, for instance, except Jacquelyn who has known him forever and if she started calling him Steve now that'd just be weird, or if she were to call him Étienne, the French equivalent of Stephen, which Mme Racicot had called him once in twelfth grade, but maybe Jacquelyn will call him that the next time they speak now that she's been in Montreal for the last couple of years, enough time to have been subject to some level of racism, even a day is enough time to have experienced racism in Montreal, even an hour, that's all it took when they took a misguided vacation there, and someone rolled down her car window and yelled at Steve, who was in the middle of crossing a street with Sam, who was teeny tiny and had just started to walk, to go back to Japan, a place he'd never visited, still hasn't visited, but has always wanted to go, probably even before he and Suzume were dating, Suzume, her again, twice he's thought of her today, maybe more, and if the two of them had gotten married their kids would have been mixed and beautiful, assuming they had kids, not as obviously mixed like Adi is—Adi, who's currently at the top of the shamrock green curvy slide, now making her descent—but their kids would have been mixed anyway, but if they had gotten married and had kids, those kids wouldn't be Sam, Daphne, or Gillian, the people he loves most in the world wouldn't exist, and the meaning of life is love, it is, it is it is it is, contrary to the message proclaimed by the truck beneath the Arthur Laing bridge, it is, that's not rubbish, though he wouldn't have known this, certainly not in the proportion he knows it now, not when he was dating Suzume, not when he was with Veronica, not in those times absent a romantic relationship when all he'd have wanted to do was stay home, open a bottle of Irn Bru, or a bottle of anything that happened to be cold, in his fridge, smoke a couple joints, but he knows it now, believes it, or thinks he does at any rate, it's the only way to explain why he has such a hard time living in the moment, because life isn't fiction, there aren't any narrative devices in real life, you can only tell the story looking backward, none of this present tense business as much as he wants to believe it, and looking back at the things and people he loves, then looking forward and seeing everything breaking apart, coming undone, going to shit, the race is not to the swift, it's not to the slow, it's not to anyone, no one wins because the race is rigged, everyone loses, and loses everything, and the only intellectually satisfying thing to do in the end is pray, again with praying, which he should do more, which he hasn't done all day yet, not since reciting the Lord's Prayer a handful of times when he woke up in the morning, he really should pray, and pray now as he senses his heart going down a hole with no end, and what he should pray in a time like this when he doesn't know what to say is the collect of the day, so Steve takes his phone from his pocket, enters his password, swipes the screen until he finds his Book of Common Prayer app, then taps it open, waits a few brief moments for it to load, and the prayer for Wednesday of Holy Week, Holy Wednesday a.k.a. Spy Wednesday, appears, and Steve reads it, quietly: Almighty and everlasting God, who, of thy tender love towards mankind, hast sent thy Son our Savior Jesus Christ, to take upon him our flesh, and to suffer death upon the cross, that all mankind should follow the example of his great humility: mercifully grant, that we may both follow the example of his patience, and also be made partakers of his resurrection; through the same Jesus Christ our Lord.

Amen.

"Mr. Halim!" A kid wearing a black PW high school hoodie is standing in front of him. It's not the first time he's been confused for Bluffwood's former computer teacher. "Mr. Halim!"

"I'm not Mr. Halim."

"Oh." The boy squints as if he thinks Steve is lying. "You look just like him."

"He must be very handsome."

"Yeah."

Steve is about to say something else, something more clever or at least biblical, like blessings aren't to the beautiful, but the p.m. bell crows Hwæt hwæt hwæt signaling the end of the day, and a moment later the outside door to Mrs. Canard's class opens, she's holding it, her back pressed against it, propping it open, and the first few students have already emerged. Steve stands and starts walking toward the school, a moderate pace to begin with, but he's picking up a little speed. He's jogging now. Sam is outside. She hasn't spotted him yet. Her head darts left and right, like a little bird searching for her father, oblivious to all the dangers in the world. She's spotted him and now she's running, too, holding something in her hand, a colorful piece of paper with what looks like a picture of a big smiling tooth. Steve's slow jog is a dead sprint now, which is undignified, perhaps, yes definitely, but he doesn't care who's watching or laughing because the race, even if it is rigged, is to the one who's willing to run.

"Daddy! Daddy!" her arms outstretched. "It fell out!" Sam's newly gap-toothed grin is wider than the heavens and the earth.

www.ingramcontent.com/pod-product-compliance
Lightning Source LLC
Chambersburg PA
CBHW051136020726
47501CB00005B/1532